Children of the Night:

Werebeasts

BY WILLIAM W. CONNORS

Credits

Design: William W. Connors ❀ **Editing:** Lester Smith
Brand Management: David Wise ❀ **Art Direction:** Paul Hanchette
Cover Artist: Robh Ruppel ❀ **Interior Artist:** Kevin McCann
Typography: Angelika Lokotz ❀ **Cartography:** Deanna Robb
Graphic Design: Matt Adelsperger

Special Thanks to Thomas Reid, Cindi Rice, Dale Donovan,
Jon Pickens, Ted Stark, Miranda Horner, and Nigel Findley.

**U.S., CANADA,
ASIA, PACIFIC, & LATIN AMERICA**
Wizards of the Coast, Inc.
P.O. Box 707
Renton, WA 98057-0707
+1-800-324-6496

EUROPEAN HEADQUARTERS
Wizards of the Coast, Belgium
P.B. 34
2300 Turnhout
Belgium
+32-14-44-30-44

9583XXX1501
Visit our website at www.tsr.com

TABLE OF CONTENTS

Introduction
For the Dungeon Master 4
Using This Book 4
The Concise Werebeast 4
The Mood of Ravenloft 7

Andre de Sang
Biography 10
Feast of the Rats .13

Angel Pajaro
Biography 19
A Night at the Opera 21

Radjiff Chandor
Biography 26
Hunter and Hunted 28

Vladimir Nobriskov
Biography 34
The Scarlet Prince 36

Meeka
Biography 41
A Cat's Revenge .43

Abu al Mir
Biography 48
Darkness and Secrets 50

Sheneya
Biography 55
Kiss of the Serpent Woman 57

Professor Arcanus
Biography 62
Missing Bones 65

Mother Fury
Biography 67
The Howling Clan .69

Henri Milton
Biography 72
A Bloody Canvas .74

Vjorn Horstman
Biography 78
The Unnatural 80

Sandovor
Biography 84
The Viper's Grasp .86

Hilde Borganov
Biography 90
The Forgotten Ones 92

The power of hiding ourselves from one another is mercifully given, for men are wild beasts, and would devour one another but for this protection.

—Henry Ward Beecher

Introduction

INTRODUCTION

FOR THE DUNGEON MASTER

ver time, any threat can lose its fearsomeness. After a party of adventurers has confronted three or four werewolves (assuming they survive!), the thought of a werewolf will have lost some of its fright.

The *Children of the Night* series offers Dungeon Masters a chance to battle this problem by introducing new and exciting variants on traditional horror monsters. The twists and turns shown in these books should catch even the most jaded heroes off their guard.

USING THIS BOOK

ver the course of the pages that follow, the Dungeon Master is presented with thirteen unique werebeasts, each with a detailed history and ready-to-play adventure. Some of these encounters are set in a specific region of Ravenloft, but most can be inserted into any campaign, anywhere the heroes happen to be. Even Dungeon Masters running campaigns based in other AD&D® settings will easily find a place for most of these adventures in their game world. With just a little effort on the part of the DM, it is even possible to insert these stories into campaigns for other roleplaying game.

Every entry in this book is divided into three subsections. The first of these, *Biography,* is a detailed description of the werebeast, its past, and its plans for the future. Also included in this section is an illustration of the character and complete game statistics. For DMs who do not want to use the adventures in this book, this makes it possible to add nearly every character into a given campaign setting.

The second section in each entry is a brief adventure. While these plots and situations are abbreviated in format, each is carefully crafted to provide a maximum of entertainment. By understanding the biography of the werebeast in question, and becoming familiar with the likely events of the scenario, Dungeon Masters will be prepared to play each story to its fullest. Of course, a campaign-oriented Dungeon Master may also interweave additional encounters and characters into the adventure to match with other events in the campaign. If the scenario makes mention of "a local priest," for instance, the DM can fill the role with an NPC cleric the party knows.

The final part of each entry is a brief section entitled "Recurrence." Here the Dungeon Master will find information about possible consequences of the adventure, and ways in which to continue using the characters or situations even after its conclusion. Often, this primarily means keeping the villain around to use

as a recurring enemy of the player characters. But many of these entries also offer suggestions for spin-off adventures, sequels, and continuing story lines.

It is recommended that the Dungeon Master not simply use these creatures one after another in a campaign. In order for them to create the best effect, they should be sprinkled like seasoning between other adventures. Otherwise, it won't be long before the players will be heard saying things like "Hmmm. Another mangled body in the woods last night. Must be another werebeast." On the other hand, it is said that every rule has its exception. If your players have just been through two werebeast adventures, and they seem certain that the next adventure *must* involve some other type of enemy, then it might be worthwhile to have them tangle with yet another werebeast. Even as they encounter evidence to the contrary, they may assume that the DM is just setting them up for a surprise. In a good horror campaign, the trick is to keep the adventurers off balance.

THE CONCISE WEREBEAST

uch of the information in the next few pages is based upon the researches of the late Dr. Rudolph van Richten, as recounted in his work, *Van Richten's Guide to Werebeasts.* For readers unfamiliar with that volume, the most important concepts are summarized below.

Important Terms

In order to discuss the nature of werebeasts, it is essential to define a few specific terms. The following are commonly used within this book.

Aspect: This word is used by Van Richten to describe each of a lycanthrope's states. For example, a true werewolf would have three *aspects:* human, wolf, and a hybrid wolfman. By contrast, most *pathologic* or *maledictive* lycanthropes have only two aspects.

Hereditary Lycanthropes: This is another term for *true* lycanthropes, as opposed to their pathologic or maledictive kindred. Hereditary lycanthropes are their own distinct race rather than humans (and the like), who have become afflicted in some way. As such, they breed true, and they generally relish their bestial natures.

Hybrid: To define the lycanthropic aspect combining the features of man and beast, Van Richten uses this term. The most familiar of these forms is certainly that of the wolfman.

Maledictive Lycanthropy: This term is used to describe those unusual persons who acquired lycanthropy via a curse or other unusual means. The term is used to distinguish such individuals from either *true* or *pathologic* lycanthropes.

Pathologic Lycanthropy: This is Van Richten's term for lycanthropes who began life as humans but who became werebeasts in the wake of an attack by some manner of lycanthrope.

Phenotype: Van Richten refers to the various species of lycanthropes as phenotypes, a term he adopted from a wandering sage. For example, werewolves and wererats are two different phenotypes of lycanthrope.

Progenitor: The progenitor is the true lycanthrope from whom a chain of infected lycanthropes is "descended." This term is used primarily in cases where the progenitor has created one or more infected lycanthropes who have, in turn, spawned more of their bestial kind.

Susceptibility: Most lycanthropes are also susceptible to certain herbs or chemicals. In order to be useful against the beast, these must be somehow introduced to its system. They might be fed to the lycanthrope or injected into its bloodstream. Examples include the werewolf's susceptibility to wolfsbane and the werebear's aversion to belladonna.

Transfiguration: This is a term used to describe the process by which a lycanthrope changes from one of its forms (or aspects) to another.

Trigger: A trigger is the event or situation that causes a werebeast to undergo an involuntary transfiguration from one aspect to another. Triggers normally apply only to pathologic and maledictive lycanthropes; true lycanthropes change only when they wish to.

True Lycanthropy: This is the accepted term for purebred lycanthropes as opposed to those who began life as humans (or the like) and then became afflicted with lycanthropy.

Vulnerabilities: Van Richten assembled quite a listing of unusual materials that can be used with great effect upon specific phenotypes. To be effective, these items must be fashioned into or employed as weapons. For example, werebats are vulnerable to weapons made from silver and weretigers to those chipped from obsidian.

Important Considerations

There are a few issues likely to surface during the course of any scenario involving shapechangers, as explained in *Van Richten's Guide to Werebeasts*. The following brief guidelines serve as a summary of that material.

Types of Triggers

There are many conditions under which the various lycanthropes of the world change their shapes. The one spoken of most commonly, at least in folk tales, is the rising of the full moon. But this is hardly universal.

True lycanthropes need not concern themselves with triggers, of course, being able to change shape at will. Among lycanthropes of the infected and maledictive kinds, there are even more types of triggers than there

are phenotypes. In fact, some triggers are specific to a particular individual, especially among the maledictive variety of lycanthrope.

Symbolic Triggers: These are triggers that, by their very nature, represent change from one state to another. Common examples include the setting of the sun or rising of the moon (the transition from night into day). Other such triggers include the changing of a lunar phase, the chiming of a certain hour, or the changing of the tides.

Physiological Triggers: These are triggers that directly relate to the physical condition of the werebeast. Common examples include extreme fear, intense pain, or even moments of consuming passion.

Other Triggers: In his notes on this subject, Van Richten makes mention of several other triggers that do not fall readily into either of the above categories. These are most often linked to maledictive lycanthropes and are tied to the curses that have made them what they are. Possible examples of such triggers include entry into a specific place, exposure to a certain individual, or even the proximity to a magical or holy aura.

Transfigurations

When a lycanthrope changes from one aspect to another, it is a traumatic and often horrifying event. For the lycanthrope, the transfiguration is an intense experience of course. For the viewer, it can be as terrifyingly mesmerizing as a cobra coiling to strike.

Pleasure and Pain: The nature of the change varies with the type of werebeast encountered. True lycanthropes find the process of transfiguration a liberating and exhilarating experience. To pathologic and maledictive lycanthropes, on the other hand, it is an agonizing and emotionally shattering ordeal. Indeed, so violent an experience is it that the latter types of werebeast must make a successful saving throw vs. death magic to avoid dropping anything held in hand during the change of aspects.

Witnessing the Change: Anyone who observes a werebeast during transfiguration must make a horror check (unless the player character roleplays effectively). If the viewer has ever before seen this particular individual undergo the change, the DM may allow a bonus to the check or even waive it altogether. If the creature is clearly assuming a more powerful and extremely dangerous form, a fear check may be in order as well.

Clothing and Armor: When a werebeast changes from one form to another, it generally alters size in the process. If the new form is larger than the old one, normal clothing and the like are ruptured and torn by the change. If armor is worn, the transforming creature suffers constriction damage during the change. The armor itself is badly damaged as well, giving way and falling off as straps break and the like.

INTRODUCTION

Use the following chart to determine the amount of constriction damage a particular type of armor causes during a werebeast's transfiguration.

Armor Worn	Constriction Damage
Leather or Padded	1d2–1
Studded Leather or Ring Mail	1d2
Scale Mail	1d3
Chain Mail	1d4
Splint or Banded Mail	1d3+1
Plate Mail	1d4+1

For other types of armor, and for heavy clothing, the Dungeon Master should decide upon a damage rating (if any), using the examples above as a guide.

Healing: Wounded lycanthropes automatically heal some of their damage during the course of their transfiguration. The process of changing forms also regenerates tissue. The amount of damage healed is 10% to 60% (1d6 x 10%) of the injury that the creature currently suffers. Thus, a wererat reduced to 1 hit point could change into its human aspect in order to instantly regain a percentage of its lost hit points. (If the creature suffers constriction damage during the change, damage and healing occur simultaneously.)

Transfigurations in Combat: Changing from one aspect to another, whether involuntarily or intentionally, is a physically demanding task. It also requires time—a full round in most cases. During this time, the werebeast cannot defend itself or attack. In addition, it is unable to employ a shield while undergoing transfiguration, and it gains no defensive bonus for a high Dexterity score. Opponents attacking a werebeast in this condition gain a +2 bonus to their attack rolls.

Painful Memories: A true lycanthrope has complete memory of all that it does in any of its aspects. However, the same is not true of pathologic or maledictive lycanthropes. Such tragic creatures only vaguely remember the crimes they committed while in their bestial forms, and then only as indistinct flashes, haunting dreams, and uneasy feelings. The reverse is also true, as the creature will not normally recall who its friends are when it enters a feral aspect.

Skills and Abilities: As a rule, any skills and abilities based upon class or race are lost when an infected or maledictive lycanthrope enters an animal or hybrid form. At this point, all of its abilities and statistics are those of the new form. True lycanthropes, on the other hand, may well have access to skills and such learned in another form. The deciding factor in each case is the shape of the creature and its ability to actually perform the action in question. A wereboar in full boar form could not pick pockets with its hooves, for instance, even though it might recall the skill.

Bloodlust

All lycanthropes, whether true, pathologic, or maledictive, have the potential to enter a sort of killing frenzy. Bloodlust is most commonly seen in the latter two types of creature, but it is not unknown in true lycanthropes (especially those who are still learning to control their natural powers).

Entering Bloodlust: Whenever a lycanthrope is exposed to the sight, smell, or taste of fresh blood while in proximity to potential prey, there is a chance that it loses itself in bloodlust. In order to resist, the creature must pass a saving throw vs. polymorph. The following adjustments are made to the die roll.

Condition	Adjustment*
Other werebeast(s) nearby already in bloodlust	–2
Each day beyond four without food	–1
Werebeast has recently tasted blood	–1
Werebeast has suffered 25% damage	–1
Werebeast has suffered 50% damage	–4
Werebeast has suffered 75% damage	–7
Pathologic or maledictive lycanthrope	–3
Werebeast is a "new" pathologic or maledictive lycanthrope**	–9
True lycanthrope during puberty (learning to control its powers)	–3

* Penalties are not cumulative.
** Has assumed bestial aspects not more than six times.

True lycanthropes generally are subject to bloodlust only when in animal or hybrid form. If reduced to 50% of their hit points in human form, however, there is a chance that they enter bloodlust. An additional –2 is applied to such a check. A true lycanthrope in human form transforms into one of its more bestial aspects if overcome with bloodlust. Infected and maledictive lycanthropes can enter bloodlust only in their animal aspects.

Effects of Bloodlust: A lycanthrope overcome with bloodlust is a terrible enemy. Such a creature enters a berserk rage that earns it a +2 bonus on all attack and damage rolls. A similar penalty is applied to the creature's Armor Class, however, making the werebeast itself more vulnerable to attack (though no more vulnerable to injury). Lycanthropes affected by bloodlust attack the nearest enemy, giving preference to those that appear to be easier prey (the weak or injured, for example).

Escaping Bloodlust: A lycanthrope can shake off an attack of bloodlust only after the creature has gorged itself on the flesh of its enemies. At that time, another saving throw vs. polymorph is made (with a +2 bonus). Success indicates that the bloodlust fades. Of the modifiers governing entering bloodlust, only those relating to wounds apply to this die roll.

Contracting the Disease

Any attack by a lycanthrope poses the danger of infection to the victim. A person who has been bitten or clawed by one of these terrible creatures is in deadly danger of becoming a werebeast himself. The following game rules apply to the transmission of what Van Richten and other scholars call the *dread disease.*

Werebeasts can pass on the infection of lycanthropy only through attacks made with their natural weaponry (claws, fangs, etc.). Obviously then, a wererat who attacks with a sword never causes his injured victims to become wererats.

There is a 2% chance per point of damage the werebeast inflicts with natural weapons that a victim will contract the disease. This check is made after the battle and against the sum total of wounds sustained, not after each exchange of blows. (It is worth noting that outside of Ravenloft, the chance of contracting lycanthropy is only half this—1% per point of damage suffered.)

Once a character has become infected with lycanthropy, it is only a matter of time before his affliction is triggered and he undergoes a transfiguration. As a rule, it takes the infection some time to spread throughout a victim. A good rule of thumb is 5d4 days. Of course, the needs of the story come before any other concerns, and the Dungeon Master should feel free to set the incubation time without resorting to rolling dice.

Curing the Disease

Not surprisingly, only pathologic and maledictive lycanthropes can be cured. As Van Richten pointed out, true lycanthropes can no more be rid of their natures than one might cure an elf of being an elf. The means by which a cure can be effected for the other types depend upon the nature of the lycanthropy.

Maledictive Lycanthropes: Lifting the curse from a maledictive lycanthrope often is a difficult, time-consuming process. Sometimes the afflicted person knows exactly what event resulted in the curse. At other times the task may involve a great deal of detective work merely to discover the cause. In some cases the only way to remove the affliction may be for the werebeast to make amends for some sinister deed that was committed.

If the curse came about because of the character's own actions or crimes, the cure may doubly difficult. First, amends must be made for the wrongs that brought about the affliction. Even once this is done, however, the character almost certainly needs to undergo a change of attitude. Failure to so can prevent the lifting of the curse, perhaps even sealing the person's doom forever.

When dealing with attempts to lift such curses, the Dungeon Master needs to judge on a case-by-case basis. What must be done should be dictated by a sense of justice (balancing the cure with the original crime) and drama (driving the story in a satisfying direction).

Pathologic Lycanthropy: If the character has contracted the disease of lycanthropy from wounds sustained in battling a werebeast, the process of healing becomes as much a medical as a spiritual one. Van Richten has detailed a series of steps that must be undertaken.

The first of these stages—and by far the most difficult—is the process of exterminating the root of the infection. This means that the true lycanthrope from whom the infection originated—not merely the werebeast who infected the victim—must be tracked down and destroyed. Van Richten refers to this original source of infection as a *progenitor.* As there are often many links in the chain of infection, finding the progenitor can be a daunting task.

Once the chain that ties the infected character to the progenitor has been destroyed, the second stage of the cure can be started. Van Richten refers to this part of the process as *revitalizing the tarnished spirit.* It is at this time that the werebeast must make amends for the wrongs that he has done, or at least come to terms with the bestial nature that dwells within him.

Van Richten refers to the third, and final, stage of the cure as *removing the blight.* At this point, a series of remedies (perhaps magical, perhaps pharmacological) must be applied. An example of such an antidote is the ability to cure lycanthropy gained by ranger characters when they reach 10th level.

THE MOOD OF RAVENLOFT

 he RAVENLOFT® campaign setting is unique among roleplaying worlds for its combination of a traditional fantasy setting with the dark moods of a gothic horror story. It has been described, not inaccurately, as *Dracula* meets the *Lord of the Rings.* The *Domains of Dread* rulebook has much to say about how to capture the mood of a horror adventure and provide players with a good helping of both fun and fright. A few words are in order, however, about the special flavor of a werebeast adventure.

Techniques of Terror

Every type of creature presented in the *Children of the Night* series is interesting in its own way. The stories of vampires presented in the first volume are very different in mood and feel from those in the second volume, which deals with ghosts and spirits. Now, with the publication of this third book, a new type of horror is presented.

Whereas ghosts are mysterious and haunting, werebeasts are often brutal and savage. Bringing these creatures to life in a RAVENLOFT adventure can be challenging, for it is all too easy for a lycanthrope adventure to become a savage chain of carnage and blood. To capture the fear and horror of a werebeast adventure without devolving into sheer slaughter, consider the following tips.

Shock Value: Despite its dark and horrific nature, Ravenloft is not a world of in-your-face gore. As a traditional, gothic setting, Ravenloft draws upon the implied and suggested for its shock value. In no case is this distinction more important than with werebeasts. By their very nature, lycanthropes are brutal creatures who tend to leave trails of blood and carnage behind them. This does not mean, however, that the Dungeon Master should have the player characters stumbling over mutilated corpses every few steps.

Consider the case of a room in which a werewolf has killed the woman he loved. There are two ways in which the heroes might discover this scene. They might just open the door and discover a grisly view of blood and entrails. Or instead, suppose that one of the heroes is reaching for the doorknob when she notices a ribbon of blood flowing out from under the door. Obviously, this example is more unnerving, for the players now have a very good idea of what they are going to find when they open that door. The scene that they anticipate is far more frightening than any description of carnage that the Dungeon Master can invent.

Bestial Fury: Another important aspect of lycanthrope adventures is the feral nature of the creatures confronting the heroes. Whereas vampires are often presented as somewhat romantic figures and ghosts as tragic characters, werewolves and their kin are viewed as animal rage incarnate. Heroes who come face to face with such a creature should be confronted with a wild opponent whose bestial energy is nearly unstoppable. In game terms, this is the purpose of the blood-lust rules presented earlier in "The Concise Werebeast." There is more to this sort of encounter than just game mechanics, however. Almost anything that the Dungeon Master can do to drive home the wild and chaotic nature of combat with a lycanthrope is a good thing.

One of the most effective ways to give a combat scene a sense of frantic activity is to move it along very quickly. The Dungeon Master can say "Quick, tell me what your character does!" and then allow only five seconds or less for the player to respond. On that same note, players might be limited to one brief sentence in describing what their characters do. And, of course, roaring really loudly before rolling the lycanthrope's attack dice doesn't hurt either.

Surprise Attacks: Another aspect of werebeast adventures is the sudden and unexpected assault of the creature. Without warning, the hulking form of a werewolf crashes through the window of a tavern to savagely attack the heroes. Or while peering down into a dark cellar, a hero is suddenly pounced upon from behind.

The nature of the werebeast goes a long way toward dictating the sorts of surprise attacks it employs. While the above examples are just fine for werewolves and the like, they don't work so well for pack-hunting wererats. On the other hand, many of the ambush and combat scenes from the movie *Aliens* work well if you use wererats and sewers in the place of aliens and space station tunnels.

"I'm Hit!": Without a doubt, the most disturbing aspect of combat with werebeasts comes not from the battle itself, but from the waiting period afterwards. If the heroes have been wounded, they now face the dreadful prospect of waiting to see if they have contracted lycanthropy and will become monsters themselves. This gives the Dungeon Master a double-edged sword to wield. On the one hand, a character who is infected may not realize it until he awakens covered in blood, or worse, in captivity awaiting a burning at the stake by irate villagers; on the other, a character who has not been infected can still be tortured with tales of recent murders that make him suspect he is cursed with the *dread disease*.

If only one member of the party has been infected, the rest of the party must somehow avoid killing or being killed by their friend while seeking out a cure. Locals won't be very sympathetic to the party's plight, however. Not only are they likely to hunt the werebeast, they will probably blame the party for harboring the creature, should they learn that it is a friend to the heroes.

All of this provides the Dungeon Master with many, many adventure opportunities. Investigation for a cure can take the party anywhere the DM desires. Avoiding hunting parties, rescuing a captured friend from otherwise innocent locals, tracking an escaped werebeast party member—all of these are full of dramatic potential.

Of course, there are some potential problems for the Dungeon Master as well. Some players just can't cope with the thought of their hero losing control or doing evil. If the DM decides to allow such a character to be infected, it may be best if the story dictates that the werebeast's first victims are animals. In this way, the player knows that the capacity for evil exists, but there is a chance for a cure before any murder is committed. Other players may have trouble playing responsible characters in the first place, and may revel in the wanton destructiveness of a werebeast. The DM can combat this by having the new werebeast destroy something it holds dear in its human form (a magical sword, perhaps), thus convincing the player that the affliction is truly a curse. (Remember, the werebeast aspect is under the DM's control.) Otherwise, the only resort may be to "retire" the character.

Obviously, then, the subject of a player character's infection is a serious one, not to be entered into lightly. Of course, the players should already understand that Ravenloft is a realm of dangerous events and dark fates. That is what makes it so thrilling!

The alleged power to charm down insanity, or ferocity in beasts, is a power behind the eye.

—Ralph Waldo Emerson

Children
of the Night

Andre de Sang

Ships are but boards, sailors but men: there be land-rats and water-rats, water-thieves and land-thieves.

—William Shakespeare
The Merchant of Venice

Biography

Andre de Sang was once a normal man, but his dark deeds and a bad turn of fortune combined to transform him into a savage monster. Formerly an infamous pirate, Captain de Sang now combines the worst features of mankind with the sadistic instincts of a wererat.

Appearance

A maledictive werebeast, Captain de Sang can assume either of two shapes. The first is his normal human form, as he appeared before his terrible curse. The second is a hybrid form, combining in equal proportion the features of his human form with those of a giant rat.

In either form, De Sang wears the garb of a ruthless buccaneer. He favors a loose-fitting blouse of crimson, laced casually up the front, and billowing black leggings. Comfortable black boots of soft leather stretch up to his calves. He wears a broad sash of yellow silk about his waist. From this hangs a razor-edged cutlass which has ended the life of countless sailors. Besides his blade, De Sang generally has a snaplock pistol tucked into his belt.

Captain de Sang favors loose garb because it does not hinder his transfigurations. In most cases, the change from one aspect to another does little more than dishevel his clothing. Only his boots are not so adaptable. These, however, are secured with a series of catches that give way easily when De Sang begins to change form. In his hybrid state, he goes barefoot.

Human Aspect

In his human form, De Sang appears as a normal man with swarthy features and short, dark hair. His brow is very pronounced, however, making his eyes look beady and giving his forehead a distinct "v" shape. His nose is long and slender but kinked in the middle, where it once was broken. He is almost always smiling, but it is the predatory smile of a carnivore rather than the reassuring grin of a friend. His jaw is sharp and almost pointed, lending the lower half of his face an angle that matches his brow.

Hybrid Aspect

In his hybrid aspect, De Sang is a chilling sight to behold. His jaw and nose distend to form the snarling countenance of a giant rat; his eyes grow even more beady; and fur sprouts from his skin. His posture becomes that of a bent quadruped unaccustomed to walking on its hind legs—the legs of a rodent. A long, whiplike tail coils out behind him, but it serves no purpose other than to lend balance as he moves about. It is important to note, however, that in this aspect De Sang appears far clumsier than he actually is. In truth, he can move quite quickly as a hybrid.

Captain Andre de Sang

Maledictive Wererat, Chaotic Evil

Armor Class	6	Str	15
Movement	12	Dex	17
Level/Hit Dice	3+1	Con	14
Hit Points	19	Int	14
THAC0	17	Wis	12
Morale	12	Cha	10
No. of Attacks	1		
Damage/Attack	1d4 (bite) or 1d6 (cutlass)		
Special Attacks	Surprise and summon rats		
Special Defenses	Hit only by silver and +1 or better magical weapons		
Magic Resistance	Nil		

Background

Captain Andre de Sang was born to a family of seafarers on the high seas of another realm. They roamed the trade lanes, carrying cargo, transporting passengers, and otherwise living up to name of their caravel, the *Sea Gypsy*. By the time he was a teenager, De Sang had become a masterful sailor. He was happy in his lot and planned to continue with this life until the day he died. Fate, however, had other plans for him.

Shortly after De Sang's fifteenth birthday, *Sea Gypsy* was hailed by what seemed to be a naval warship. The ship signaled that it bore important news. Fearful that *Sea Gypsy* might have found herself caught in the midst of a war, De Sang's father struck his sails nevertheless and waited for the warship to come along side.

At the last instant, the approaching vessel lowered its flag and hoisted a pirates' banner. *Sea Gypsy's* captain and crew were caught completely unawares. The elder

De Sang signaled the other ship that *Sea Gypsy* would offer no resistance.

At first, it appeared that this was good enough for the pirates. They emptied *Sea Gypsy*'s hold, cleaned out the weapons locker, and helped themselves to anything else of value on board. That done, however, they then took axes to the ship's masts and knives to the sailcloth.

Most of *Sea Gypsy*'s crew was left to die aboard the crippled ship. But De Sang's mother and the half-dozen other women aboard were carried off, to serve as a harem for the pirates until a port could be found where they could sold, or their new masters lost interest in them.

Adrift without food, water, or other supplies, *Sea Gypsy*'s crew quickly began to perish. With each new death, the hope of rescue faded further. But lack of provisions was not the worst peril to beset the dying men.

Like all ships, *Sea Gypsy* had her compliment of rats. Without food stores to pilfer, they became emboldened. Soon it was necessary to post watches to prevent the rats from feeding upon on sleeping bodies.

In order to prolong the lives of the crew, De Sang's father made a difficult decision. By his order, the bodies of those who died were converted into rations for those who remained alive. Many of the hands cast themselves into the sea rather than become a party to cannibalism, but the worst of the horror was not that the living should sustain themselves on the flesh of their shipmates. Rather, it was that some concession must be made to the rats. To that end, a portion of each body was left in the hold—an offering to the rats who might otherwise have proved more deadly than the elements themselves.

Despite the time purchased by these measures, rescue did not come. In the end, with the death of his own father, Andre de Sang was the last survivor. No longer the light-hearted boy he had been when the corsairs struck, De Sang carried out his father's orders grimly. He butchered the captain's body, setting aside a portion for the rats, and began to count off the hours until he himself would become a meal for them.

Once the improvised provisions were exhausted, the rats again became dangerous and aggressive. De Sang was forced to battle them for his life. He took to sleeping in naps, constantly wary lest one of the filthy creatures should nip at his exposed flesh. When possible, he killed the rats, feeding on them as they had fed on his shipmates.

Days later, when the last of his stamina was spent, De Sang collapsed on the deck. It seemed the time had come for him to die.

When next he opened his eyes, however, De Sang found himself in a comfortable bed. His bites had been bandaged, and wholesome food waited nearby. *Sea Gypsy* had been spotted and salvaged by a passing carrack. His saviors took *Sea Gypsy* in tow, escorting both ship and her sole survivor to the nearest safe port.

Andre de Sang

Once there, they placed the boy in a sanitarium and turned his ship over to the harbormaster.

For several weeks the young man battled a violent brain fever. On more than one occasion, the healers despaired for his life. Once he came to himself, however, De Sang recovered quickly. Still, the ordeal had certainly changed him. No longer was he a young lad content with the life of a sailor. Now he longed only to find the men who had shattered his life and destroy them.

Unable to raise by legal means the money he needed to repair his beloved *Sea Gypsy,* De Sang agreed to smuggle illegal cargoes in order to secure patrons who could provide him with the necessary finances. Over the course of the next several years, the new captain became a most skilled smuggler. With a swift ship and loyal crew, he quickly amassed a fair amount of wealth.

Not a day passed, however, during which he failed to search for the pirates who had destroyed his family. Informants were paid, agents hired, and every resource applied to this task. Still, days became months became years with no sign of the villains. In an effort to find them, De Sang himself turned to raiding. Ships were halted, their cargoes seized, and their crews interrogated (even tortured) as his search for revenge became more frantic. In time, *Sea Gypsy* herself became the most dreaded ship to ply the waves.

ANDRE DE SANG

Finally, nearly a decade after he began his quest, De Sang found the lead he was looking for. He set sail at once and came upon his enemies unawares. Under the pretense of forming a brotherhood of pirates, he lured them into an ambush and took their ship with no more effort than that with which they had themselves claimed *Sea Gypsy*.

Rather than simply putting them to the sword, however, Captain de Sang vowed to see his prisoners suffer as he and his shipmates had. One at a time, the brigands were lashed to the deck. Then, as their peers were forced to watch, starving rats were released to feed upon the screaming prisoners.

As the captain of the pirates breathed his last—the man who had ordered *Sea Gypsy* crippled and its women stolen—he fixed De Sang with a terrible glare. Invoking the name of a malevolent sea god, he laid a venomous curse on his captor. "May the rats take you!" he hissed. De Sang laughed, thinking this nothing more than the idle threat of a helpless prisoner. Only in the months to follow would he realize its true import. By the time De Sang's vengeance was complete, a thick mist had risen around the ship. For many days, *Sea Gypsy* lay becalmed within these rolling vapors. When they finally parted, it was to reveal a brilliantly blue sea in an unknown land.

Their vengeance complete, De Sang and *Sea Gypsy* returned to a life of piracy. Soon they became infamous in all the ports bordering the Sea of Sorrows. The fact that he had now become every bit as vicious and sadistic as the men he destroyed was lost upon De Sang.

It quickly became apparent that the curse laid upon De Sang had indeed taken effect. Whenever he led his crew into battle, he would undergo a terrible transformation. The rats had indeed taken him, for he had become akin to them. Captain de Sang was now a wererat.

De Sang's transfigurations are not voluntary. Nor are those of his crew, all of whom are infected lycanthropes. So long as they stay aboard *Sea Gypsy,* they remain in their primary aspects. For De Sang, this means human form; for his crew, it means a form of hybrid rat-man. The moment that De Sang or his men leave their ship, they transform to their secondary aspect: De Sang to his hybrid form and his crewmen to huge (though not giant) rats.

Current Sketch

In the years since *Sea Gypsy* carried Captain de Sang into Ravenloft, his bestial nature has become more and more dominant. He has infected his entire crew with lycanthropy, so they are to a man wererats as he is. His crew is as corrupt and cruel as he (though not as fiendishly clever), and their loyalty to him is absolute.

Although he has avenged himself on the pirates who destroyed his life, De Sang now has a new goal. He fervently believes that his mother is still alive, and he has vowed to find her. The fact that he no longer sails the same seas he once did makes this virtually impossible, but he does not see this as the case. De Sang is convinced that his mother preceded him into this strange land and fate has carried him here that they might be reunited.

Personality

If there is a truly bloodthirsty pirate anywhere in Ravenloft, it is Captain Andre de Sang. He is a brutal man, savoring the pain he inflicts on his enemies before he tosses them to his crew.

Because he cannot leave his ship without undergoing the agonies of transfiguration, De Sang is denied the ability to move about in human society. The same is true of his crew, although they can go ashore as rats if there is a need to obtain information and the like. Although he is loath to admit this, De Sang feels this aspect of his curse very keenly, as it greatly hampers the search for his mother.

Combat

Captain de Sang lures his victims by setting *Sea Gypsy* adrift near the shipping lanes. When a vessel comes to investigate, he looses his crew upon them.

Human Aspect

When pressed into battle in his human aspect, De Sang tries to bring his pistol, Scorpion, into play, discharging it at the most dangerous foe he sees.

Scorpion is a snaplock pistol which has a speed factor of 6 (1 if it was ready to fire at the start of the round) and inflicts 1d8 points of damage. If the damage roll comes up an 8, the die is rolled again and the new result added to the previous total. This continues as long as the damage die rolls an 8. Short range for this weapon is 15 yards, medium is 30 yards, and long range is 45 yards.

After discharging his pistol, De Sang draws his cutlass. This blade inflicts 1d6 points of damage in his hands.

Hybrid Aspect

In his hybrid aspect, De Sang uses the same techniques described above. Both his pistol and cutlass are designed to be used in either his human or hybrid form.

When facing an unarmed or helpless opponent, however, De Sang generally attacks with tooth and claw. While this inflicts only 1d4 points of damage, he savors the terror that grips the victims of such attacks.

Sea Gypsy's Crew

The tactics used by De Sang's crewmembers depend upon the current situation. When defending *Sea Gypsy* against a boarding action or the like, they are always encountered in their hybrid aspects. In this case, they do battle with cutlasses and pistols, just as their leader does.

If De Sang's crewmen are attempting to board or take another ship, their lycanthropy forces them into the shape of huge rats, unable to use weapons in combat, of course. The following game statistics can be used for the crewmembers of *Sea Gypsy* when they are in rat form.

> **Wererat Crewman:** AC 7; MV 12, Sw 6; HD 1/2; hp 4 each; THAC0 20; #AT 1; Dmg 1d3; SA disease and lycanthropy; SD hit only by silver and +1 or better magical weapons; SZ T (2[FM] long); ML Elite (13–14); Int Low; AL CE; XP 120.
> Notes: Anyone bitten by one of these creatures has a 2% chance per point of damage inflicted of becoming a wererat. In addition, each bite has a 5% chance of infecting the victim with a horrible disease with the same effects as the fatal version of the *cause disease* spell.

FEAST OF THE RATS

his adventure can be set on any ocean, sea, or great lake. Although the locations given in De Sang's biography and the following scenario are specifically in Ravenloft, there's no reason that these events couldn't take place on Oerth, Faerûn, or any other world. Indeed, with a little work, they might even be set on the Silt Seas of Athas.

In running this adventure, the Dungeon Master should take full advantage of the nautical setting. Player characters at sea are isolated from normal society, beyond the reach of help from shore. They are in an environment that hems them in, preventing their escape from any calamity that might befall. Make sure to convey that sense of hazard to your players; don't let them act as if their characters are out for a simple pleasure cruise.

Introduction

The adventure can begin whenever the heroes are at sea. They might be voyaging from port to port with a valuable cargo in their hold, or perhaps they might be on some manner of military patrol. Theirs might be a mission of mercy or an exploratory expedition into unknown waters. They might own their ship, merely serve as crew, or simply be traveling as passengers. It is best, however, if their vessel visits more than one port along the way, so that the heroes can hear dark rumors of a ghost ship before they actually encounter De Sang's vessel.

For the purposes of this adventure, the ship upon which the characters are traveling is known as *Seafarer*. The Dungeon Master can change the name of the craft, of course, to suit the needs of the campaign.

Scene I: The Ghost Ship

Late one afternoon, the player characters' ship makes port at a new city. (Choose any seaside city you wish, near your group's current location.) Taking this opportunity to stretch their legs, the heroes go into town, perhaps hoping to make some purchases. Before long, they come to realize that something isn't right about this port city.

Entering the city, you begin to notice a certain grimness settled upon the locals. In previous ports you have visited, the townsfolk have been happy to talk with strangers, learn some news from afar, and trade fresh food and cool drinks for a sailor's coin. Here, however, people watch silently as you pass, a guarded expression in their eyes. When they think you are not looking, some even make a sign to ward away evil. Shopkeepers grunt prices if you ask but strangely don't try to talk up the value of their wares.

Strangely, the town itself doesn't seem to fit with the wariness of its inhabitants. The buildings are well constructed and gaily painted (though that paint could use touching up here and there). The people are as well dressed as any you have seen (though again, even the best of those clothes show some signs of wear). It seems as if a sudden poverty has settled upon the place.

Food and drink here are three times the cost of the last port of call. Worse, it is all pretty plain fare. There's nothing fancy for sale in this town, nor are these people willing to dicker. If the heroes try, they are met with a curt, "I've named my price; now pay it or go away!"

Wherever the heroes wander in this town, they are met with surliness (though not outright hostility). All the locals are touchy, as though their pride has been offended somehow. Perceptive player characters will note that, given the down-at-the-heels appearance of even the most prosperous buildings, the town is suffering from some sort of recent ill fortune. Equally clear, from the bearing of its citizens, is the fact that they aren't used to the situation, and that they resent it.

Charismatic player characters can discover the reason, if they are careful not to offend the townsfolk's pride. A friendly, commiserating comment goes a long way here. But offers of money for information, or any other ostentatious show of wealth, offends the locals' pride.

Assuming they are careful of the inhabitants' feelings, then, the heroes eventually hear the following tale from one of the local merchants in the trade square. Read this text aloud to your players.

"You're right in thinking this town's not always suffered such poverty." The merchant gazes about the market square, casting his memory back to better days. He absentmindedly draws a pipe from a pocket, clamps it between his teeth, and draws upon it. At the hiss of air through its empty bowl, he frowns, snapping out of his reverie, and puts the pipe away again.

"Until just this year, we've seen lots of sea trade all up and down this coast. Coin used to pour into our coffers, I can tell you. Our inns were always full of sailors making merry on shore leave.

"But now the sea has sent a wind of ill fortune blowing our way. One of our local ships, the Moondancer, *set sail from here early this spring, for a quick trip up the coast and back. But no sooner had it left than the mother of all storms broke loose—a last gasp from winter, I suppose. Nobody expected it.* Moondancer *was never heard from again. The captain's widow lives over yonder; you can see the house among the trees up on that hill..*

"Well, since that time, several other ships have gone missing, though the weather has been fine all along. Some folks say Moondancer *has become a ghost ship, and she prowls about the seas, preying upon vessels that rode out the storm safe in harbor. If you ask me, that's a load of nonsense. Still, it has put a crimp in the local business. We don't see a quarter the trade we used to. Your ship is the first to land here in a month. That's why the rest of the townsfolk are surly-like. They aren't used to hard times, and most of them think there's a curse hanging over all our heads."*

"I will tell you this: There's definitely something amiss out there among the waves. I'd be careful if I was you, the next time you sail."

Scene II: Sea Gypsy

For *Seafarer*, the visit to this port proved hardly worth the trouble. Little of the ship's cargo could be sold in town, and there was even less to buy in return. Even simple supplies were hard to come by. Fortunately, enough food and fresh water was available to carry the vessel to its next port of call.

Days pass, with fine weather. The crew goes about its duties smoothly. It is a fine time to be sailing, and spirits aboard the ship are high.

Then, late one afternoon, as the sun is sinking, *Seafarer's* lookout gives a sudden cry. Read the following text to the players.

"Ship on the horizon!" the lookout cries. As all eyes turn toward the west, where he points, a strange image comes to view.

The setting sun grows swollen and bloody as it sinks beneath the waves. Starkly superimposed upon it, magnified with the sun to enormous proportions, is the silhouette of a two-masted ship, with a man's shape hung upon the foremast, crucified.

Aboard Seafarer *several sailors gasp, and a murmur passes through the crew. Within the space of moments, the sun slips below the horizon, and the crucified image seems to sink along with it.*

Of a sudden, a chill evening breeze passes across the waters, and a mist begins to shroud Seafarer. *From the crew's muttering, it does not promise to be a happy night.*

Rumors fly among the crew members that night. Many suggest that the image was a visitation of the ghost ship they heard about in town. Others argue that the man on the mast might still be alive, and that it's every sailor's duty to come to the aid of a ship in distress. If there are wounded men aboard that vessel and *Seafarer* fails to render aid, then its crew is no better than murderers.

As the next morning dawns at last, the sun burns away the mists, and the other ship is revealed once again. But now it is much closer. Although the man on the mast hangs lifelessly, it can be seen that he is merely tied there. As no gulls are feeding upon him, it would seem that he is still alive! Assuming *Seafarer* moves closer to investigate, more details become evident concerning *Sea Gypsy*. Read the following text aloud.

As Seafarer *approaches the drifting ship, it becomes clear that there is no sign of movement aboard the vessel, which is being tossed to and fro by wind and wave alike.*

The bow of the ship has been carved in the likeness of a beautiful woman. Her dark hair and complexion combine with the bright colors of her clothes to mark her as a Vistani maiden. Her dark locks flow back to form the words Sea Gypsy *in a golden script.*

Curiously, there is neither sign of damage to the ship nor any indication of misfortune. Her sails are

carefully furled and tied, and her rigging is taut. There is only one thing missing from the mysterious Sea Gypsy: *her crew—all, that is, except the one man bound to the mainmast.*

If the heroes are to learn any more, they'll have to board the other ship. Depending upon the desired pacing of the adventure and the tastes of the players, the Dungeon Master can make this rendezvous as hazardous or as easy as he likes. Heavy waves may toss the two vessels, threatening to crash them together, or gentle winds may ease *Seafarer* to *Sea Gypsy's* side.

Once aboard *Sea Gypsy,* the heroes will probably want to rescue the hanging man before anything else. Climbing the mast, cutting him loose, and carrying him safely back to the deck is not an easy task. Several crewmembers step forth willingly to do this—those most at home in the rigging of a ship. While they go to work, the heroes can explore the rest of *Sea Gypsy,* seeking to learn what has become of its crew.

The man on the mast is, of course, Andre de Sang. He had his crew tie him there briefly the evening before, to serve as a lure, when he spotted *Seafarer* on the horizon. Just before dawn, he had them do so again. De Sang takes great pleasure in playing the part of a victim being rescued. While he delays his saviors aboard *Sea Gypsy* and the heroes go about exploring his ship, his crew slips overboard from the ship's hidden gun ports and swims to board *Seafarer.*

The following descriptive sections of boxed text are keyed by number to the map on page 17. The Dungeon Master should read each section aloud as the player characters enter that part of the ship. As they explore, especially once they are below decks, the DM should do everything possible to play up the tension. He might suggest that they feel that they are being watched, for example. Further, the motion of the ship might cause something to topple from a shelf, or a shadow might seem to move unnaturally when they enter a room. None of these encounters is legitimate, of course, but an empty ship will play tricks on anyone's mind.

1. Anchor & Capstan

At the bow of the mysterious ship, two heavy anchors hang from thick chains. The latter are wound evenly about sturdy capstans. Both are well maintained and show every indication of being ready to use at a moment's notice.

2. Masts

A pair of tall masts rise above the deck, each bearing furled sails. Atop each mast stands a crow's nest, from which a spider's web of rigging descends to the deck. These wooden spires creak with each gust of wind, and the rigging hums eerily, filling the air with a sound that serves only to magnify the unnatural silence aboard the vessel in the absence of her crew.

3. Cargo Hatches

Two large, wooden hatches dominate the center of the deck. These are worn around the edges, showing that they have often been removed for the loading and unloading of cargoes. Undogging these bulkheads would take some time, but there seems to be no reason why the holds could not be exposed within the space of an hour or so.

4. Ship's Wheel

If *Sea Gypsy's* crew had been aware that some misfortune was about to befall them, it might be reasonable to expect that they would have secured the ship's wheel. Oddly, this has not been done. As the vessel shifts to and fro in the waves, the wheel rotates freely. Leather lashes dangle from the framework that supports the wheel, indicating that only a few seconds of effort would have been required to check the ship's random movements. Yet no one took the time to do so.

5. Ship's Rudder

If a hero looks down, over the aft railing, it is clear that the rudder is intact and operating smoothly. Any movement from the wheel is instantly echoed by this heavy wooden construction, and vice versa.

6. Canvas and Rope

Coils of rope, bundles of canvas, and other important supplies are stored neatly in this room. Various tools are secured here as well. The air here is heavy with the smell of cloth and oiled rope, making the place feel extremely confining. Judging from the fact that this room is only about half full, it seems logical to assume that *Sea Gypsy* had been away from port for some time before her mishap.

7. Armory

The door to this room is locked tightly. If the heroes wish to enter it, they'll need to pick the lock, force the door, or otherwise bypass this safeguard. There is no trap on the door.

Racks of gleaming sabers and metal breast plates line the walls of this room. All told, there is enough equipment here to outfit 15 men for battle. A like number of snaplock rifles, each stored with a powder horn and pouch of shot, stands ready.

8. Brig

Like the armory (area 7), this door is locked though not trapped.

This room is appointed only with three uncomfortable looking bunks. Each of these has shackles anchored to it, making it clear that those who found their way into this room did not remain here voluntarily. Exactly why the *Sea Gypsy* would need such a place is difficult to imagine.

9. Officer's Cabin

These are well-appointed rooms that provide quarters to the ship's officers. A small writing desk folds out from the wall of each, opposite an equally tiny bed. A cedar chest stands in each as well, secured by a rather unimpressive lock.

There is nothing in these rooms to make the heroes suspicious, unless they notice what is missing. Although there are writing desks here, and each is stocked with quill, ink, and paper, none of *Sea Gypsy's* officers appears to have kept a journal of any sort. In fact, there doesn't seem to be so much as a letter or note in any of these rooms. Captain de Sang does not allow his officers to keep written records of their travels, for fear that they will fall into the wrong hands.

10. Captain's Cabin

There can be little doubt that this cabin belongs to *Sea Gypsy's* master. It is well appointed and seems as comfortable as possible for a shipboard cabin.

A writing desk is folded down from the wall, with a journal of some sort standing open upon it. A quill stands in an ink well next to it, as if the captain had just gotten up for a moment and expected to return promptly.

The discovery of this journal is all part of De Sang's plan, of course. If the heroes read through the journal they learn nothing of any importance. The records indicate that *Sea Gypsy* is a trading vessel that travels the Sea of Sorrows, carrying various cargoes from port to port. There is nothing to indicate that anything unusual ever happens aboard this ship. This in itself could be a cause for suspicion. After all, who ever heard of a ship, or any other business, in which everything always goes as expected. If anything marks this book as a work of fiction, that's it.

Reading the last entry in the book, the heroes find that the captain, whose name is clearly and properly recorded, was suddenly called to the deck. No reason is given for this summons, but it is clear from the writing that the captain didn't think anything of it.

11. Chart Room

The walls of this room are lined with shelves holding dozens of rolled parchment maps. One such chart is spread out on a table in the center of the room. It depicts the area in which the ship currently sails but shows the marks of many revisions. The charts are very detailed but are of little use because they depict the seas from De Sang's native realm. The map on the table shows De Sang's attempts to map the Sea of Sorrows, which is proving to be an impossible task. De Sang has drawn the western coastline of Lamordia, Dementlieu, and Mordent with some confidence. But the center of the map is a mess of islands sketched in, scratched out, and resketched in increasingly erratic lines, demonstrating his growing frustration with this mist-clad sea.

12. Magazine

A heavy latch and a sturdy lock secure this room. Getting into it requires the characters to pick the lock or, perhaps, the use of a bit of magic. There are no traps on the lock or door.

A bitter smell fills the air of this room, reminiscent of sulfur. The source of this odor is clear enough as the heroes notice several large kegs marked "black powder." Crates of cannon balls line one wall, making it clear that this ship is not without its defenses.

The most curious thing about this room is that the ship shows no indication of having cannons from the outside. *Sea Gypsy's* cannons are stored below decks, hidden behind hatches that are all but invisible from outside until they swing open. It's no wonder that the heroes didn't notice them as the two ships drew near each other.

13. Cannon

There are eight cannons secured in this hold, with half facing port and the rest bearing starboard. The muzzles of these deadly bombards face seemingly unbroken stretches of hull, but hinges show that the gun ports are very well concealed.

It doesn't take much imagination to hear the thunderous report of these cannons in the low, crowded confines of the ship. The smell of powder and hot iron seems to hang in the air here, even though the guns show no sign of having been fired in recent history.

Although *Sea Gypsy* is seldom called upon to use her guns, De Sang keeps them well maintained. On more than one occasion they've meant the difference between freedom and destruction for him, having been used to drive away both military pickets and other sea raiders.

Sea Gypsy

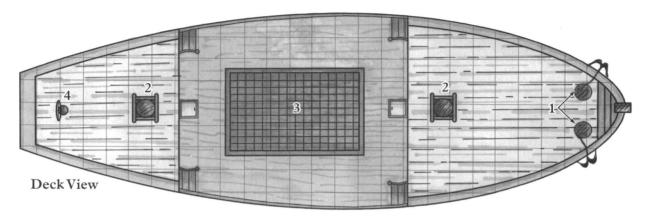

Deck View

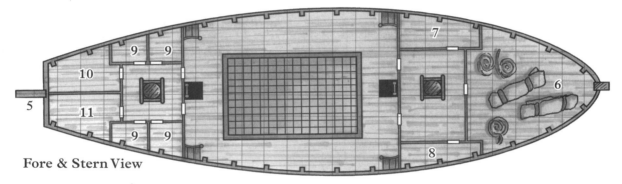

Fore & Stern View

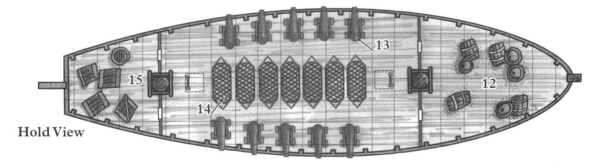

Hold View

1. Anchor and Capstan	6. Canvas and Rope	11. Chart Room
2. Mast	7. Armory	12. Magazine
3. Cargo Hatch	8. Brig	13. Cannons
4. Ship's Wheel	9. Officer's Cabin	14. Hammocks
5. Ship's Rudder	10. Captain's Cabin	15. Cargo Hold

14. Hammocks

Twenty-one hammocks are stretched across the hold, hanging three high between *Sea Gypsy's* cold metal cannons. A coarse blanket of gray wool is thrown or folded on each hammock, but it is impossible to say how long it has been since these beds were last slept in.

15. Cargo Hold

This section of the ship is clearly intended as a cargo hold. Kegs of fresh water stand in one corner, and a large wooden shelf holds tinned provisions. For all these stores, however, this room is still mostly empty. Clearly, *Sea Gypsy* was not carrying any cargo on its current voyage. Either that, or someone has removed it.

Scene III: Attack of the Rats

After the heroes have had a chance to explore the ship, at a time that seems dramatically appropriate, the Dungeon Master should launch the next part of the adventure. De Sang's crewmen, having found their way aboard *Seafarer,* are rousing that ship's rats to the attack.

Aboard Seafarer, *a sudden commotion is heard from the hold. It begins with the howling and spitting of the ship's cat, accompanied by an odd rustling noise. Suddenly, the cat comes bolting onto the main deck, bleeding from dozens of ragged wounds.*

Another cry of pain and agony is heard from below, but this time it is human. It is quickly matched by other shouts of alarm and fear. Scant seconds later, a bulkhead door bursts open and one of Seafarer's *crew staggers onto the deck. A dozen rats cling to his body, their jagged claws and teeth cutting bloody gashes in his flesh.*

Scores more rats follow onto the deck, chasing crewmen before them. In their midst are nearly twenty rats of exceptional size. They are bigger than the ship's cat! And they attack with a human cunning.

From his resting place on the deck of *Sea Gypsy,* De Sang watches the turmoil with barely concealed humor. He waits for everyone else aboard his ship to rush back to join the battle aboard *Seafarer,* then he follows, stabbing the rearmost sailor from behind. Then, giving a wild yell of battle lust, he leaps across the gap between the two vessels. Of course, the moment De Sang leaves his own vessel, he begins to transform into his hybrid aspect.

The supposed victim from Sea Gypsy *leaps, with a fierce grin on his face and a bloodied blade in one hand, headed for* Seafarer's *deck. But even as his foot leaves the rail of the other ship, he howls in apparent agony, his body wracking with convulsions. He hunches over in mid-leap, bones popping and shifting, then lands aboard* Seafarer *down on one knee. Before the horrified eyes of* Seafarer's *crew, coarse hair sprouts from his arms and face. His jaw stretches forward, as does his nose, the latter twitching as his eyes shrink and transform into tiny black orbs. His boots split, revealing the scaly feet of a giant rat, and a fleshy tail lashes out behind him.*

With a feral snarl, the beast draws a pistol and fires at the nearest member of Seafarer's *crew.*

Wrapping Things Up

The battle for *Seafarer* and *Sea Gypsy* can end in any number of ways. Of course, the Dungeon Master will certainly want to give the heroes every chance to triumph over their enemy. But really bad die rolls or poor planning on the part of the characters can make that impossible.

If the heroes do manage to triumph over the rats, they have at their disposal both vessels. At some point in the closing moments of battle, however, De Sang should be wounded and sent overboard. His body should be lost at this point, with the players free to assume that he is either dead or alive. One or more of his crewmen might go with him into the drink.

If the battle is going against the heroes, the PCs can attempt to flee in a long boat. Captain de Sang does not pursue them, being too busy overseeing the taking of *Seafarer.*

Recurrence

If the heroes have not defeated Captain de Sang, the dread pirate can return to torment them time and again later. Any ocean voyage can serve as an excuse to bring *Sea Gypsy* out of a fog bank. (The same is true, of course, if the dread pirate was defeated but not slain.)

If the heroes destroyed Captain de Sang, he could return as the master of a ghost ship. This craft, which is swarming with spectral rats, sails the Sea of Sorrows in search of vengeance upon those who laid him low. Being pursued by their own private ghost ship is certain to excite any player character!

Cenors are noble, pure and heroic and get the soprano, if she has not tragically expired before the final curtain. But baritones are born villains in opera.

—Leonard Warren
New York World-Telegram and Sun

BIOGRAPHY

 ngel Pajaro plays supporting roles at the venerable Port-a-Lucine Opera House in Dementlieu. Although she is a favorite among male patrons and critics, her singing is not the equal to that of Maria Diosa, diva of the company. Angel longs to replace Maria, whose father owns the theater, and she has undertaken a nefarious plan to do so. The fact that Maria and others may have to die in order for Angel to fulfill her dreams is of no consequence to her.

Appearance

Most of the world knows Angel Pajaro as a stunningly beautiful elf maiden with exotic features. She is tall and statuesque, with perfectly formed features combining the full lips of a human beauty with the almond eyes and delicate angles of elvish grace. Her smile is dazzling, if somewhat predatory, and her hair hangs in waves of silvery tresses to her waist.

Around the opera house, Angel is as likely to be caught in costume as any other garb. Thus, her wardrobe varies drastically depending upon the opera currently under production. Outside of the theater, she always wears clothes of elegant design, favoring white and silver fabrics accented with reds and greens. Although her attire is never less than exquisite, it is always a bit more provocative than modesty might dictate. Many a married man has suffered a stormy argument at home after an evening of glances in Angel's direction. Angel is well aware of her effect on such men, and she delights in the trouble it creates.

In her hybrid, or *vixen,* aspect, Angel appears as a mixture of elf woman and silver-haired fox. In this form she seems slightly shorter because of a tendency to stoop forward. In addition to the pointed ears and long snout of a fox, Angel sports a bushy tail in this shape.

Angel's tertiary aspect is that of a large, silver-haired fox. Other than this exotic coloring, she appears to be a normal fox in this form. Her great speed and the glow of intelligence in her eyes, however, are clues that there is something unusual about this animal.

Angel Pajaro

Pathologic Werefox, Chaotic Evil Half-elf

Armor Class	2, 4, or 6	Str	14
Movement	24, 18, or 12	Dex	17
Level/Hit Dice	8+1	Con	14
Hit Points	65	Int	14
THAC0	13	Wis	12
Morale	13	Cha	20
No. of Attacks	1		
Damage/Attack	1d2 (fox's bite) or 2d6 (vixen's bite) or 1d4 (silver dagger)		
Special Attacks	Charm and wizard spells, poisoned dagger		
Special Defenses	Silver or +1 or better magical weapon to hit		
Magic Resistance	90% to *sleep* and *charm* spells		

Angel Pajaro

Background

Angel Pajaro was born to a family of entertainers in Kartakass. Like many folk in that domain, she was blessed with a love of music and an extra share of talent.

Angel's father, Pietro, was a handsome and talented singer and masterful teller of tales, quite popular with the ladies even after he took a bride. He met his wife, Ellestra, while the two were both performing at a festival. While Pietro professed a strong love for his bride, the sizable dowry she brought certainly made her more appealing.

Eventually, Pietro's wandering eye came to rest upon a beauty who called herself only Karino, a traveler from another land who claimed to be merely passing through Kartakass. Karino seduced the more-than-willing Pietro, then threatened to reveal his infidelity to Ellestra. The price for her silence was Angel.

Reluctant to give up his daughter but unwilling to lose his comfortable life style should his indiscretions be revealed, Pietro agreed. With the next dawn, Angel was gone. Pietro acted the role of an anguished father at first, but soon returned to his previous ways.

Angel grew up under the protection and tutelage of Karino, a foxwoman. She soon embraced her new life and the powers that came with her own rebirth as a werebeast. She remembers her parents with disdain, for Karino made sure that she knew the circumstances of her "adoption." Over the years, she began to think of humans in general, and men in particular, as mere playthings for her pleasure.

In time, Angel left Karino and made her way to the city of Port-a-Lucine. Like all her wanton kind, she hungered for nothing so much as the adoration of men and the gratification of her ego. Moving like a predatory shark through the sea of humanity in this city, she took many lovers, all of whom ended up as meals when her fleeting interest in them had passed.

Angel's childhood fascination with music and theater was reborn when she took an apartment near the famed Port-a-Lucine Opera House. A talented singer by any measure, she would have been able to join the opera company even without her ability to *charm* males.

Her ego led her to assume that she would become the diva in no time. What Angel did not anticipate, however, was the fact that the current diva, Maria Diosa, was truly a legendary performer. That Maria's father, Ricard, was the owner of the opera house further prevented Angel from ascendance. The pride and love of Ricard for his only daughter allowed him to resist Angel's charms. The foxwoman found this resistance a new, and intolerable, experience. Unwilling to admit defeat in this matter, she began to hatch a fiendish plan.

Almost since the day the opera house was built, rumors had circulated that a ghost haunted it. Ricard found the idea amusing, believing that it lent an even more dramatic air to the building. But Angel decided to use the story to her benefit. Through magic, she would make the haunting seem both real and dangerous. Her plan would culminate in the tragic death of Maria Diosa, leaving the path clear for her own ascension as diva.

Current Sketch

Angel is a vain and bitter woman, possessed of a fiery temper that can be used against her. It is her belief that no man can resist her charms. With the exception of Ricard Diosa, she has always been proved right.

Angel will let nothing stand in the way of her becoming diva. She is aware, however, that the sudden death of Maria Diosa might be blamed on her, as Diosa's chief rival. So she works carefully to disguise her true nature. In public, she takes care to praise the voice and talents of Maria Diosa. She also reins in her vampish tendencies unless she is alone with someone she intends to either enslave or devour. She does her best to appear delicate and gentile. Only in moments of stress or passion does her disguise slip.

Combat

Angel Pajaro is a spiteful, cunning, and deadly opponent. In all forms, she has infravision that allows her to see heat sources at a distance of up to 60 feet. Only silver and +1 or better magical weapons can harm her.

Elf Maiden Aspect

When in the form of an elf maiden, Angel uses a thin-bladed, silver dagger that inflicts 1d3 points of damage. Occasionally she coats the blade in a deadly poison (Immediate/Death/0) made from nightshade, belladonna, and monk's hood.

Angel's incredible beauty has the same effect as a *charm* spell and automatically affects all males with a Wisdom score of 13 or less. (Males with a higher Wisdom score are not affected, though they still find her a most enchanting woman.) Although this *charm* is not magical, it can be countered in like fashion as the *charm* spell.

In elf maiden form, Angel has the ability to cast spells as a 4th-level wizard. Her spells are primarily from the schools of Enchantment/Charm and Illusion/Phantasm. She normally has memorized *blur, improved phantasmal force, phantasmal force, spook,* and *scare.*

As an elf maiden, Angel has a Movement Rate of 12 and an Armor Class of 6. She also has the normal advantages of an elf, including a +1 bonus with bows and swords and a 90% resistance to *sleep* and *charm* spells.

Vixen Aspect

In her vixen (hybrid) form, Angel is a dangerous opponent. Her bite inflicts 2d6 points of damage. Human or elven women who lose half or more of their hit points to her bite, if not slain, become werefoxes in three days. This can be prevented if a priest of at least 12th-level casts a *cure disease* and *remove curse* spell, by a ranger's ability to cure lycanthropy, or by other means the DM deems appropriate. Females of other races and males cannot contract lycanthropy from a werefox.

In vixen form, Angel has a Movement Rate of 18 and an Armor Class of 4.

Silver Fox Aspect

As a silver-haired fox, Angel attacks by biting her enemies. She inflicts only 1d2 points of damage with her jaws, and she cannot transmit lycanthropy. In this form, Angel has a movement rate of 24. This gives her an excellent Armor Class of 2 and enables her to move through underbrush and the like without being detected 90% of the time. While in this aspect, she is treated as if benefiting from a *pass without trace* spell.

A Night at the Opera

This adventure brings the heroes to the great opera house in Port-a-Lucine, at the point where Angel Pajaro's plan to destroy Maria Diosa is at its zenith. If they are quick and cunning, they can thwart the actions of the werefox and save the life of a very talented diva. If they fail, they will almost certainly be lucky to escape with their lives.

Introduction

While the adventure is set in the city of Port-a-Lucine, it could just as easily be moved to any major city known for its culture and cosmopolitan atmosphere. How or why the heroes are in this city is unimportant. It is probably best, however, that they begin the scenario between adventures, so that no pressing business hangs over their heads.

There is an intentional similarity between the situation in this adventure and the traditional story of the *Phantom of the Opera*. The major difference, of course, is that there is no "phantom" seeking to elevate the young star above the established diva. Instead, Angel is behind the events herself. The Dungeon Master's task is to lead the player characters to believe in a hidden agent. If their energies are focused upon discovering that third party, they will not be likely to suspect Angel until late in the game, if at all. Thus, when the truth of the matter is revealed, it should come as quite a shock to the players.

Scene I: Accidents Will Happen

The player characters are initially drawn into this adventure by a simple twist of fate. It just so happens that as they are wandering through the streets of the great city, an accident occurs that very nearly claims the life of Maria Diosa and her father before their very eyes. Read the following text aloud to the players.

A gentle snow flutters down from the sky, drifting to and fro in the gentlest of breezes. Street lamps illuminate the white flakes, filling the air with a wash of sparkling stars. Well-dressed people move about, bundled in warm clothes. Their voices and laughter seem hushed by the soft beauty of the falling snow.

Out of the corner of your eye, you notice that this tranquillity is suddenly threatened. A large carriage, drawn by a pair of strong horses, is thundering down the street. No one else around seems yet to have noticed the renegade vehicle, particularly not the wealthy looking man and woman who have stepped into the street in front of it.

It is assumed that the player characters will take some sort of action to save the couple—Maria Diosa and her father—from being injured or killed. The Dungeon Master must adjudicate exactly how successful the action turns out to be.

A quick and clever plan, matched with a good die roll, should result in the heroes saving the Diosas without any injury to anyone. A somewhat less auspicious outcome might see Maria spared any injury, while her father is bruised and shaken, and one or more player characters suffer a broken arm or similar wound.

If the heroes delay too long, or otherwise foul up this encounter, the couple can still be saved, but both the heroes involved and Ricard Diosa should receive some fairly major injury. The damage should not be life threatening, but it ought to throw a kink in the actions of the party. A broken leg (or two) certainly qualifies.

Should the heroes opt to do nothing at all, they see Mister Diosa notice the carriage at the last second. Pushing his daughter clear, he is run down and mortally wounded. Only the quick use of healing magic can save his life. Presumably, the heroes will supply such spells. If they fail to help the couple and then don't even provide care after the injury, one has to wonder why they consider themselves heroes at all.

In any case, the end result of the encounter should be to introduce the Diosas and put them somewhat in the heroes' debt. While Maria behaves haughtily, acting every bit the prima donna, her father acts more politely.

As a reward for their efforts, he offers the heroes passes to the opera for that night.

Scene II: The Show Must Go On

Depending upon the reactions of the heroes to a the prospect of a night at the opera, the Dungeon Master can play this scene as either a great privilege or a toilsome hardship. If they demonstrate a clear dislike of such theater, then it can be looked upon as something to be endured rather than something to be enjoyed.

The fact that the seats provided are among the best in the theater, however, should make the invitation tempting to even the most scornful of player characters. If this still isn't enough to make them want to attend, remind them of the beauty and fame of both Maria Diosa and the young Angel Pajaro.

Once the heroes arrive for the performance, they discover that the opera house is truly a grand place. The building is ornate, richly decorated, and well designed. The seats are comfortable and the acoustics splendid. If the heroes are even the least bit cultured, they should have the time of their lives as the show unfolds before them.

About half way through the performance, however, a most macabre thing happens. Read the following aloud.

The opera, which tells the story of a young princess who gives up her heritage to marry a handsome beggar, is a wonderful affair. Maria Diosa, the diva, is one of the most talented singers you have ever heard. The other members of the cast are nearly as splendid, and one of the other performers, a young elf maiden with silvery-white hair, is perhaps the most ravishing woman you have ever seen.

As Maria Diosa takes the stage alone and begins to sing her aria, however, a frightening transformation falls over the theater. As one, the stage lights are extinguished, plunging the opera house into an eerie twilight. Then, as if from nowhere, a cold and commanding voice fills the air with chilling speech:

"People of Port-a-Lucine, mark my words. For as long as Maria Diosa continues to profane this stage with her pitiful performances, the opera house will be a place of death. You have heard my words of doom, now learn them to be true!"

While the echoes of this threat yet hang in the air, an ominous groan of tortured metal echoes through the near-darkness. High above the audience, a great chandelier—one of three that provides light to the opera house—now hangs at a peculiar angle, swinging slightly back and forth. One of the three chains by which it was supported has broken. From the groaning sound, it seems that the other two are about to give way as well!

Although the player characters are not in any direct danger from this looming disaster (they are in a box and the chandelier hangs above the floor seating), if they wish to minimize the danger to those below, they must act quickly. Even then, they likely won't be able to save absolutely everyone below from harm. But any action they take to lessen the extent of this disaster is recognized.

Scene III: A Plea for Help

Following the accident at the opera house, Ricard Diosa requests that the player characters come speak with him privately. Once they are gathered in his office, he begins by thanking them for their efforts and acknowledges that he is, once again, in their debt. With these formalities out of the way, he then relates to them the story of the opera house's resident ghost, and he asks for their help in defeating it. The story he tells is as follows:

"For as long as the opera house has stood, there have been rumors of a ghost. To this point, these stories have been harmless, and they may even have helped business.

"I, for one, never believed these tales. I've owned the opera house for almost a decade and have seen no evidence of anything supernatural associated with it. At least, that was the case until a month ago.

"When last the moon was new, the voice you heard tonight spoke for the first time. It promised that death and destruction would visit the opera house if my daughter, Maria, was not removed from the company. I was given until the moon was new again—one month—to comply.

"I had the company search the building high and low, but we found no sign of the speaker, no clue as to who he might be. Some among the troupe murmured of a haunting, but I forbade them to speak in that way. I told them it must be the work of a prankster. To give credence to his words would be to encourage further mischief.

"Since that time, I have kept an eye open for signs of our 'ghost,' seeking to reveal the culprit behind the affair. Until tonight, there had been no further signs. I had almost begun to hope that the matter was closed.

"Now that a tragedy has occurred, I must take serious action. I hesitate to presume, and yet my need is great. Will you help me to discover the truth behind this matter?"

Presumably, the heroes accept this request and begin an investigation of the matter at once. If they seem reluctant to do so, Ricard Diosa is more than willing to pay for their aid. (In fact, he'll insist on doing so even if they volunteer their help freely). He is a wealthy man, with much influence in Port-a-Lucine, and can well afford to pay for their aid. Further, to count themselves among his friends will do well for the PCs in the future.

Scene IV: The Investigation

Exactly what the heroes learn over the course of the next few days and nights depends upon the actions they take. The Dungeon Master should play these scenes by ear, using the following guidelines to resolve matters.

The Chandelier

An examination of the fallen chandelier reveals that its collapse was no accident. The bolts that held it in place were cut through. This sabotage was done from a crawlspace above the auditorium and required a person of above average strength with a good pair of cutters. If the theater is haunted, the ghost is a particularly material one.

The Stage Lights

Exactly what caused these to be extinguished is not clear. In actuality, Angel used her magical powers for this trick (just as she did for the voice). Unless the heroes have some way of determining this, however, they find this avenue of investigation a dead end.

Ricard Diosa

Most of what Ricard Diosa has to say has been covered above. He puts no stock in the idea of a ghost and can offer no reason for recent events. He is somewhat blind to the fact that his daughter is more than a bit snobbish and rude. She is the apple of his eye and he won't tolerate anything said against her.

If the matter comes up of who would replace Maria should something happen to her, Ricard does not hesitate in his answer. Only Angel Pajaro has the talent to replace his daughter. She is such a sweet thing, however, that it is impossible for him to believe that she has anything to do with "the ghost."

Maria Diosa

Maria Diosa treats the heroes with a minimum of politeness and spends as little time answering their

questions as possible. She clearly considers them to be beneath her and wants nothing to do with their investigation.

If asked who she believes is responsible for the threats and mayhem at the opera house, Maria wastes no time in accusing Jean Pierre Cambier. He plays the male lead in their current production, she says, and he is quite madly in love with Angel Pajaro. (This infatuation is due to Angel's magical and nonmagical charms). Maria believes that Jean Pierre would wish to see Angel replace her as the opera house's star. (Questions asked of other company members reveal that Jean Pierre and Maria Diosa used to be lovers. Their relationship ended very shortly after Angel came to the opera house.)

As for Angel, Maria thinks of her as a sweet young thing who has some talent, but who gets by primarily on her looks. She would probably think even less of the beautiful elf maiden, but Angel is always praising the diva's talent. Consequently, Maria does not blame Angel for stealing Jean Pierre away from her. Rather, she considers the young man a woman-chasing fool who didn't realize when he had a good thing.

Jean Pierre Cambier

Jean Pierre has been with the Port-a-Lucine company for just over four years. He is a talented, handsome man who has left a trail of broken hearts in his wake. In many ways, he is exactly the woman chaser that Maria believes him to be. Currently, however, his eye does not wander from Angel. Her magical power binds him tightly, and his loyalty to her is absolute. The rest of the company and crew view this sudden fidelity as evidence that Jean Pierre has finally found the right woman.

Jean Pierre is arrogant and self-impressed but willing to deal with the player characters. He treats them as fans, however, making the assumption that they are constantly in awe of his good looks, talent, and very presence. This sort of treatment can get old very quickly, but that's the way he treats everyone.

If asked who he blames for the "accident" and threats, Jean Pierre considers the matter for a moment and then points his finger at Maria's father. It's no secret that the opera's patronage has fallen off over the last few years. Almost certainly, this is an attempt to restore the theater to the forefront of the public's mind and to lure those with a morbid curiosity back into the seats. "After all," Jean Pierre asserts, "they say that any publicity is good publicity. Who wouldn't want to see a bunch of theatergoers get killed?"

Angel Pajaro

When the heroes approach Angel, she assumes the mask of a polite, almost shy, woman. She answers all their questions without seeming to accuse anyone else of being involved with recent events. She says she is certain that Maria Diosa and her father are innocent, and she praises both of them to some extent. If asked about Jean Pierre Cambier and her relationship with him, Angel blushes prettily and acts the part of a young maiden caught up in her first true love.

Angel takes steps to support the idea that there is a ghost in the theater, although she won't directly say so. If she believes that the heroes are starting to suspect one of the other members of the cast, she'll try to lead them back to the idea of a haunting. After all, she wishes to be the star of the show, and a major scandal could close the whole place down.

The Cast and Crew

Interviews with the rest of the cast and crew can be used by the Dungeon Master to sew confusion and mystery. A few other NPCs, all of whom are minor players in the company or who work as stage hands, can lead the heroes on any number of wild goose chases.

Along the way, these misadventures should begin to reveal to the heroes that Angel is not the blushing innocent she seems to be. It should become apparent that she has seduced more than a few of the men in the opera house. Further, it quickly becomes obvious that anyone who speaks against her is treading on thin ice with the rest of the troupe. The speed with which everyone else comes to her defense ought to provide an indication that all is not what it seems to be.

Other Accidents

As the heroes are conducting their investigation, which is assumed to take several days, the Dungeon Master should toss a few accidents in their way. These might include falling sandbags, fires in their hotel rooms, or even "accidental" gunshots during a re-hearsal. All in all, however, these mishaps should be of a physical nature and offer no indication of the super-natural. The intended purpose of these events, from Angel's standpoint, is to discourage the heroes from investigating any further into the mystery at the opera house. Of course, this discouragement is certain to fail, player characters being the stubborn creatures that they are.

At the same time, more macabre events also begin to manifest themselves around the theater. These include shadowy shapes, spectral lights, and similarly eerie visitations. The Dungeon Master should use care in detailing these, however, for they must all be the sorts of things that Angel's magic could accomplish. The purpose of these events is to put even more of a scare into the members of the theatre company, which in turn puts pressure upon Ricard Diosa to give into the "spectral" demands.

Scene VI: Lair of the Ghost!

Eventually the player characters should come to suspect that something is not quite right about Angel Pajaro. If they decide to search her dressing room, a careful inspection reveals a sliding panel in the wall beneath her makeup table, leading into a set of forgotten catacombs below the opera house. It is here that the foxwoman has made her lair.

Assuming that the heroes decide to investigate the catacombs, they find a virtual labyrinth of tunnels. The walls are lined with burial niches, holding the bones of people from long years ago. If the party is yet unsure as to whether the opera house is haunted, it would not be at all difficult to believe that more than one ghost dwells in this subterranean maze, any one of which might be offended at having a busy theatre built atop its resting place.

Proceeding further, the heroes discover alcoves and side passages where bones litter the floor in untidy piles. A clever character may note that all of these bones are relatively fresh compared to those in the niches. Worse, they are show signs of having been chewed by very sharp teeth, and many of them have been cracked and their marrow sucked out. Although the party has no way of knowing it at present, these are the remains of some of Angel's more recent victims.

A few minutes later, the heroes catch a glimpse of a pale figure flitting through the tunnels ahead. Given the setting, they might assume this to be a ghost. In actuality, it is Angel in her vixen aspect. Spotting the player characters in turn, she flees at once, attempting to escape before she is recognized. She uses her magic as needed to conceal her identity from the group.

What happens next depends upon what the heroes decide to do. If they pursue Angel, she leads them on a merry chase—merry for her, that is. Because she knows the catacombs well, she is able to lure the party into hazardous stretches where walls collapse upon them, floors give way beneath their feet, and bats, snakes, and spiders swarm. (The DM should set the deadliness of these encounters to suit the abilities of the party.) While the party is occupied with these hazards, Angel herself attacks without warning, then flees before the group can retaliate. If events turn against her, Angel tries to escape back to the opera house, using what magic she has left and her superior speed.

Crafty groups of heroes might choose to avoid pursuing this elusive figure, deciding instead to exit the tunnels and guard the entrance to Angel's dressing room while sending someone for help. Angel is forced to attack these heroes to avoid being trapped in the tunnels and hunted down by a mob of locals. When it comes, her attack is calculated and savage. Then, at the first opportunity, she flees the opera house, convinced that there is little time before reinforcements arrive.

If this battle ends with the death of Angel, the heroes learn the her identity when she reverts to elf maiden form. Even if she survives this battle, her secret may be out. Unless she manages to kill the entire party of heroes, she knows that they will report what they have seen, and a scholarly friend of Ricard Diosa will make the connection between werefox and elf maiden. Convinced that her secret is soon to be revealed, then, Angel flees into the night, away from the city. The "haunting" of the opera house is ended.

Recurrence

Although her efforts to destroy Maria Diosa come to an end after the battle in the tunnel, Angel can still return to torment the heroes again (assuming that she wasn't killed).

Once she has put a safe distance between herself and the opera house, Angel certainly swears to avenge herself on the heroes. Convinced that success was within her grasp, she blames their meddling for her failure.

Through the use of magical spells like *change self*, she'll return to the heroes at a later date and try to win over one of the male characters. In this form, she can be introduced by the Dungeon Master as a minor love interest. After several adventures, during which she is of genuine assistance to the heroes, her true nature will be revealed. Angel will pick the moment when the group least expects to be betrayed, and can least afford it. Only in this way can she gain satisfaction against these heroes.

RADJIFF CHANDOR

There is a passion for hunting something deeply implanted in the human breast.

—Charles Dickens
Oliver Twist

BIOGRAPHY

 adjiff was born a normal baby in the domain of Sri Raji, a land recently assimilated into the Steaming Lands Cluster. He grew to adulthood in the city of Muladi, learning the craft of hunting from his father, Jahmid. Now that he has become a werebeast, he uses those skills to hunt the most dangerous quarry in all the world: human beings!

Appearance

Radjiff has only two aspects: the form of a normal man and the shape of a great tiger. He does not have the ability to become a hybrid.

In his human aspect, Radjiff appears small and timid. His features are friendly, but his watery brown eyes give the impression of a man lacking in courage. His mouth is slender, with jagged teeth that give him a crooked, almost comical smile. All in all, Radjiff is the sort of man that many dismiss without a second thought. A member of the *Vaishya,* Sri Raji's lowest cast, Radjiff wears drab gray robes that, in addition to marking him as a man of little importance, allow him to transform without interference.

In his tiger aspect, Radjiff is a nearly nine feet long and every bit the nightmare of the jungle. His dangerous claws and keen emerald eyes make his a deadly hunter and dangerous opponent.

The only jewelry or ornamentation that Radjiff wears is a large gold loop in his right ear. This brightly polished trinket is a relic of his departed wife. This ring remains in either aspect, unaffected by the transfiguration process.

Radjiff Chandor

Maledictive Weretiger, Chaotic Evil

Armor Class	3	Str	12
Movement	12	Dex	17
Level/Hit Dice	6+2	Con	10
Hit Points	42	Int	18
THAC0	15	Wis	17
Morale	14	Cha	10
No. of Attacks	1 (human form) or 3 (hybrid form)		
Damage/Attack	By weapon (1d6) or 1d4+1/1d4+1 (claws) and 1d12 (bite)		
Special Attacks	Rear claw rake (1d4+1/1d4+1)		
Special Defenses	Hit only by silver and +1 or better magical weapons		
Magic Resistance	Nil		

Background

Radjiff was born in the city of Muladi, Sri Raji. Like many members of the Vaishya, he had little or no health care and suffered greatly from the plagues that periodically swept in from the jungles to torment the poor.

His father pushed him to learn the huntsman's craft, although it was not one that came easily to Radjiff. By the time he became an adult, however, by sheer determination he had learned to be a skilled hunter. While his frail health still persisted, his keen mind more than made up for any physical shortcomings. By age 18, he was considered the shrewdest hunter in all of Sri Raji. No beast, not even the mighty tiger, could escape him.

Radjiff's life was more or less a happy one for many years. His parents had arranged his marriage to Meedga, a young woman who proved a good and loving wife. She

Radjiff Chandor

bore him two sons and he earned a comfortable living by leading hunting expeditions and acting as a guide for occasional explorers of the Sri Raji's steaming jungles.

In time, however, Radjiff began to tire of his profession. His skills had become so great that nothing in the jungle presented him with any challenge. Even as the numbing hand of despair gripped him, however, a new quarry came to his attention.

His discovery came when a woman hired him to track down and capture a fugitive named Jahed. What he was not told about this task, however, was that his patron was a priestess of Kali in the service of Arijani, the Dark Lord of Sri Raji, and that Jahed was the leader of a secret society known as the Stalkers. Only when he found his quarry did Radjiff learn that one vital fact had been denied him: Jahed and his companions were weretigers.

Radjiff managed to escape the Stalkers, but he was badly wounded. He spent the next few weeks hiding in the jungles to recover. Once he returned home, however, he found that the Stalkers had exacted their revenge. What remained of his beloved wife and two young sons was barely enough to identify and bury.

Between his injuries and this mental shock, the huntsman was nearly driven mad. He eventually wound up at the temple of Rudri on the shores of Lake Veda, although how he came there he could not recall.

The temple priests nursed him back to health and kept him hidden. Both the Dark Sisters—who believed Radjiff had failed them—and the Stalkers—who hated him as an enemy—now hunted him. If it were not for the temple's protection, Radjiff's life would surely have been lost.

While the followers of Rudri were able to restore Radjiff's body to health, they could do nothing for his tormented spirit. By the time he was ready to leave them, Radjiff was a bitter man, determined to take his revenge on both the Dark Sisters and Stalkers.

Upon leaving the temple, Radjiff discovered that his encounter with the Stalkers had left him profoundly changed. As he was hunting for an evening meal, his heart began to hammer in his chest. He cried out in pain as his body seemed to be tearing itself apart. At that point, he lost consciousness. Hours later, when he awoke, Radjiff found that he was covered in blood. The half-eaten body of a wild ape lie on the ground beside him. From that day forward, a similar fate befell him whenever he hunted.

In time, Radjiff was able to reason out that the injuries he sustained at the hands of the Stalkers had left him like them. At first, this was a revolting thought. But in time he began to savor the power and exhilaration that came with his new form. It is now impossible for Radjiff to hunt anything, even a rabbit, without assuming his tiger aspect.

Current Sketch

Radjiff has made a home deep in the jungles of Sri Raji along the banks of the East Damuhm River. He has assembled a menagerie of deadly animals in the wilderness around his home, making this by far the most hostile part of the Sri Rajian jungles.

When he is not actively working against the interests of the Dark Sisters and the Stalkers, Radjiff hones his hunting skills in the jungle. At times, he lures adventurers into his lands and then hunts them himself. When he is able to capture one of the Dark Sisters or Stalkers, he brings them back to his home and then allows them to "escape." The hunt that follows invariably ends up with the death of his quarry and a temporary feeling of victory over the people who directly or indirectly destroyed his family.

Personality

Beneath his innocuous exterior, Radjiff is constantly sizing up those around him, viewing them as potential prey. Radjiff recognizes that he does not look the part of a great hunter. This mild and unassuming appearance, however, makes him even more dangerous.

Combat

Radjiff never assumes his tiger aspect until he is about to begin hunting. In other words, he does not transform at the beginning of combat; it is the anticipation of the chase and kill which triggers his change. If his enemy should turn and flee, however, Radjiff may well assume his hunting form.

In either of his forms, Radjiff can be hit only by silver weapons or those with a magical enchantment of +1 or better. In addition, he has keen night vision that allows him to see as well by the moon's glow as normal men do in full sunlight. His senses of hearing and smell are also acute; it is possible to surprise Radjiff only on a roll of 1.

Human Aspect

While in human form, Radjiff favors crossbow and scimitar. He is so highly skilled with both that each receives a +1 bonus to its attack roll. This does not, however, qualify them as magical weapons or enable them to strike what normal weapons could not harm.

Even an unarmed Radjiff can be very dangerous. Despite his slender frame, his punches are extremely powerful. This enables him to strike twice in a given round, inflicting 1d4 points of damage with each blow that finds its mark.

Radjiff is also skilled at setting wilderness traps. The jungle around his home is filled with spiked pits, concealed nets, and the like. As a rule, these are designed to capture or incapacitate. Radjiff prefers to make the kill in person.

Sometimes Radjiff uses a paralyzing toxin that he brews from jungle fruits and snake venom, then applies to blowgun darts. Anyone hit by one must make a saving throw vs. poison. Success indicates that the victim is unaffected. Failure causes the victim to collapse in one round. Although aware of all that transpires around him, the victim cannot take any action, including speaking, for a time. These effects wear off after a number of minutes equal to 60 minus the victim's Constitution score.

Tiger Aspect

Radjiff begins any attack in tiger form by striking with his front claws. This deadly pair of attacks inflicts 1d4+1 points of damage each. He can also bite for 1d12 more points of damage. On any round in which both front claw attacks hit, he can also to rake with his rear claws. Each of these attacks inflicts another 1d4+1 points of damage.

HUNTER AND HUNTED

 his adventure casts the heroes as members of a dangerous expedition into the jungles of Sri Raji. If the scenario is placed in another campaign setting, any region of tropical jungles will serve nicely.

Introduction

The adventure begins when the heroes are invited to join Raja Mahanda Gee, a minor nobleman of Sri Raji, on a hunting expedition. He has heard tales of a great tiger who stalks the banks of the East Damuhm. It is his desire to find this beast, kill it cleanly, and return home with the hide as a trophy. Unfortunately, there are three important facts of which the heroes and their host are unaware as the adventure begins.

The first is that the beast they are hunting is none other than Radjiff Chandor, who is not only a weretiger but also a master huntsman himself. No matter how well things go during the start of this adventure, the PCs are almost certain to end up in a face-to-face encounter with that deadly predator by adventure's end.

The second fact, of equal importance, is that the unwitting raja is acting under the influence of the *Dark Sisters*. This secret society has long desired Chandor's death and is using Mahanda as a weapon against him. The raja's advisor, a slender woman named Tomor Ahmanja, is a member of that clandestine order. During the adventure, she continually spurs the hunting party toward an encounter with the weretiger.

The third fact is that Chandor himself has infiltrated the raja's party, assuming the role of guide, which the great huntsman finds highly amusing. He looks upon the whole operation as little more than a game and plans to have a good time with the expedition before he wipes it out to a man. Chandor doesn't suspect that Tomor is a Dark Sister, however; nor does she know who he really

is, although both are destined to learn the other's identity by adventure's end. Tragically, the heroes are equally destined to be caught in the middle of this feud.

Scene I: The Great Adventure!

Getting the player characters involved in this adventure should be a fairly easy task. If it is being played after another adventure in Sri Raji (or some similar location), the raja can be replaced with some noble familiar to the heroes. In that case, they can be invited to join the hunt as honored guests. Refusing such an invitation would be insulting to their intended host, so the party should feel obliged to accept.

If, on the other hand, this adventure is being played without any such connection to the current campaign, there is another easy route that can be taken to involve the player characters: Simply have them hired on as body guards. In this case, the raja explains that he has tried to hire local guards, but they are afraid to travel on this particular expedition. According to the locals, the beast the raja now hunts is no ordinary tiger, and only a fool would pursue it. Raja Mahanda scoffs at these stories, but he still wants to have a few extra guards along just in case there is some unexpected trouble.

Whichever the case, once the heroes have agreed to join the expedition, they'll have a day or two to prepare for it. If they sniff around the city, they learn that the locals believe the expedition to be doomed. The creature it is to hunt is not a natural beast, everyone says. The locals believe it to be some sort of a vengeful spirit of the jungle. They say that this *ghost tiger* can run as fast as the wind and move unseen through the jungle shadows. While not technically true, these rumors do serve to foreshadow the trouble the player characters are destined to face.

It should also be clear to the heroes that Raja Mahanda looks forward to this expedition as a grand adventure. In fact, he has the same enthusiasm for this hunt that a skilled angler might have for a much anticipated fishing trip. The fact that his quarry is a ferocious tiger, a known man-eater, seems to mean nothing to him. He bears an almost childlike enthusiasm which other members of the expedition do not share.

As the expedition begins, read the following text:

The raja's expedition is nothing if not grand. As it prepares to leave the palace, you, like Mahanda himself, are all comfortably seated in elephant-borne howdahs. (Of course, the raja rides alone while your group travels two to an elephant.) A dozen bearers walk behind these beasts, carrying water, provisions, tents, and other supplies. Colorful banners snap in the wind and scores of well-wishers fill the city streets with shouts and cheers.

It's difficult not to be swept up in the festivity of the moment, even though you know that many of the well-wishers secretly believe this expedition to be doomed. But as you leave the city, and the dark canopy of the jungle spreads around you, quickly screening all traces of civilization from your sight, you are taken by the feeling that you have been swallowed alive by some great, green behemoth.

Still, the raja grins excitedly, obviously delighted to be hosting this expedition.

Scene II: The Jungle's Wrath

The jungles of Sri Raji are filled with danger for the unwary. They are even more deadly for those who put their trust in the wrong hands.

During this portion of the adventure, Radjiff uses his role as guide to lead the expedition into trouble with some of the jungle's more dangerous denizens. In this way, he can judge the mettle of the group, sizing up his prey for later, while reducing its ranks at the same time. Of course, he doesn't perform this treachery in any obvious manner. Radjiff doesn't want to tip his hand to the raja just yet. So as each new misfortune occurs, when the raja berates him for not having anticipated the trouble, the guide responds by explaining tersely that the jungles are not a playground and suggesting that perhaps the raja would like to turn around and return home. His pride thus stung, the raja insists upon proceeding, charging Chandor to be more watchful from this point on.

The Dungeon Master should use these encounters to kill off one or two of the raja's native bearers at a time. While the players should feel that their characters are at risk, in actuality the heroes have every opportunity to escape these hazards while lesser characters are dying.

Dangerous Animals . . .

The first encounter the heroes have with the wilds of Sri Raji features a deadly predator. This is exactly the sort of thing they should be expecting, although the nature and size of their first attacker may come as something of a shock. The following text sets up the scene and should be read to a randomly determined pair of characters.

As the caravan presses on, each elephant takes its turn in the lead. The turn for your own mount comes near the end of the day's travel, as the gloom of the jungle is starting to deepen toward the darkness of night. The endless swaying of the flora and shifting of the shadows makes it seem that an attack could come at any time.

When it does come, the attack is not from the jungle around you. Instead, without warning, the ground collapses under your mount. The great pachyderm cries out in shock as it crashes into a five-foot-deep pit. An unlucky bearer to your left slides in as well, shouting and striving to avoid being crushed by the panicked beast. At first, this seems to be the extent of the danger, but then the man begins to scream in pain, and the animal beneath you bellows again, thrashing about wildly. At its feet, you spot something that makes your flesh crawl.

The bottom of the pit is aswarm with hundreds of six-inch-long centipedes. They have already started to strip the flesh from the screaming bearer and the elephant's legs, and they are quickly swarming up onto the body of the beast. In only a few seconds, the entire animal—along with its riders—is covered with the things.

The creatures in the pit are normal huge and giant centipedes (as described in the *Monstrous Manual*). There are about a hundred of each type.

Give the heroes a chance to leap from the pit before they are swarmed by these horrific creatures. None of the PCs should die in this encounter, but a few nasty bites aren't out of the question. The elephant and the unfortunate bearer, of course, are almost certainly doomed. Unless the heroes act so swiftly and decisively that it would be entirely unreasonable for them not to rescue these two, simply assume that both are eaten alive, before the very eyes of the PCs.

Linger on their deaths long enough to horrify the heroes, at least a little. But be careful to convey horror rather than revulsion. Instead of describing the gruesome sight of these deaths, then, rely upon the sounds—the steadily weakening screams of the victims, the frantic rustle of the centipedes, the hushed cries of "Merciful gods!" from the raja, the piteous gurgling of the bearer's last breath, and the final silence that settles.

When the encounter is over, Chandor stands at the edge of the pit, staring into its depths. He looks up to meet the eye of the raja, smiles grimly, and says, "The jungle is unforgiving of those who do not know its ways. Your men are as ignorant children out here. We will lose many more before this journey is over. Ah, but the tiger you seek is a wonder, is it not? Killing the beast will be worth however many lives it takes."

"From now on, you will lead," is the raja's response.

. . . And Dangerous Plants

The next deadly encounter takes place near noon the next day, when the expedition stops to rest. Read the following text to your players.

Just after midday, the raja calls for a halt, to rest and eat. The guide points out a large tree just ahead, with wide-spread limbs sheltering a clear stretch of ground. Once there, the raja is helped from his mount, and camp tables are set up and laid with victuals. Many bearers toss their bundles down and lie against them, determined to use this time to nap before the march resumes. While everyone relaxes, the guide leaves to scout around for tiger spoor.

With the raja's troupe settling down to rest, you notice again just how much noise surrounds you from the jungle itself. It is filled with a cacophony of sound. Birds cry, monkeys howl, insects rasp, and the foliage rustles here and there with the passage of small creatures.

Suddenly even all this noise is eclipsed by an agonized cry ringing through the camp. This shout is quickly joined by another, and then a third. A trio of bearers has been caught up in the snaking vines of a carnivorous plant!

It quickly becomes obvious that caravan is camped in the very clutches of a choke creeper (or, at least, it's tropical cousin). This deadly menace is described in the MONSTROUS MANUAL™ tome under the "Dangerous Plant" entry. The Dungeon Master should decide the size of the plant based upon the strength of the adventuring party.

Players commonly being suspicious sorts, their characters may take it into their heads to accuse Chandor of laxity in his duties, or even of purposely sabotaging the hunting trip. If so, the guide faces them down, suggesting that perhaps they would like to take his job. He asks if they have no common sense themselves, to watch for danger, and insists that he alone cannot baby-sit every member of the expedition every day.

Chandor acts so self-assured during his self-defense and so quickly turns any accusations back upon the heroes, that his forcefulness alone should carry him through. If not, he leaves the caravan in a seeming fury at this point, resigning his position as guide. (After all, he has the expedition deep enough into the jungle by now that its members could not likely find their own way back. Indeed, the raja's party is now within the borders of Chandor's own domain.) If, on the other hand, the PCs push this conflict to the point of a fight, Chandor does not back down, but (for sake of the plot) the raja certainly intervenes, demanding that there be no brawling among the members of his caravan. "Save your hot blood for my tiger," he says. Chandor shows a thin smile at these words, interpreting them in his own way.

Ghost in the Night

Among the members of the caravan now, morale is low and tension is high. What began as a festive jaunt into the jungle to kill a single tiger shows every sign of becoming a grim death march. As the sun sets and camp is pitched, the bearers move about their evening tasks solemnly, casting frequent glances toward the dark foliage outside the light of the fires. To add to the tension, a tiger roars eerily in the jungle from time to time—sometimes nearby, sometimes from a distance.

For his part, the raja continues to smile and speak with cheeriness, but even he seems a bit forced in his manner. Sensing the mood of his servants, he has extra rations of wine passed about, and he calls for an early retirement to bed, insisting that everyone get a good, long night's sleep. To keep watch during the night, four guards are posted around the camp, one at each of the cardinal points.

At some point during the night, while the player characters sleep, Chandor decides to strike at the caravan himself, to increase its fear level to a fever pitch. Read the following text to the players.

The evening is quiet and tranquil (or as much so as it can be in a jungle teeming with tiny, nocturnal creatures). Even the roaring of the tiger, somewhere in the darkness, has abated. The hours pass, and most of the camp sleeps fitfully. Out at the limits of the firelight, the sentries stand their posts, vigilant to protect the camp from surprise.

At last the dark sky starts to slowly lighten toward morning. It seems the night has passed without event.

Abruptly, a scream of terror rises from the western guard post. In the dimness of false dawn, you vaguely spot the guard's shape, frozen against the dark wall of the jungle. A rumbling roar sounds from that direction, the distinctive cry of a great hunting cat. Something huge leaps onto the guard, and horrible ripping sounds ensue. The guard's cry abruptly changes from terror to agony. Although it is too dim for you to see what is happening now, the roaring and screaming begin to fade into the jungle undergrowth.

All this occurs within bare seconds. By the time you grasp your weapons and run to the guard post, the guard is gone, a dark, wet trail the only evidence of his passing.

The great hunting cat is, of course, Chandor in his tiger form. Rapidly dragging the guard some distance into the jungle, he then tears the unfortunate man to pieces, leaving them scattered about a clearing. His bloodlust momentarily sated, Chandor reverts to human

form, takes a quick dip in a nearby stream, then retrieves his clothes from the bank where he left them earlier. By the time the player characters arrive to investigate, he is waiting there for them, "investigating" the gruesome scene for himself.

"I sensed the beast was near," he explains, "and I rose to track it. But like you, I was too late to save this man."

The raja then arrives, accompanied by a quartet of tense-looking guards.

"It would seem we have found our tiger," Chandor tells him.

The raja turns his head away from the carnage, his face pale. "This beast *must* die," he states, his voice a shaky whisper. "It has too great a taste for human flesh. It must be destroyed."

"As you command," Chandor replies, his eyes glinting coldly in a hard face. "We must follow it west."

Scene III: The Killing Zone

After returning to the camp, it takes some time for Raja Mahanda to convince his shaken followers that the caravan absolutely must pursue the man-eater. Many bearers, in particular, are loath to hunt the thing any further.

The raja begins by trying to raise everyone's spirits with his usual joviality. When this doesn't work, he resorts uncharacteristically to simple bullying. He states

that any who wish to return now can do so, but they must leave without weapons or supplies, as these belong to him. At that, even the most fearful cease their complaints. Soon, the caravan is packed and on its way once again, in pursuit of the deadly tiger.

But now Chandor has the troupe on his own lands, where he has prepared many a nasty surprise for them all. It is time for Dungeon Master to pull out all the stops. Terrible things should spring up to challenge the player characters and wipe out the expedition. In addition to throwing a little fear into the heroes, these encounters should also begin to it clear to them that there is more to this expedition than they might have suspected. This revelation begins with the first encounter, in which Raja Mahanda himself is killed.

Deadly Intentions

As it nears his home, Radjiff begins to lead the caravan into traps that he has set around his territory. It is this act that may well give him away. Any hero who is familiar with traps or snares has a chance of noticing that the guide is missing some pretty obvious things.

A good rule of thumb is to allow such characters to make a Wisdom check. Success indicates that they have perceived something suspicious. For example, they might notice Radjiff stepping over a trip wire or

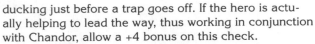

ducking just before a trap goes off. If the hero is actually helping to lead the way, thus working in conjunction with Chandor, allow a +4 bonus on this check.

The following description can be used when the first trap is triggered.

As your caravan wades through the sweltering heat of the jungle, suddenly you hear a series of sharp cracking sounds and the whistle of a dozen spears taking flight.

One after another, these deadly projectiles find their mark. The screams of bearers are choked off as blood wells up in their lungs, and elephants roar mightily as razor-tipped shafts sink into their flanks.

Even as all this chaos runs through the caravan, an even more upsetting sight greets your eyes. High atop the largest elephant, Raja Mahanda has met his own end at the point of a spear. Pinned to his seat in the howdah, transfixed by the shaft of that spear, he seems to be grinning down at you, jovial even in death.

In addition to learning that their guide is not reliable, the heroes now also have a chance to learn that Tomor has a secret of her own. In the wake of the raja's death, as the rest of the caravan prepares to turn back, she steps forward to insist that the party continue.

In so doing, however, Tomor lets slip a few secrets. It soon becomes clear that she knows the nature of the beast they seek and perhaps even its name. Indeed, clever player characters might learn even more from her—especially if they surreptitiously use magic.

Of course, Radjiff tumbles to the truth of Tomor's identity at the same time. And as soon as he realizes that she is a member of the Dark Sisters, he decides to end things a little more quickly.

Other Traps and Attacks

Some of the other traps that can be thrown at the player characters now include poisoned darts, spiked pit falls, and spring-loaded spikes that suddenly snap out to impale the unsuspecting. Radjiff is a master huntsman and has had plenty of time to both build and conceal these traps that surround his lair. Because of this, anyone attempting to find or disarm them suffers a –20% penalty to his die rolls. Magical detection functions normally.

In addition to these mechanical menaces, some very unusual (and, of course, dangerous) creatures can attack the party. These include such horrors as ankhegs, violet fungi, and maybe even a fire lizard or wyvern (all of which are described in the *Monstrous Manual*). The Dungeon Master is reminded that Radjiff

is a collector of deadly plants and animals, so just about any manner of creature might be found here.

Dwindling Numbers

The DM should keep hitting the caravan with these attacks until only Tomor, Radjiff, and the PCs are left alive. Then the adventure can continue with the events of the next act.

Of course, the players may force matters to a head by calling Radjiff to account for his actions, or pinning Tomor down about her own secrets. In either case, the Dungeon Master needs to guide things along as best he can to get the adventure back on track for the events in Scene IV.

Turning Tail

There is a pretty good chance that the characters will reach a point where the idea of returning to civilization now seems a good one. There are a few things that can be used to keep them from escaping, however.

First Tomor insists that they press on. She claims that this is to avenge the death of the raja, but of course that isn't her true motivation. She is determined to find Radjiff Chandor and destroy him for his crimes against the Dark Sisters.

Second, keep in mind that the party is being guided by Radjiff. He doesn't intend to allow any of the characters to leave the jungle alive. Because of this, he'll lead them around in circles if need be. While he's doing this, of course, he'll also be enjoying the sight of bearers and elephants being torn apart by his deadly traps and vicious menagerie.

Scene IV: Radjiff Strikes

Once the party's numbers have been cut to almost nothing, Radjiff decides to take personal action against Tomor. Waiting for a moment when the heroes aren't watching (such as during a battle with one of his monsters), he kidnaps her and drags her off to his lair. As for the heroes, Radjiff is certain that his deadly jungle will finish them. He does, however, leave them a note of explanation.

Worthy survivors,

I have determined that the woman Tomor is not what she seems to be. She is a member of the Dark Sisters, an order which would like nothing more than to see me dead.

Since I cannot allow that to happen, I have taken her away to my home. Once she is fed and rested, I will release her into the jungle again and hunt her. If she can escape me, she will be the first.

The rest of you are consigned to the tender mercies of my jungle. I hope your deaths are not too painful.
Radjiff Chandor,
Ruler of the Jungles

This note is a simple statement of truth. Radjiff has taken Tomor and intends to savor the hunt as she tries to escape his gleaming claws. He doesn't assume that the heroes will have anything more to do with him and expects never to see them again.

Of course, the average band of heroes isn't going to accept defeat so easily. In fact, there are a number of things the party can do at this point. The biggest problem with any of these, of course, is that the jungle in this area has been groomed to be deadly.

Raiding Radjiff's Lair

While raiding Radjiff's lair is certainly a possibility, it won't be an easy task. After all, it requires the heroes to penetrate even deeper into Radjiff's deadly jungle. Even then, they must find the weretiger's home, which is pretty well hidden. In other words, unless the Dungeon Master wants to design Radjiff's lair and run an adventure into it, this course of action can justly be discouraged.

If the DM decides to run a lair adventure, there are two different approaches to designing that hideaway. The first approach assumes that Radjiff now follows his bestial nature and dwells in a lair that is little more than an animal den. All the heroes find when they enter this lair is the bones of the weretiger's kills and a few makeshift tools. The second approach assumes that, just as in his former life as a huntsman, Radjiff now keeps an estate full of trophies from the hunt. In this case, the lair might include all manner of rooms, numerous traps, and even a menagerie of dangerous animals and plants. (There might even be some well-trained animal servants.)

Turning The Tables

Knowing of Radjiff's plan to release Tomor and hunt her, the heroes may decide instead to lay in wait for the weretiger. If they are careful, they can survive the jungle long enough for Radjiff to release Tomor back into the wild. Then, once the hunt is on, they can move against him with surprise. After all, he assumes that the heroes are dead.

How long will the weretiger keep his prisoner before releasing her? That should be dictated by the condition of the party. If the group is badly wounded, the Dungeon Master should allow the heroes enough time to get back on their feet. This way, he can throw all manner of deadly encounters at them as they hunt Radjiff, making this task truly memorable for them.

Keep in mind that the player characters may not realize that Radjiff is a weretiger. If this is the case, they may be caught off guard when they try to surprise him. Of course, if they find Tomor first, as she is fleeing, she'll tell them everything she knows. She's well aware that there is no point in keeping secrets any longer.

Fight or Flight

Once the heroes have found Tomor (either in the wilds or on the run), they'll need to decide where to go from there. They can either stand their ground and battle Radjiff, or they can make for civilization at top speed.

In the former case, the Dungeon Master should do all he can to play up the savagery of the weretiger's rage. The battle should be a frantic sweep of claws, fangs, roars, and blood. The great size and cunning of Radjiff Chandor should be apparent at every turn. When the battle comes to an end, the heroes should be in pretty rough shape. Compared to this fierce enemy, the other hazards of the jungle should seem insignificant.

On the other hand, given the deadliness of the weretiger, there's something to be said for turning tail and running. The group's flight from Radjiff should not be an easy one, of course. He'll strike from the shadows whenever he can, trying to kill or cripple individual party members each time. The Dungeon Master can use Tomor to play up the severity of these encounters. When Radjiff attacks, she can be badly injured or even killed. If she dies, however, the DM should have her pass along some token of friendship so that the other Dark Sisters won't blame the heroes for her death.

Recurrence

If Radjiff survives, he does not take his defeat well. He'll recognize that the heroes are worthy enemies, and he won't rest until he is able to hunt them again. After all, this was hardly a fair match—he didn't begin to understand the sport they would offer him.

The Dungeon Master needs to give some thought as to how the weretiger might lure the party back into the jungle. Radjiff would be only too glad to simply invite the group, but he knows that isn't likely to work. Thus, he'll be more than willing to kidnap a close friend of the party or otherwise constrain them to return as he wishes.

The Dark Sisters can also be used as a motivation in this matter. They might hire or otherwise persuade the heroes to hunt the weretiger again. That is especially true if the heroes brought Tomor out of the jungle alive.

Even if Radjiff did not survive this adventure, the Dark Sisters might contact the heroes with other missions from time to time. Again, if Tomor survived or managed to mark the heroes as her allies, this helps matters.

Of course, if Tomor didn't survive and the heroes have no way of proving that they befriended her, the Dark Sisters won't take so kindly to them. In fact, the Dungeon Master might even arrange for them to encounter Radjiff again, this time as allies against a common enemy.

VLADIMIR NOBRISKOV

And oft, though wisdom wake, suspicion sleeps
At wisdom's gate, and to simplicity
Resigns her charge, while goodness thinks no ill
Where no ill seems.

—John Milton
Paradise Lost

BIOGRAPHY

Vladimir Nobriskov, also known as "The Scarlet Prince," is a nobleman who resides in the domain of Borca. He is a dashing and charismatic figure, the sort of man who draws all attention to him when he enters a room. Men of Borca respect and admire Nobriskov's physical strength and keen mind. Women, on the other hand, are easily won over by his smile, wit, and chivalrous demeanor.

Vladimir Nobriskov

What few realize, however, is that Nobriskov is a deadly predator feeding on the blood of Borca's people. He is a werebat who looks upon all folk of that domain, both gentry and commoners, as little more than food.

Appearance

In his human aspect, Nobriskov is one of the most handsome men in all of Borca. His features are clean and aristocratic, his build athletic without being muscle-bound, and his gaze captivating. He wears his black hair short in the front and in a braid at the back. His eyes, which are every bit as dark as his hair, sparkle in even the faintest light. Nobriskov's only apparent physical flaw is a slender dueling scar on his right cheek, but even this seems to accent his handsomeness rather than detracting from it.

While most of Borca's aristocracy wear somber clothes of black and gray, Nobriskov does not. Indeed, it is his taste for clothes fashioned from red silk that earned him his nickname, "The Scarlet Prince." He does favor a long black cape, but even this is lined with crimson satin.

The Scarlet Prince is also well known for the sword cane that he carries with him. It is roughly a yard long, and he keeps its blade razor sharp at all times. Its grip is fashioned from pure gold in the shape of a crescent moon.

When he assumes the shape of vampire bat, however, there is nothing about his appearance to suggest that he is anything other than a normal bat. Only the fact that this bat is so difficult to kill gives away its unusual nature. (Like all werebeasts, he retains his immunity to most weapons in every shape, and retains his normal hit points.)

In his hybrid form, the Scarlet Prince is a truly horrific creature. His arms distend and transform into leathery wings. His normally attractive face twists into the pug-nosed snout of a bat, and his teeth become needlelike fangs. Coarse fur covers his entire body, and his feet become curved talons. In this aspect, his hands are useless for grasping but sport dangerous claws.

Vladimir Nobriskov

True Werebat, Neutral Evil

Armor Class	5	Str	15
Movement	9, Fl 15 (D)	Dex	16
Level/Hit Dice	4+2	Con	14
Hit Points	38	Int	17
THAC0	17	Wis	16
Morale	12	Cha	18
No. of Attacks	1 (human or bat form) or 2 (hybrid form)		
Damage/Attack	By weapon (1d4) or 1d4/1d4 (claws)		
Special Attacks	Bite (2d4)		
Special Defenses	Hit only by silver and +1 or better magical weapons		
Magic Resistance	Nil		

Background

Nobriskov's ancestors have lived in Ravenloft almost since the day Barovia emerged from the Mists. If asked about his heritage, Nobriskov says only that he is of Barovian descent but was born in Borca. What he omits is that he was born in a bat cave on the slopes of Mount Gries.

When Nobriskov was but a teenager, his parents were killed by a traveling adventurer named Rudolph van Richten. This tragedy taught Nobriskov to be wary of humans. He decided that there were two ways to protect himself. The first was to live among humans, as if one of them. Thus it was that he insinuated himself into the gentry of Lechberg. By adopting a flamboyant lifestyle, he hoped that none would suspect him of any dark nature.

The second thing he learned from the encounter with Van Richten was that some men are far more intelligent and deadly than others. To defend himself from the bright ones, he determined to act the dandy, so that even should they suspect his secret, they would still underestimate his own intelligence. Further, if discovered, he would lead them to conclude that they faced an undead vampire. Only when it was too late would they realize their folly.

Current Sketch

Nobriskov enjoys his life among humans. He favors the blood of young women when feeding but drinks from the veins of men when necessary. Usually, the Scarlet Prince is wooing one member or another of Borca's nobility. He is careful not to claim the lives of his loves, to avoid drawing too much attention. Once a lady begins to grow too weak from his feedings, he ends the relationship. Usually, he arranges for the poor thing to catch him with another woman. Thus, he has earned a reputation as a heart breaker. Those who

look closer, however, find that most of his former girlfriends died within 18 months after the relationship ended—the werebat hates loose ends.

Personality

Nobriskov favors the finer things in life and takes no pains to hide the fact. The flamboyant manner that he has adopted has led nearly everyone to assume that the Scarlet Prince is nothing more than a pampered dandy.

In his heart, Nobriskov believes that he will one day meet a woman he can truly love. When that happens, he will transform her into a werebat, and they will dwell together in the night. To date, however, he has had only contempt for the women upon whom he preys.

Combat

Like all lycanthropes, Nobriskov is immune to injury by weapons that are not made of silver or imbued with a +1 or better magical enchantment.

In all his forms, his eyes are so keen that he can see to a full 120 feet in all but total darkness. He can also use echolocation to "see" out to 30 feet in bat form, or 60 feet in hybrid form, even in pitch darkness.

Human Aspect

The Scarlet Prince is a masterful fencer uses the blade of his sword-cane whenever he enters battle in human form. This weapon is treated as a rapier, having a speed factor 4 and inflicting 1d6+1 points of damage. His skill with it is such that he receives a +1 bonus on all attack rolls made with it and a +2 bonus on all damage rolls.

Vampire Bat Aspect

In vampire bat form, Nobriskov can bite for a single (though painful) point of damage. Those who face him while he is in this form discover that he retains his full normal hit points despite his small size.

As a rule, Nobriskov uses this form when he wishes to sneak into an area unobserved or to retreat from battle. He is well aware that people who see him transform into this shape might mistake him for a vampire.

Hybrid Form

The Scarlet Prince is most dangerous in this form. When fighting as a hybrid, he is able to strike twice per round with his claws, inflicting 1d4 points of damage with each successful blow. Should both of his claw attacks score hits, he is able to bite with his needle-like teeth for an additional 2d4 points of damage.

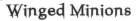

Winged Minions

The werebat is also able to telepathically command the bats that share his lair. Typically, there are 20d10 common bats and 1d10 large bats. When called, they arrive within 2d10 rounds, adjusted for the current distance to his lair. These minions have the following game statistics.

> **Bats (20d10):** AC 8; MV 1, Fl 24 (B); HD 1/4; THAC0 20; #AT 1; Dmg 1 point; SA Swarm; SZ T (1' wingspan); ML Unreliable (2–4); Int Animal (1); AL N; XP 15.
>
> Notes: If at least 10 bats are attacking, they do so in a swarm. As such, they have a 1% chance per bat of putting out torches and the like. In addition, they disrupt spellcasting, requiring anyone attempting magic use to pass an ability check on Wisdom. Attacks made within a bat swarm suffer a –2 penalty on all attack rolls. Under ideal flying conditions (DM's judgment) the Armor Class of the bats improves from 8 to 4.

> **Bats, Large (1d10):** AC 8; MV 3, Fl 18 (C); HD 1/2; THAC0 20; #AT 1; Dmg 1d2; SA Rabies; SZ M (5' wingspan); ML Unsteady (5–7); Int Animal (1); AL N; XP 35.
>
> Notes: If a large bat is attacked with missile weapons by foes with a Dexterity of 13 or less, its AC improves by 3 points. There is a 1% chance per point of damage inflicted that those bitten by a large bat are infected with rabies. After 1d4+6 days of incubation, the victim has 10 days to live unless a *cure disease* or similar spell is cast on him. Rabid characters cannot eat or drink and are prone to violence. Whenever under stress, they must attempt an ability check on Wisdom. Failure means they attack in a berserk rage until dead or unconscious.

The Scarlet Prince

This adventure ensnares the heroes in a web of courtly intrigue and murder within the domain of Borca. As these events unfold, the heroes brush elbows with nobility, so they should be on their best behavior.

Introduction

The key to this adventure, at least from the Dungeon Master's point of view, is some clever misdirection. In addition to playing up the pomp and circumstance of court life, the DM will present the player characters with a number of leads and suspects surrounding the murders. Only at the end of the matter should the truth become clear to them.

This scenario is set in Lechberg, a well populated city in the domain of Borca. If the Dungeon Master wishes to place the adventure elsewhere, he should choose another city where the heroes can rub elbows with the gentry.

Besides Vladimir Nobriskov, there are four other major characters involved in this adventure. (Of course, if the DM wishes, others could be included to add even more confusion to the lives of the players.) Those four characters are as follows.

Lady Monique

This young lady is a slip of a girl. While she is fairly attractive, true beauty is something she will never know. She and her sister, Lady Gennifer, are lesser members of the gentry, and both are fairly well off, thanks to an estate managed by their uncle Count Pretorius.

Monique plays the part of an innocent young girl, but in truth she's had her share of sweethearts. In fact, some twelve months ago, she was regularly seen on the arm of the Scarlet Prince himself. This fact, however, should not be revealed to the heroes until indicated in the adventure.

Baron Amthor

Amthor is Monique's current sweetheart. He's quite smitten with the young woman, and popular rumor says that they'll be married within a few months. This is certainly what Amthor has in mind, because his own inherited money is near to running out.

A handsome young man, though a trifle slow in his thinking, Amthor possesses two other major personality traits that the player characters may come to note. First, he is something of a hot-head. Second, he has a great deal of pride. Considering his dwindling finances, that pride is easily offended, leading Amthor into many a heated confrontation over an imagined insult. To be fair, however, Amthor does love Monique. His monetary trouble is merely a red herring to be used by the DM during the course of the adventure.

Lady Gennifer

Gennifer is the Scarlet Prince's latest conquest. He has been keeping company with her for the last month or so. She is a good deal more attractive than her older sister, but also much less personable. She isn't rude, exactly, but should come off as fairly impressed with herself.

Gennifer is not at all prone to feign maidenly innocence, especially if left alone with a character she finds attractive. Her relatively wanton ways are just one reason that the Scarlet Prince was drawn to her. At the same time, of course, they can lead the heroes to suspect that she's a vampire, succubus, or other such creature.

Count Pretorius

The Count is an older, distinguished, gentleman. He carries himself well, always dresses very sharply, and has the air of old money about him. His aloof attitude causes him to keep his distance from the player characters, almost certainly giving them the impression that he has something sinister to hide.

Pretorius takes his role as custodian of Monique and Gennifer's money very seriously. He isn't happy with their current behavior, believing them both to be too flighty.

A clause in the papers that make him their guardian also states that he loses access to their money if they both marry. This might seem suspicious to the players if they discover the fact (which they certainly should), but again, it is nothing more than a decoy. The truth is that Pretorius has his own money and doesn't really need the girls'.

Scene I: A Lady in Need

This adventure begins with the heroes in some manner of social setting. It can be dictated by their own actions or brought into play by chance. For the purposes of this scenario, the assumption is made that the characters are in a fine restaurant known as The Black Pearl.

The Dungeon Master can get things moving by reading the following boxed copy aloud.

It would be difficult to imagine better fare than that offered at The Black Pearl. An outstanding meal of bitter-glazed lamb is accompanied by an outstanding wine. Fresh bread, a delicate onion soup, and an intriguing assortment of side dishes have each come to your table with flourish and elegance. To be sure, this will be an expensive evening, but for now the cost seems inconsequential.

Just as your desert arrives—a beautifully arranged assortment of fruits and cremes—a cry of alarm goes up from a table near yours. As the four patrons seated there were rising to depart, one of them, a young lady, suddenly fainted to the floor.

Even as the call goes out for a doctor, her companions rush to lift the woman back into a chair. She is a slender thing with light auburn hair arranged in delicate curls. Her ill health is clear, for her complexion is no less pale than the white satin band that encircles her throat or the shimmering ivory gown she wears.

This woman is, of course, Lady Monique. The others at the table are her date (Baron Amthor), her sister (Lady Gennifer), and the foppish Vladimir Nobriskov.

As luck would have it, none of the restaurant's other patrons is familiar with the healing arts. Any player character who has any training in medical care, even merely the Healing proficiency, will find himself pressed into service.

Fortunately, Monique's life is not in danger. She is weak, however, and should be taken somewhere to rest as soon as possible. A few questions reveal that the young woman had certainly taken her share of wine with dinner, but she wasn't intoxicated. Clearly, that is not the cause of her collapse.

In fact, the woman's weakened state and pale complexion combine to suggest only one thing to a skilled healer: Lady Monique appears to be suffering from a great loss of blood, perhaps some variety of anemia.

At this point, the heroes will probably suspect the work of a vampire. If they look beneath the satin sash on Lady Monique's neck, they'll see just what they expect: a pair of puncture wounds. These may be taken as evidence that the woman has been visited by a nosferatu. In truth, of course, they show the feeding of Vladimir Nobriskov, the werebat.

If this injury is pointed out to the others at the table, they make nothing of it. "Vampires," they all scoff, "may be found in the wilds of Barovia, but here, in the heart of Lechberg, such things are hardly likely to be found." They insist that there are any number of ways in which Monique may have injured herself. As to her having covered the wound, would the player characters rather that she had left such a blemish uncovered for all the world to view?

Once things have calmed down, the heroes are offered the thanks of Baron Amthor. He introduces himself and his companions at the table, and asks the player characters to help get Monique home. As a token of his thanks to the heroes for their aid, he settles their tab, paying their own bill as well as his own.

The Dungeon Master should play the events of the next few hours by ear. What's most important is that the heroes are brought into Monique's home. Once they have seen the slender woman safely to her bed, they have a few moments to relax with Nobriskov and Lady Gennifer.

This is an excellent time for the Dungeon Master to play up the characters of the Scarlet Prince and his companion. Nobriskov should be presented as a foppish dandy with a taste for wine, good food, and the easy life. (A good model for this character would be Sir Percy Blakesly from *The Scarlet Pimpernel*.) Lady Gennifer, on the other hand should be shown to combine the features of an elegant lady with those of a vamp. While she doesn't actually flirt with any of the player characters, she does devote all her attention to the most charismatic member of the group.

During the heroes' conversation with these two characters, an important fact should emerge: This is not the first time that Monique has suffered from this mysterious anemia. It has happened before, just over a year ago. At the time, the ladies' father had just died, and Count Pretorius been appointed as guardian to the pair. Nobriskov deftly works the conversation so that the heroes are led to believe that the Baron appears to be suspicious.

It is also possible that the player characters will come to suspect that Monique's father has risen from the grave to prey upon his own daughters. Nobriskov certainly encourages this thinking, should it be mentioned. (If the heroes pursue this line of investigation, the DM should toss a few encounters their way that hint at vampires and such. For his part, Nobriskov does what he can to lay such hints at their feet. Before long, however, it should become apparent that the girls' father still rests peacefully in his grave.)

Throughout this conversation, Baron Amthor salts his speech with a tone of simpleminded ridicule. By cleverly making light of the situation, and jesting about any theory put forth to explain what has happened, he hopes to lead the heroes to assume that he is a scatterbrained fool.

Scene II: Count Pretorius

The next step in the heroes' investigations (at least, the next step that brings any results) is to learn more about Baron Pretorius. Besides actually speaking with him, the player characters can learn much by asking questions around the city and among the gentry.

The heroes can easily discover that the Count is not a native of Borca. He was born in Barovia and came here only after Monique and Gennifer lost their father. Locally he is respected, although perhaps not well liked. The Count is certainly a distinguished man, but he holds himself above the local gentry.

Pretorius does not live with his nieces. Rather, he has his own residence on the outskirts of the city. This is an old estate that has seen better days. The Count has men working on it, but he seems in no great haste to have the place repaired. Rumors abound that the manor is haunted. The fact that Pretorius himself appears gaunt and cadaverous has only served to further these tales. At the same time, it should move the players to suspect that the Count is himself the vampire they seek.

When approached, Pretorius grants the characters a short audience, though he certainly shows no interest in talking with them. While he is thankful that they came to the aid of his niece, he resents their intrusion into his personal life. This becomes even more pronounced as the interview goes on or if the questions asked by the heroes become too pointed.

This interview with the Count should reveal that he has little liking for either of the men with whom his nieces have been keeping company. It is through him that the heroes first learn of Amthor's dwindling wealth.

As for Nobriskov, the Count makes it clear that he hold this womanizing dandy in complete contempt. It won't be possible for the heroes to learn here that Nobriskov and Monique were once lovers, however, as the Count himself is not aware of the fact.

The interview matter should come to an end with the heroes being shown out of the house by Pretorius' butler. In fact, if things get too heated, the Dungeon Master might even have the count loose his hounds on them. These are trained hunting dogs who are only half domesticated. In game terms, they have the same characteristics as wolves.

Scene III: Dust to Dust

When the heroes return to their rooms after their interview with Count Pretorius, they find a message waiting for them. This very brief missive is written in a rushed script and reads as follows: "Come at once. Monique has had another attack. Your aid is imperative. Baron Amthor."

No matter how swiftly the PCs get to Monique's house, however, they are too late. When they arrive, they find Nobriskov comforting Lady Gennifer in the parlor while Amthor paces wildly, trying to regain his own composure. From the three, the heroes learn that Monique has died.

Another examination of the woman reveals that the cause of death is exactly what the heroes most likely expect. She has lost a great deal of blood, though there are only a few crimson droplets on her pillow cases.

This evening offers the characters another chance to converse with Amthor, Gennifer, and Nobriskov. The Dungeon Master can make use of this time to let the heroes see that Amthor's grief is very real.

Shortly afterward, the Count arrives. He says that he has just learned of Monique's death and made haste reach her side. He asks to spend a few minutes alone with the body. In all likelihood, the heroes will be uncomfortable about this, but there is little that they can do to prevent it. After all, Count Pretorius is the woman's uncle.

If the heroes somehow spy on the count, they see the following. After sitting beside his niece for a while, the count begins searching about the room. He puts away a hat that rests on Monique's vanity and returns some of her jewelry to a case near where it lies. As he does so, however, he suddenly stops, reaches into the case, and draws out a slender book. This is Monique's diary. With trembling fingers, Pretorius flips through the book, perusing the last few pages, then drops it into his pocket.

Although the heroes have no way of knowing, it is the count's intention to read the book for clues about his niece's death. He is a native of Barovia, a land where stories of vampirism are taken seriously. He has seen the mark of the nosferatu, he believes, on her throat. This is a matter he wants to investigate for himself. Most likely, however, the characters will assume that he is taking the book to cover his tracks, that it implicates him in Monique's death.

Having taken the book, the count departs. He says very little as he leaves; with an almost cursory pause to offer Gennifer his sympathy, he opens the door and heads out into the night.

Once the count has gone, Nobriskov leads the conversation toward that worthy's curious behavior. "Duced odd, that fellow," he says. "You'd think he has more care for the dead than the living." If he earlier jibed the heroes about their vampire theory, now he winks and adds, "Maybe he's your vampire, eh?"

Scene IV: Dead Woman's Tale

At some point over the course of the next day or so, the heroes receive a letter from Count Pretorius. It arrives just before sundown, delivered by an unimportant message boy. Its text reads as follows.

Friends,
I have discovered something of utmost importance about Monique's death. Please come to see me tonight at 8:00.
Tell no one that you have received this missive or that you are coming to my home. Secrecy is essential in this matter.

Your servant,
Count Pretorius

There is no deception in this communiqué. An examination of Monique's journal has revealed to Pretorius the identity of her killer and the circumstances of her death. It has also served to convince him that the player characters were not involved and, more importantly, that their aid may be vital if matters are to be resolved for the good.

The player characters, on the other hand, are likely to believe that they are being lured into the hands of a vampire. They will probably begin to make plans for confronting and destroying him. It matters little how they prepare for their meeting with the count, however, as the following text reveals. Read it aloud to the players when their characters arrive at the count's home.

You are led into the dark interior of the house by the count's slender, handsome butler. "The master has been in his library for many hours," he says. "He left word that you were to be shown in as soon as you arrived."

Vladimir Nobriskov

As he finishes speaking, your party comes to a halt before a large double door. The butler reaches out to swing the great portal slowly open. He begins to announce your presence, then stops, gasping in horror.

The count's body lies in the center of the floor, a great pool of crimson spreading out over the carpet around him. His head is twisted at an odd angle, indicating that his neck is most assuredly broken.

Even a casual examination of the room reveals that it has been searched. The drawers have been pulled from the writing desk and their contents dumped onto the floor. Books lie scattered about the carpet, indicating that the shelves lining the walls also have been ransacked.

If the count's body is examined, a terrible wound is discovered on his throat. Some deadly claw or fang has torn open his neck, spilling his blood on the floor.

There is one other clue here that the heroes must find somehow. It is a page from Monique's journal which the count tore out prior to his death. The Dungeon Master should handle things so that the group discovers this document. Exactly where it is found should depend upon where the heroes look. It might be concealed in the hollow shaft of a walking stick or pinned to the underside of a desk drawer. When it is found, however, the heroes should be very pleased with themselves for their cleverness. While this page doesn't give away the nature of their enemy, it certainly makes his identity clear.

Vladimir has returned to me! He has not paid me much attention since my father's death, although his romance with Gennifer has kept us in close company. He tells me now that we can be together again and that his days as a lady's man are at an end. I have won his heart, as I always knew I would.

I must keep our nightly rendezvous secret for now, he says, although he does not explain why. "In time," he whispers, "you will understand."

I suppose that he's right about this. He always seems to know best.

Scene V: The Scarlet Prince

Having learned that their enemy is none other than the Scarlet Prince, the heroes will certainly begin to make plans to move against him. Exactly what these are, however, depends upon the nature of the party and the research they have been able to do.

A search of Nobriskov's home reveals that it is actually little used. While the place contains a wealth of luxurious items, a thick layer of dust covers everything, and only a little food is on hand. Obviously, the place is not truly where the Scarlet Prince dwells. A trap door in the floor, however, opens into a vast cavern beneath the house. It is here that the werebat makes his lair.

Within this cavern, the heroes find numerous bats. These are loyal followers to the werebat and certainly come to his aid if he is attacked. Other such guardian creatures may be encountered, as desired by the DM.

The final confrontation with the Scarlet Prince will be shaped by the party's preparations in advance of this meeting. If the heroes expected to encounter a vampire, the battle may not be a pleasant one. Indeed, they may be caught completely off guard. On the other hand, if they have managed to ready themselves (even accidentally) to face a lycanthrope, they should stand a good chance of emerging victorious. Of course, if events turn badly for werebat, he seeks to flee the caverns in bat shape, through a crevice too narrow for the heroes to follow.

Recurrence

Assuming the heroes survive their encounter with the Scarlet Prince, however else it might turn out, there are several possible plot threads for the Dungeon Master to weave into another adventure.

If Nobriskov was destroyed or chased away, Lady Gennifer and Baron Amthor are destined to fall gradually in love and be married. The heroes are invited to the wedding. If the DM desires, however, there is no reason why Lady Gennifer might not have contracted the Dread Disease from her one-time lover. In this case, the heroes may find themselves facing a whole new series of mysterious deaths, leading to another adventure. Given their fledgling friendship with the lady and her new husband, the discovery of her disease could be quite tragic.

For his part, if Nobriskov escapes the party, he puts a few miles between himself and Borca, seeking out another city where he can return to the posh life. The heroes might run into him again in any major city, although only the most luxurious of places appeal to him. Naturally, he will be eager for revenge upon these people who meddled in his affairs in Borca.

On the other hand, if the heroes barely escaped their first encounter with the Scarlet Prince, he takes pains to fortify his lair with further guardians and traps, and does what he can to discredit the heroes with the locals, portraying them as foreigners and madmen. How long he can maintain this charade depends upon the manner in which the heroes handle themselves in the face of these accusations. Of course, he continues to court the Lady Gennifer, as well, at least until he tires of her. . . .

As the cat lapses into savagery by night,
and barbarously explores the dark,
so primal and titanic is a woman with the love-madness.

—Gelett Burgess
The Romance of the Commonplace

BIOGRAPHY

eeka is an unusual creature, for she is not a human who has been infected with lycanthropy. Rather, she was born a common house cat and contracted lycanthropy from a werebeast in its animal aspect. Shortly afterwards, this quiet, black cat developed the ability to change shapes, assuming the form of a beautiful, raven-haired woman. Although Meeka is not an evil creature, her natural predatory nature has made her into a deadly enemy.

Meeka

Pathologic Catwere, Neutral

Armor Class	5	Str	1 or 14
Movement	18, Climb 9	Dex	15
Level/Hit Dice	5	Con	1 or 14
Hit Points	30	Int	12
THAC0	15	Wis	13
Morale	Average (10)	Cha	17
No. of Attacks	3		
Damage/Attack	1d2/1d2/1d2 (2 claws/1 bite)		
Special Attacks	Surprise, rear claw rake (1d2/1d2)		
Special Defenses	Surprised only on a 1 or 2, hit only by silver and +1 or better magical weapons		
Magic Resistance	Nil		

Appearance

In her normal form, Meeka appears as a slender cat with a glossy coat of short hair the color of midnight. Her eyes are emerald green, ringed by a flickering halo of gold. A series of scars runs down her right flank, reminders of the wound that made her what she is today. Although mostly hidden by her fur, these blemishes are still visible as defects in an otherwise perfect coat of black.

Meeka is as graceful and elegant in her human aspect as in her feline one. Her delicate body stands just an inch or so over five feet, but it is supple and well proportioned. Although her eyes are those of a human woman, they retain a cat's green color. Her skin is dark and her features almost oriental. All in all, her unusual heritage gives her an exotic look that most men find alluring.

When moving about in human society, Meeka favors sarongs and similar loose clothes. Yellow is her favorite color, but she sometimes wears green and red fabrics. She never uses any manner of jewelry or cosmetics, although her beauty certainly does not suffer from these omissions.

Background

Meeka was born to a comfortable family of innkeepers in the village of Briggdarrow, Tepest. The family kept cats to hunt the rodent population of their inn and were delighted when blessed with a new litter. While they embraced her half dozen siblings, however, they did not welcome Meeka. A black cat, as everyone in Tepest knows, is an omen of great ill fortune.

Meeka

Meeka

The innkeeper's wife insisted that they keep the kitten for a time, hoping it would develop a patch of white somewhere. After three months, however, when no such blaze surfaced, she allowed her husband to rid them of the ill omen. He placed it in a burlap sack along with a pair of heavy rocks, then tossed it into the chill waters of Lake Kronov. In a matter of days, he had driven the incident from his mind. Fortune was with the black kitten, however, for the innkeeper's knot slipped loose and the feline swam ashore.

In the months that followed, the cat became feral, surviving on a diet field mice, small birds, and the like. As winter set in, however, food became scarce, and the cat grew thin. If not for a chance encounter, she might well have died. Instead, she was befriended by Anjornio, a black-hearted darkling. He saw in the cat a kindred spirit, an outcast forced to survive as best she could.

Meeka seemed to share the darkling's feelings of kinship. Though wild, she returned to his fire each night, often bringing a mouse or bird as a token of friendship. When Anjornio traveled, Meeka followed. In time, the darkling named her with the Vistani word for midnight.

Eventually Anjornio traveled into the domain of Valachan. One night, in the light of a dancing campfire, while Meeka sat cleaning herself, a pair of men arrived to meet with the him. After their business was done, they turned on the darkling. Transforming into werepanthers, they attacked. When Meeka rushed to Anjornio's aid, one of the werebeasts slapped her away. This blow opened a trio of wounds in her side and forever changed her life.

For several days, Meeka was on the verge of death. When she finally began to recover, she went back to her feline ways, unaware of the changes that were taking place inside her. As the wounds faded to scars, the dread disease spread throughout her body.

Two weeks later, when the moon grew bloated and amber in the sky above Valachan, Meeka underwent a transformation. No longer did she move about on four legs, slipping quietly from shadow to shadow as she hunted. For the next three days, she had the form of a human woman. Only the scars on her side remained to remind her of what she truly was.

Along with this change came a great increase in her mental faculties. Meeka was now as clever as any human. Her natural hunting instincts, however, had not changed. Within hours after her transformation, she made her first kill in human form.

In time, Meeka learned to be careful in her dealings with the human race. She soon learned some of their languages and customs, enabling her to move about in their society. She grew more careful in making her kills, aware that a trail of bloody bodies could lead to her doom.

Meeka also learned the nature of the rhythms that now control her life. Most of the time, she would remain in her feline aspect. But during the three nights of the full moon, she would become human from the moment the moon rose until the instant its last rays vanished.

Current Sketch

Meeka now travels the Core, much as she did in the days before her transformation. In feline form, she is a menace only to mice, chipmunks, and the like. When she is transformed into a human woman, however, she preys upon larger creatures—often the citizens of Ravenloft.

Personality

As a cat, Meeka is a solitary creature. She enjoys exploring, basking in the sunlight, and all other things common felines take pleasure in. She takes pleasure in the thrill of the hunt and loves to pounce at things even if she has no intention of killing them.

In her human aspect, Meeka retains something of her feline manner. This can lead others to believe that she is a pampered, almost spoiled, woman. Her aloof nature and exotic looks often cause those she meets to speculate that she is an exiled princess or other such soul.

Perhaps the most disturbing characteristic that Meeka carries over into her human form involves her hunting style. Like all cats, she likes to play with her food before she kills and eats it. While these games of cat and mouse might seem cute for a tiny cat, they are nothing short of horrific in a human female.

Meeka has little interest in human society, except as an idle curiosity. She finds the men and women of Ravenloft dirty and more than a little offensive. Her lack of experience with people makes it difficult for her to hide her contempt, something that even her exotic good looks cannot always make up for.

Combat

Meeka is really only a dangerous enemy in her human form. As a cat, she shies away from human contact. In either of her aspects, Meeka is immune to damage by any weapon not made of silver or endowed with at least a +1 magical enchantment. She is also able to move with great agility and in almost total silence, imposing a −3 penalty on the surprise rolls of her victims. Her own keen senses make it possible to surprise Meeka only on a roll of 1 or 2.

Cat Aspect

While most cats have only a single Hit Die, Meeka's intelligence and unusual physiology give her 5 HD. In her cat form, Meeka attacks with her front claws and keen teeth. Each of these attacks inflicts 1d2 points of damage. If both front-claw attacks find their mark, Meeka can then rake with her rear claws. Each successful attack with these inflicts an additional 1d2 points of damage.

In cat form, Meeka is able to climb trees and other such surfaces at half her normal movement rate. She does so to escape from danger or to set up an ambush.

Human Aspect

When in human shape, Meeka is a far more dangerous creature. The long fingernails, which appear at first glance to be the mark of a pampered woman, are actually deadly claws. In any given round, Meeka can attack twice with them, inflicting 1d4 points of damage with each blow that lands. She can follow up these attacks with a dangerous bite that inflicts an additional 1d4 points of damage.

Meeka never makes use of weapons. She is a natural hunter, and the use of knives, daggers, and the like is foreign to her. She is still very agile in her human form, having a movement rate of 18. While not as quick a climber in this aspect, she can scale surfaces like trees at one third her normal movement rate.

A CAT'S REVENGE

s this scenario unfolds, the heroes become entangled in a series of killings. At first, they'll probably be blamed for the crimes. In actuality, however, these are just loose ends being tied up by Meeka.

The nature of Meeka's curse means that the heroes must act fast if they are to solve the mysteries to follow. After the three nights of the full moon, she'll be locked in her normal cat form for another month. During that time, she'll leave the scene of her crimes far behind.

Introduction

This adventure takes place in the village of Briggdarrow, on the shores of Lake Kronov in the domain of Tepest, not far from the Shadow Rift. If the Dungeon Master wishes to move the scenario to another location, perhaps even one outside of Ravenloft, a similar setting should be chosen. In this case, the assumption must be made that the new location is also Meeka's town of birth.

There are a few important characters in this story, although their occupations are fairly generic. If the Dungeon Master wishes, they can easily be replaced by similar characters familiar to the player characters.

Barthol

Barthol is the owner and keeper of The Wayfarer's Friend, a small tavern and inn on the road leading into Briggdarrow. He is a round man with a jolly temperament and a great white beard. As a matter of fact, he looks an awful lot like Santa Claus and even shares the robust laugh one associates with that winter visitor.

Barthol's role in this adventure is, sadly, that of the victim. It was he who once threw a black cat into the chill waters of Lake Kronov and whose image has burned forever since in the mind of Meeka the catwere.

The Dungeon Master should go out of his way to portray Barthol as a really nice guy. He worries about the comfort of his guests, charges a fair rate for room and board, and is an excellent host. The more the heroes like him, the greater the impact of his death.

Wanada

This charming woman is Barthol's wife. She has elegant features and dark hair, shot through with silver. A careful look reveals that she is, in fact, a half-elf. She met Barthol many decades ago and decided to stop her nomadic wandering and assume the role of a wife. The two are happy together, and she is every bit as pleasant a host as her husband.

Denton

There are few men in Briggdarrow as physically powerful as Denton, the massive smith who fashions and mends the assorted tools required to keep the village running.

Denton is arrogant and proud. He's an easy man to dislike, prone to taking too much drink and getting into brawls. If the players suspect that they are involved in an adventure that features a werebeast, it won't be hard for the Dungeon Master to portray the blacksmith as a wereboar. This is especially true because of the tale he tells at the start of the adventure.

Several years ago, Denton spent some time as a wandering man at arms. In those days, he began to collect knives and swords. He has continued to do this ever since, which is another trait that may draw suspicion to him during the first part of the adventure.

Clandon

A stern and quiet man, Clandon is the head of Briggdarrow's city watch. He's not a man to be crossed (treat him as a 5th-level warrior) and has astonishingly little sense of humor. In many ways, Clandon can be run as the medieval equivalent of a western sheriff.

Still, despite his grim demeanor, he's an honest man who wants only to see justice done. From time to time, when witch hunts break out or other such things threaten his town, he tries to keep things calm. He doesn't always succeed, but he's always ready to clean up whatever mess such incidents might result in.

Clandon doesn't like outsiders, a trait he shares with almost everyone else in the town. He won't go out of his way to help them, but neither will he stand by and watch them blamed for a crime he doesn't think they committed.

Scene I: The Wayfarer's Friend

This adventure begins when the heroes reach the outskirts of Briggdarrow. It is assumed to be near the end of the day and a light, chill rain has come from off the lake. The warm lights of The Wayfarer's Friend beckon, as does the smell of a good meal and the promise of a warming drink.

The following narrative can be read to the players when their characters enter the tavern.

Amber light and the warmth of a blazing hearth fire embrace you as the door of The Wayfarer's Friend swings shut behind. Several tables, some occupied, are spread out before a wide bar, and the smell of roast pig hangs in the air. At the table nearest the bar, a great bear of a man with a flat-featured face is in the midst of a tale.

"Ne'er before have I seen such a creature," he says in a heavy voice slightly tainted by drink. "It were no normal boar—'twas twice the size of any I've set eyes on afore."

His companions laugh good-naturedly at this tale, jesting that his encounter was with a keg of ale rather than a wild boar. The man responds by opening his shirt. A red gash, crusted with blood, runs across his belly. It is indeed an angry wound, one sure to leave lasting scars.

At that point, the place falls quiet. The characters have been noticed and are being examined by cold eyes. Not the least curious of the tavern's patrons is Denton the Blacksmith, whose tale the heroes caught near its end. The Dungeon Master should make the most of this scene, letting the characters know from the start that this inn obviously does not hold as much hospitality as its name promises.

Then, as this cold reception is beginning to make the heroes uncomfortable, Barthol comes to their rescue. He waves them over to the bar with a big smile. The following text introduces the heroes to this friendly fellow.

"Welcome my friends!" comes a booming voice from behind the bar. "There's a storm coming in off the lake an' I can't imagine you'll be headin' out again tonight, eh? But I've room enough for you here, an' stables in the back fer horses if you've got 'em. Come o'er here and dry yourselves off. The first round is always on the house at The Wayfarer's Friend."

Angry Words

The Dungeon Master can carry on the happenings of the evening more or less as he sees fit. There are, however, a few important things that must be woven into the tapestry of events before the PCs call it a night.

As the evening goes on, the heroes are subjected to more and more hostility from Denton. He doesn't actually go so far as to start a fight on this chilly evening, but he does come pretty close to it. In fact, events proceed to the point that it seems he's about to come to blows with one of the heroes, when Barthol steps in to put an end to the matter. Or, at least, that's his plan. What actually happens next is that Denton turns his anger on the jovial innkeeper. He grows more and more hostile, though still stopping stop short of actually throwing a punch.

This whole matter comes to an end when Clandon enters the tavern. He announces that he could hear the blacksmith all the way down the block. He suggests that the burly man call it a night and head home. For a moment, it looks as if Denton is going to lash out at Clandon, but then he backs down. Cursing and grumbling under his breath, the blacksmith storms out into the night.

Clandon excuses himself as well at this point. He wants to follow Denton home and make sure the fellow doesn't get into trouble on the way. In the wake of his departure, the heroes are given the impression that this behavior is somewhat unusual. Although Denton often drinks and lets his temper get the better of him, he's never come so close to getting into a brawl with Clandon or Barthol.

Most of the locals put this down to irritability due to his injury. After all, he's a proud man and the boar that wounded him was never found. This is, in fact, exactly what happened. Of course, the heroes may well leap to some more sinister conclusion, that the boar was a werebeast, and Denton has been infected with its curse.

Cats, Cats, And More Cats

It also becomes quite apparent over the course of the evening that Barthol and his wife keep a good many cats around The Wayfarer's Friend. All told, there are about a dozen of the animals, all wandering about the place at will. The cats seem to know better than to leap onto tables or the bar but otherwise have their run of the place.

The Dungeon Master can use these animals to introduce Barthol's wife. She has a great affinity for the animals and, although her husband is fond of them as well, thinks of them all as hers. Although she acts in no way suspicious at this time, the Dungeon Master can rest assured that her love of these animals will bring her to mind when her husband is discovered murdered.

The Dungeon Master should also work in mention during the evening that a black cat has been seen around town. Briggdarrow's people as a superstitious lot, and they all make signs of protection when the creature is mentioned. Again, later in the adventure, further mention of a black cat being associated with the killings will help to point a finger of suspicion toward Wanada. Whether the PCs think that she is able to become a cat, or that she is some manner of witch herself (remember, the lords of Tepest are hags) is unimportant. All that matters is that these seeds of doubt and fear are planted.

Scene II: The First Night

Several hours later, after the heroes have retired for the evening, Meeka strikes. Tonight is the first of the three nights when the lycanthropic blood in her veins changes her to the form of a human woman. It is the night when Barthol pays for the attempted murder of a small kitten many years ago.

Meeka strikes a little before midnight. She starts by making a slight racket outside of Barthol's window. As the rain outside falls steadily and the wind howls in the darkness, the innkeeper is awakened. Concerned that something might be amiss in the stable, he dons a robe and wanders out to investigate. In the stable, he is attacked.

Meeka strikes without warning, opening a nasty gash in Barthol's face with her long fingernails. She doesn't follow this up with a killing blow, however, but torments him with several other cuts first. She eventually tires of this game, however, and ends the matter.

Barthol's death scream wakes the heroes from their sleep. Read the following text aloud to detail this event.

In the dead of night, as a steady rain dapples the window panes and a chill wind howls through the trees, a horrible scream startles you from your sleep. It is a sound so full of fear and pain as to make your blood run cold.

This dread cry is followed quickly by the sound of a woman's voice. You recognize it as Wanada's. "Barthol!" she yells. "What has happened? Are you okay?"

Having heard the scream, you know she will receive no answer.

Outside, in the yard that separates the stables from the inn itself, is the body of Barthol. It is not a pretty sight, for the flesh has been nearly flayed from his bones in places. The following text can read aloud to describe what the heroes see that night.

Barthol's body lies face down in a broad puddle that seems composed of equal parts water, mud, and blood. The innkeeper's rounded shape is oddly contorted, with ribbons of flesh hanging from great wounds, and one knee clearly broken. His hand is outstretched, as if he were grabbing at the inn's door when he cried out. A more gruesome sight would be difficult to imagine.

Clandon's Investigation

In the wake of this attack, Clandon arrives to investigate the matter. He is be quick to suspect the newcomers but won't insist on locking them up right away. He warns them not to leave town, however, and sets about trying to figure out what went on.

Even a casual investigation of the area reveals that the attack began in the stables. This is evident from the splashes of blood on the walls, a few broken tools with which Barthol tried to defend himself, and the general scattering of just about everything else inside.

A more detailed investigation enables the characters to determine that the wounds inflicted on Barthol were caused by very sharp claws. Exactly what type of animal might have made them is unclear, however.

The Blacksmith

Some suspicion also falls on the blacksmith. After all, Denton and Barthol did quarrel earlier that night. In addition, the blacksmith is known to keep some fierce dogs. While it seems unlikely that Barthol's wounds were caused by anything canine, still the corpse is in pretty rough shape, so Clandon won't rule anything out.

If the heroes go to visit Denton, they find that he denies all knowledge of the killing. He doesn't seem too surprised by it, though. Like most of the folk in Briggdarrow, he's always assumed that something like this would happen to Barthol. No good can come of catering to strangers.

While they're looking around at Denton's shop, which is also his home, the heroes can hardly help noticing his collection of knives. Most of these are in excellent condition, razor sharp and well polished. The wounds suffered by Barthol are long, parallel gashes, however—not the sort of injuries that a common knife inflicts.

A closer look, however, reveals one weapon that just might have been used to cause the types of wounds found on Barthol. Hanging on one wall is a weapon that looks like a metal gauntlet with short blades projecting from between the knuckles. It's similar to the tiger claws worn by assassins in certain oriental cultures.

Any interview or meeting with Denton should end with him losing his temper and chasing the heroes away. He may even loose his dogs on them or threaten other violence. This sets the stage for the next killing.

Scene III: The Next Night

Meeka's next victim is the Blacksmith. At first, however, she intends only to kill his dogs. A bad turn of events, however, costs Denton his life as well.

Shortly before midnight on the second night of the full moon, Meeka makes her way to Denton's home. She breaks into the pen where his trio of dogs is kept. As she rips them apart, they raise a terrible ruckus. The noise soon arouses Denton from his deep slumber.

When the blacksmith goes to investigate, Meeka has no real choice but to kill him. His body, as well as those of his dogs, is found in the morning. Following this, Clandon is notified and he, in turn, sends for the heroes. When they arrive, read the following narrative.

At first glance, everything looks normal enough at the Blacksmith's shop. His bellows and other equipment stand ready, finished tools are offered for sale, and those in need of repair await Denton's attention.

Behind the shop and the small cottage to which it is attached, however, things are quite different. There, beneath a peaceful blue sky, lies a scene of bloody carnage and death.

The blacksmith's body lies in the center of a large dog pen. Three parallel gashes cut across his face, splitting it open to the bone. A thick, white blanket has been thrown over his body. This is almost certainly a merciful thing, for great crimson stains have soaked through it. Clearly, Denton's wounds must be nothing short of horrific.

The bodies of three dogs lie near that of their master. Great wounds crisscross their bodies, making it obvious that their killer had a most savage disposition. These animals are clearly half-wolf, and they certainly didn't go down without a fight.

It should be clear from the questions he asks that Clandon suspects that the player characters are his murderers. Not only does he conclude matters by reminding them that they are not to leave town, he also has their horses (if they have any) rounded up and transferred to his own stables. He then assigns three men (all 1st-level fighters) to watch The Wayfarer's Friend that night.

The PCs have the day to look around and conduct their own investigations, but they are under strict orders to be back in their rooms by sunset. If they don't agree to these terms, the constable has them arrested and held in the town jail. He's willing to give them the benefit of the doubt for the moment, but he won't stand for anyone challenging his authority.

Wanada's Thoughts

Barthol's wife is doing her best to hold things together in the wake of her husband's death. She loved him dearly and can't believe that he's been taken from her. For the time being, she tries to lose herself in keeping the Wayfarer open and running.

She also pays a lot of attention to the cats. In fact, this is something that the PCs may well read the wrong way. After her husband's death, she is never to be encountered without one of the felines in her arms. Often, she can be found brushing them or whispering softly in their ears. She also seems a bit distant and lost.

All of this is normal enough considering what she has been through. To the PCs, however, it's likely to raise suspicions.

Scene IV: The Last Night

The third night of the full moon finds Meeka returning to the scene of her first crime. It is her plan to put an end to the life of Wanada, who shares Barthol's guilt in her attempted killing. This time, however, the PCs will be alarmed before the killing and ought to arrive in time to save Wanada's life.

In order to get into the house, Meeka must get past the man stationed outside. This isn't too difficult for her. All she has to do is sneak up on him and slash open his throat with her deadly claws. Apart from a gurgled cry of alarm, which can't be heard more than a few yards away, there is no other warning of her entry into the inn.

Read the following narrative aloud some time after the heroes have retired for the night.

At first, the sounds that reach your ears in the dead of night don't seem at all unusual—especially in The Wayfarer's Friend. A single cat hisses and lets out a low growl of warning. This primal alarm spreads from one animal to another until the whole of the night is filled with feral sounds. In fact, so disturbing is this caterwauling that it hardly seems surprising when a woman's scream is added to the chorus.

Meeka has made her way into Wanada's bedroom (where nearly all the cats in the house sleep) and now crouches at the foot of the bed. Her eyes blaze with the fury of an untamed animal. There can be no doubt that the heroes are in the presence of the killer.

Fighting Meeka

In the battle that follows, Meeka fights valiantly. She focuses her attention on Wanada, however, eager to destroy the woman who was a party to her attempted murder. In this skirmish, the Dungeon Master should do everything in his power to play up the cat-like nature of this enemy. She leaps about, hissing and snarling, throughout the whole encounter.

This battle almost certainly ends with the characters dispatching Meeka. After all, she isn't a particularly deadly opponent (at least, not as far as lycanthropes go).

Loose Ends

The Dungeon Master must use some care at the end of this adventure. If it ends without the PCs learning why Meeka has been killing the people of Briggdarrow, the players won't feel the scenario was anything more than a random collection of killings. There are a number of ways in which they can learn about the events that led to this tragedy, however.

After her death, the Meeka reverts to her cat form. If Wanada is still alive, she recognizes the animal and

gasps out the revelation in horror, speaking as if to her dead husband. For the moment, she seems to have forgotten altogether the presence of the heroes.

If instead Meeka manages to kill the innkeeper's wife, she can be allowed to spit out a few seconds of vengeful explanation before an attempted escape. Her words make it clear that Barthol and Wanada once tried to kill her, although the rest of her story remains untold.

In either case, or if both of the women are killed, the players can learn about what has gone before in any number of ways. They might use a *speak with dead* spell or perhaps piece together the facts from someone else in town. As a last resort, the Dungeon Master may assume that that Wanada has kept a journal in which an account of the black cat's birth and presumed death is recorded.

Slipping Away

It's quite possible that the characters will be the inn's only survivors of this encounter. If this happens, they'll be right in the middle of things again. Or so it seems. The folk of Briggdarrow are so superstitious that they are more than willing to blame a black cat for what has happened. However, they're also going to be pretty quick to link the cat to the heroes. This is especially true if one of the party is a wizard or other spellcaster. After all, is there anything more common for a wizard or a witch to have than a black cat familiar?

All in all, the best thing for the heroes to do at the end of this adventure is pack up their gear and get out of town as quickly and quietly as possible.

Recurrence

Even if this adventure ends with Meeka's death, there are other ways in which these events might further torment the heroes.

It is possible that one of the other cats in the room was injured by Meeka during the fight. In this case, the animal could become a catwere as well. The same thing could happen if one of the cats laps at Meeka's wounds or tastes her blood. If the heroes managed to save Wanada's life, the newly afflicted cat might even be made a gift to them at the end of the adventure, with no one realizing its deadly potential.

At the very least, this adventure can be mirrored if the heroes ever return to Briggdarrow. As soon as they ride into town, the villagers begin to whisper behind their backs. If this is coupled with another mysterious killing or two—whatever the reason—the heroes might find themselves in danger of being hanged or burned at the stake.

Abu al Mir

It is a matter of regret that many low, mean suspicions turn out to be well founded.

—Edgar Watson Howe
Ventures in Common Sense

Biography

Abu al Mir was once a young priest of Anubis in the distant domain of Har' Akir. His parents headed an order of werejackals who had built a hidden temple to their god. In the wake of Senmet's attempt to destroy the domain's lord, the temple's priesthood all perished, with the exception of young Abu. Stripped of many of his powers as a result of the temple's fall, al Mir now wanders the Mists of Ravenloft, a broken man with little hope, struggling merely to survive.

Appearance

As a werejackal, Abu al Mir is able to take either of two forms. The first is human; the second is a hybrid aspect of human and jackal.

Human Aspect

In human form, Abu al Mir is a slight man, standing perhaps five and a half feet tall. He is very slender—so much so that he looks distinctly unhealthy. His leather-brown skin is mottled here and there with darker splotches, and his hair is ragged and unkempt. His eyes are cold and black but so watery and weak that all who look into these orbs cannot help but realize that they are in the presence of a broken man.

Although he has left behind the domain of his birth, al Mir normally still wears the traditional clothes of that desert land. These consist of a loose tunic of creamy yellow cloth upon his upper torso, above a snug robe of the same material around his hips and legs, bound at the waist with a black sash. He also wears a tightly wound turban of like color. An unusual bronze dagger with a large, wickedly curved blade rests in a sheath in his belt.

Hybrid Aspect

Al Mir's hybrid aspect is a horrific combination of jackal and man. At first glance, al Mir seems a terrifying and deadly creature. A second look, however, reveals that his fur is uneven and dirty—giving off an odor that is both distinctive and offensive—and his eyes are as every bit as watery and weak-looking as in his human form. While he is clearly a monster, he is a pitiful example of one.

Abu al Mir

True Werejackal, Neutral Evil

Armor Class	5	Str	10
Movement	15	Dex	10
Level/Hit Dice	6	Con	10
Hit Points	45	Int	16
THAC0	15	Wis	16
Morale	Steady (12)	Cha	8
No. of Attacks	2		
Damage/Attack	1d6/1d6 (claws)		
Special Attacks	Bite (1d10), Spell Use,		
Special Defenses	Hit only by bronze and +1 or better magical weapons, Turn Undead		
Magic Resistance	Nil		

Abu al Mir

Background

Abu al Mir's parents were the founders of a hidden temple to Anubis, built somewhere in Har' Akir. They were rewarded for their devotion with a transformation into werejackals. When their son was born in 725, they discovered that he too shared the gift of their god.

In 738, when Senmet attempted to destroy Ankhtepot, the lord of Har' Akir, he sought to enlist the aid of al Mir's parents. They agreed to help, but never even had the opportunity to enter into the fray. The very night of their agreement, a raging fire swept through the hidden temple of Anubis. Al Mir's parents were destroyed, along with all the other priests there. Only Abu survived.

The young boy was terrified. He believed that Anubis was angered by the deal his parents struck with Senmet. Certain that the wrath of this god would soon fall upon him as well, he fled into the desert. He had not gone far into the wastes around Muhar when a savage sandstorm whipped up. Abu found shelter in a the lee of a small outcropping of stone and fell asleep as the storm raged all around him. When al Mir awoke, the storm was ended, and he was in a land unlike any he had ever seen before. Instead of yellow sand, he saw only lush green vegetation. The young man was no longer in Har' Akir but had made his way into Nova Vaasa.

From that point on, al Mir has lived as a fugitive, convinced that the wrath of Anubis follows close upon his heels. The fact that his own powers are greatly reduced in this new land has served only to confirm his belief.

Current Sketch

Al Mir has become a coward and a scavenger in his new life. He uses his magic to learn secrets, then sells these to the highest bidder. He is very comfortable with blackmail and other such crimes, though he is careful that no one pays him off with a dagger instead of a gold piece.

Sometimes al Mir will come to the aid of a party of adventurers, if they can meet his price. He has provided crucial information to Alanik Ray, the master detective, on many occasions. What he received in the way of payment for these services is unknown.

Al Mir works from the shadows, never allowing anyone to know more about him than is necessary. He trusts no one but occasionally strikes up a short-term relationship with someone he perceives as useful. He almost always ends such arrangements with the flash of a bronze dagger in the dead of night.

Personality

Al Mir is a coward, plain and simple. He is constantly on the move, fearing that the agents of Anubis or Senmet are not far behind him. Whether he is actually being hunted is anyone's guess, but there is a good chance that the only hounds on his scent are in his imagination.

There is another reason, far more immediate, for al Mir to be afraid, however. Over the years he has made many enemies, and more than a few would like to see him dead. Al Mir knows this all too well and treats every new encounter as a potential trap. The truth is, he is ruthless and without compassion. Those who refuse to settle with him when he comes into possession of incriminating information soon find their secrets spread all over town.

For some odd reason, however, al Mir does maintain a modicum of integrity in his business dealings. He never sells information that he believes to be untrue, and if his silence is purchased on a given matter, that is the end of the matter. He never returns to demand additional payments from a "client" for the same bit of blackmail. This is not to say, however, that new information will not merit another call from the werejackal.

Combat

When al Mir expects to enter combat, he usually arranges to be in his hybrid form because it is his most dangerous. As he is very cowardly at heart, however, he goes out of his way to avoid conflict whenever possible.

In either of his forms, al Mir remains immune to harm from any weapon that is not either made from bronze or endowed with a +1 or better magical enchantment. Silver weapons, which are anathema to most werebeasts, have no special power against al Mir.

After each round of combat, al Mir must make a morale check. Failure indicates that his natural cowardice takes hold and he must flee the area at once (if possible). It takes him 5d4 rounds to recover his courage, and he may return to the fight at that time. In most cases, however, he simply considers the encounter closed and plots some sinister revenge against those who drove him away.

Most werejackals can cast spells as 6th-level priests with an 18 Wisdom. Because of his cowardice, however, al Mir can no longer work magic that well. He now casts spells as a 3rd-level priest with a 16 Wisdom, using these powers primarily for information gathering and protection. Typically he has the following spells ready: (1st level) *detect magic, detect poison, detect snares and pits, invisibility to undead;* (2nd level) *augury, find traps, wyvern watch.* If he expects to be in a dangerous situation, he alters his chosen spells, replacing *augury* with *barkskin,* for example.

Although al Mir retains some mastery over the undead, this power has also been weakened. Instead of commanding them, as he could while in Anubis's service, he can now only turn them. Further, he uses this power as a 3rd-level priest, able to turn only skeletons, zombies, ghouls, shadows, wights, and ghasts.

Hybrid Form

In hybrid form, al Mir strikes first with his sharp, curving claws. Each successful blow inflicts 1d6 points of damage. If either attack finds its mark, al Mir is assumed have drawn close enough to bite his enemy. A successful biting attack with his keen ebony teeth and powerful jaws inflicts 1d10 points of damage. Those injured by al Mir are not at risk of becoming lycanthropes, however, for the ability to create others of his kind has been stripped from him.

Human Form

When forced to do battle in his human form, al Mir normally attacks with a large dagger with a blade that curves like a hawk's beak. This weapon inflicts 1d4+1 points of damage and is fashioned from bronze so that it can be used against other werejackals. Al Mir has been known to use a variety of deadly poisons on this blade.

DARKNESS AND SECRETS

This scenario can be run as a one-shot adventure, luring the player characters unknowingly into a confrontation between a greater mummy and a desperate werejackal. If the Dungeon Master desires, however, the scenario can instead become merely a launching point for an entire mini-campaign into the domain of Har' Akir. Notes for both approaches are included within the adventure text. In either case, the scenario works well to introduce the heroes to Abu al Mir, who potentially could become a regular source of information for them.

Introduction

This scenario can be set within any city sufficiently large to contain something of an underworld (a thieves guild, for instance). For the purposes of this text, the adventure is set in Port-a-Lucine.

At the start of the scenario, the heroes come into contact with a woman who calls herself Madame LaFontaine. Her true identity—that of a greater mummy—is hidden by a series of illusions. If the PCs have some means of penetrating them, the Dungeon Master needs to counter that ability, at least for a while. The DM might choose a time when they have decided to memorize other spells, for instance, to introduce her, or drop a magical item into the player characters' path that neutralizes the ability to detect her true nature.

Over the course of this adventure, the characters run into (and perhaps afoul of) three important characters on their path to finding Abu al Mir. Brief descriptions of these persons and the roles they play are detailed below.

Madame LaFontaine

The woman who goes by the name of Madame LaFontaine carries herself with the class and sophistication of a noble lady. She has dark hair, an olive complexion, and intelligent eyes. Her features never betray the slightest hint of emotion. Her clothes, jewelry, and other adornments are all valuable antiquities.

In actuality, however, this woman is not at all what she appears to be. Madame LaFontaine is actually a greater mummy named Lef Ahmnet. (Game statistics for greater mummies are presented in the *Monstrous Manual*.) A devoted servant of Ankhtepot, the darklord of Har' Akir, she has disguised her true features by means of several magical spells. The DM should decide her age (and thus her strength) based upon the abilities of the party.

Lef Ahmnet has been sent by Ankhtepot to track down and destroy Abu al Mir. The role al Mir's parents intended to play in Senmet's abortive attempt to destroy Ankhtepot has come to that lord's attention of late. Assuming that al Mir is his enemy as well, Ankhtepot has decided to trim this loose end.

Unfortunately for the player characters, Lef Ahmnet is uncomfortable dealing with cultures outside her own. Her unfamiliarity with the ways of Dementlieu has proven to be a great handicap. Consequently, she has decided to recruit some local help—which is where the heroes come into play. Once they have located al Mir, she intends to dispose of them along with him, in order to protect her secret and avoid discovery by Dementliue's darklord, Dominic d'Honaire. She assumes that no darklord would take kindly to another's agent working within his realm.

Black Pieter

Black Pieter is an accomplished rogue and master assassin who heads an order known as *The Circle Sinister* in Port-a-Lucine. Through this group of murderers and cutthroats, he has a finger in almost all illegal activity within the city. In this adventure he serves as a source of information for the heroes, because he also has some interest in Abu al Mir, although it is of a more businesslike nature.

Captain Dupree

If Black Pieter has an opposite in the city, it is Captain Dupree. Dupree is in charge of the city watch's night shift. From just before midnight to shortly after sunrise, the entire city is in his hands. Like Black Pieter, Captain Dupree appears in this adventure primarily to help the heroes in their search for Abu al Mir. While the werejackal isn't currently wanted by the police, they always watch with interest the comings and goings of such folk.

Scene I: A Grand Lady's Plea

To begin the adventure, the heroes receive a short letter, requesting a meeting in *The Blue Crescent*, one of the city's most expensive restaurants. The letter is delivered by a messenger boy who can only say that it was given to him by "a great lady, very proper-like." Other than that, he has no other information to reveal. Of course, the "great lady" is none other than Lef Ahmnet, in her disguise as Madame LaFontaine. Her letter is on expensive stationary and reads as follows.

My Friends,
*   We have never met, but word of your bravery and resourcefulness has reached my ears. I am in need of the services of heroes such as you, and will gladly pay you a considerable fee for your aid. Please meet me at 10:00 tonight at The Blue Crescent. A private room has been reserved there in my name.*
*   This is a matter which is at once very important and of the most sensitive nature. Please tell no one that you are to meet with me.*

*   Madame LaFontaine*

The Dungeon Master should do all that he can to convey the posh nature of this place to the players. At the same time, however, it should be made clear that the help is being paid a great deal of money to forget that any of this is taking place. (If a similar setting has been previously established in the campaign, the Dungeon Master can substitute it instead.)

Madame LaFontaine arrives shortly after the heroes do. The following text can be used to introduce her.

*   The Blue Crescent is as fine a restaurant as you have ever seen. The wine that awaits you upon your arrival is obviously of superb vintage and quite expensive. Never before have you tasted its equal. As the first bottle gives up the last of its crimson contents, the door to the private room opens, and a slender figure enters from the shadows beyond.*
*   She is an elderly woman, who moves with some effort. Her clothes are dark blue and elegant, speaking of wealth and distinction. Her gray hair is bound back from her narrow face by a silver ribbon. With keen eyes, she looks you over carefully. Then, with a nod of satisfaction, she takes a seat.*
*   "I thank you very much for coming," she says in a dry voice. "I am Madame LaFontaine."*

This meeting need not be a protracted one. Madame LaFontaine has, for all intents and purposes, no personality at all. She is as dry and distinguished as might be. Her story is a short one, and she relays it without any evidence of emotion.

*   "Not too many days ago," Madame LaFontaine says hoarsely, "I received a letter demanding one thousand gold pieces. If this payment is not made, certain information of a most delicate nature will be made public. In common terms, I am being blackmailed.*
*   "While I can easily afford to make the payment, I am loath to do so. Instead of giving my gold to some black-hearted rogue, I prefer to give it to you. All I ask in return is a simple service. Find the man who is blackmailing me and persuade him that it is in his best interests to drop the matter. How you convince him is of no interest to me."*

Madame LaFontaine does not offer any advance payment for this service unless the heroes demand it of her. If pressed, she offers half the payment up front. While she doesn't have the cash with her, she gives the party an ornate golden ring as a retainer.

This is a most curious item, which she claims to have been given by a dignitary from a distant land. It is covered with hieroglyphs and made of solid gold. Madame LaFontaine says that she's never had it appraised, but it must certainly be worth several hundred gold pieces. Anyone who examines it with a knowledgeable eye recognizes that this is the case.

As a starting point for their investigation, Madame LaFontaine hands the heroes a creamy white envelope. It has been cut open, leaving the wax seal on its back intact. This seal bears the imprint of a jackal's head. Although LaFontaine states that this is the envelope in which the blackmail note was received, that is not the case. It's actually a forgery she created to support her story. The imprint on the wax, however, is an excellent imitation of that produced by Abu al Mir's own signet ring.

Scene II: The Investigation

The heroes can set about their investigation however they see fit. If they are familiar with the city, they may have contacts to check with for a lead on the wax imprint they possess. If they are new to the city, however, they may need to do some careful asking around to determine who might know something about their man.

There are two basic directions to go in seeking Abu al Mir. One is to check with the city's authorities. The other is to contact the seamy underbelly of the city.

Checking with the authorities eventually leads the heroes to Captain Dupree. But along the way, they meet various other personalities, from honest, hard working officials to petty bureaucrats. The Dungeon Master will have to invent these individuals on the fly, depending upon where the heroes start. Many of the people they meet should be gruff, even threatening, wanting to know why the party is seeking such a low-life. By evening, however, the heroes should be directed to the city guard, where they are told that Captain Dupree is the best man to talk to about scum like al Mir. They just have to wait until near midnight, when he comes on duty.

If the heroes choose to check the less scrupulous side of the city, they should get the same sort of runaround for a while—though the personalities they meet in this case range from nervous, penny-ante crooks to hard-eyed ruffians—before they are finally ushered in to meet Black Pieter himself.

In the end, it doesn't really matter which path the heroes follow first. From that source, they learn the name of the likely blackmailer: Abu al Mir. By the time they are finished, however, the players should feel like clever detectives—easily the equal of Alanik Ray, Rudolph van Richten, or Sherlock Holmes.

The First Encounter

When the heroes finally meet Black Pieter or Captain Dupree, whichever they see first, read the following text:

"I recognize that sign," he says, with a slow nod. "It belongs to a weasel named Abu al Mir. I don't know where he's from, but he's been living in the city for the last year or so. He deals in information, dabbles in blackmail, and maybe does some spying on the side. I don't know where he lives, though. His kind keeps a very low profile."

The Second Encounter

When they finally reach the second of these two men, the heroes receive a few more pieces of the puzzle.

"Abu al Mir? Yeah, I know the little rat. He lives down on the waterfront. Last I heard, he was renting a place above Novak's Rentals on Harbor Street. Stay clear of Novak—he's a tough customer. I don't think he'll get involved unless you force the matter, though."

Black Pieter's Final Words

The meeting with Black Pieter, whether it is the first or second trail the heroes pursue, can be concluded with the following bit of information.

"When you find al Mir," says Black Pieter in a smooth, measured voice, "tell him that his time is running out. He's fallen behind in his payments to the Guild and my patience is exhausted."

Captain Dupree's Final Words

When the heroes talk with Captain Dupree, the conversation can be wrapped up as follows.

"Do me a favor," says Captain Dupree coldly. "When you talk to al Mir, tell him that I'm going to be keeping an eye on him. If he takes a single step out of line, I'll see to it he doesn't have time to take a second."

A Sinister Shadow

After the party has had its second meeting, one of the heroes should notice a mysterious figure tailing the group. The PCs are free to speculate about the nature of this figure and to take whatever steps they wish to elude it.

In all probability, heroes will assume that the tail is an agent of the Thieves Guild, although they might also suspect a member of the town watch. The truth, however, is that the figure shadowing the group is actually the mummy Lef Ahmnet (a.k.a. Madame LaFontaine). By means of her magical abilities, she is tracking the group so that she will know the instant that they discover al Mir's location. While the heroes can lose this tail without too much effort, turning the tables on her is a different story altogether.

Scene IV: Abu al Mir's Lair

The next scene begins as the heroes make their way along the waterfront in search of al Mir's lodgings. These are dangerous streets, and strangers (like the heroes) are likely to find trouble within them. The group might set off a brawl by saying the wrong thing to a drunken sailor, bumping into a dock worker who's carrying a heavy burden, or unintentionally offending a woman looking for some companionship. Given the fact that they're snooping around, the locals may take an instant disliking to them no matter how well they behave.

Sooner or later, however, the heroes find their way to al Mir's apartment. It's an attic room three floors above street level, poorly furnished and filthily maintained.

Abu al Mir's apartment is revolting. The air inside is thick with the smell of rotting food and moldering cloth. A pitiful excuse for a hearth holds a dismal fire, adding a sour smell of smoke to the atmosphere.

Al Mir himself is hardly more impressive than his lodgings. He looks—and smells—as if it's been far too long since his last bath. Indeed, one would imagine that even getting caught in the occasional rainstorm would keep a person cleaner than he is.

The man regards you with fearful, guilty eyes. The way they shift makes him seem spineless and weak. It's easy to believe that this cowardly little man is nothing more than a parasite. Still, something inside reminds you that parasites have a way of killing their hosts.

Al Mir acts guilty from the moment the heroes meet him—before they even tell him why they've come. Obviously, he has many sins weighing on his

conscience, and he automatically assumes that the party has come to bring him trouble. Even as the player characters speak, al Mir edges toward a window, obviously ready to take flight at a moment's notice.

When the heroes mention the name of Madam LaFontaine, however, al Mir looks honestly confused. He swears that he has never heard of such a person. Sure, he admits to procuring and selling information, and sometimes selling his silence—after all, everyone needs a trade—but in this case he insists the group has found the wrong person.

Assuming the heroes show al Mir the envelope with the jackal symbol imprinted into its wax seal, he gives it a startled glance, begins to say "But I didn't. . . ," then shakes his head in disbelief, a trembling grin slowly growing on his lips.

"This looks like mine, but it isn't," he says. "See how crisply etched the jackal's teeth are? Now look at my ring. My jackal lost a tooth some years ago." Sure enough, the signet ring on al Mir's finger is missing a tooth from its jackal emblem.

"Someone went to a lot of trouble to make up this false signet and have you seek me out," the little man says. Then, as the implication of that statement set in, his eyes grow wide, his face turns pale, and a trembling begins to sweep over him. "They must have followed you!" he says. Fearfully, he turns to gaze at his apartment door, edging away from it slowly.

At this moment, as if summoned by al Mir's words, the mummy Lef Ahmnet makes her appearance.

The door to the apartment swings slowly open, as if propelled by a gust of wind. From the darkness beyond, a strange, stale scent of exotic spices wafts into the room.

"You have done well, my little detectives" a dry voice rasps from the doorway. It is instantly recognizable as that of Madame LaFontaine. "For many years I have searched for this offensive little creature, and now you have delivered him into my hands."

She steps forward out of the darkness, and stands there for a moment, as prim as ever, but somehow seeming to radiate a smug satisfaction. Then, without a sound, her shape begins to ripple as if viewed through heat waves off of desert sands. The features of the old woman dissolve away to reveal a thing so utterly horrific that your heart seems to stand still in your chest.

Where once stood a frail old woman, you now see a withered brown corpse. Funereal cloths are wrapped tightly around its torso, but dangling loosely from the arms and legs. A faintly glowing ankh hangs from a brass chain around its neck. Cold evil seems to glow in the mummy's eyes as its ominous laughter echoes in your ears.

The creature that was Madame LaFontaine does not intend to let anyone leave this place alive. Casting a *blade barrier* on the doorway, she then moves forward to attack, focussing on al Mir first. The Dungeon Master should choose other spells for her appropriate to the party's level of ability, keeping in mind that she avoids conjuring magical flames, because of their potential danger to herself. Otherwise, she is content to destroy the entire building, if necessary, in order to kill her enemies inside.

For his part, at the end of the first round of combat, al Mir transforms into his hybrid shape. He and the player characters should fight side-by-side against the mummy for a few rounds. Then, when the heroes seem committed to the battle, al Mir takes the opportunity to flee, diving out a window. If any of the heroes are close enough to watch, they notice that he catches hold of a rope he has strung from just below the window to the roof of a neighboring building. Transforming back to human shape, he scrabbles hand-over-hand along that rope, soon reaching the other building and disappearing from sight.

Frustrated at having lost her primary quarry, Lef Ahmnet now focuses her attacks upon the player characters. Given her fearsome power, it shouldn't take

long for them to decide that al Mir had the right idea in fleeing. Perhaps if they were better prepared to battle a mummy they might have a chance of winning. But given that Lef Ahmnet has caught them unawares, their hope of beating her now should be slim.

The heroes can escape by following al Mir's route out the window and along the rope, though the mummy tosses magic after them with abandon. As they near the other roof, she severs the near end of the rope, hoping they will fall when they strike the far wall. The Dungeon Master should arrange this to seem a very narrow escape.

With this, the scenario is ended. While the heroes may not have defeated their enemy and gained great treasure, the fact that they have escaped with their lives should seem a not inconsequential reward.

Recurrence

If the player characters are inclined to cut their losses and get out of town, that's fine. In this case, however, the Dungeon Master can keep Abu al Mir in reserve, as a recurring character when the heroes need information. Al Mir might turn up in any town they visit, as he is always on the move to avoid being found by Lef Ahmnet or other agents of Ankhtepot. For that matter, the heroes might stumble across Len Ahmnet again as well, perhaps in another guise than that of Madame LaFontaine. While she is not actively seeking them, she will not pass up an opportunity to destroy them should they meet again.

If, on the other hand, the heroes are of a mind to resolve the loose ends of this scenario, the Dungeon Master can use this as an opportunity to lure them into Har' Akir. In this case, immediately after the heroes escape the mummy's attack, they find al Mir waiting for them. He explains that Lef Ahmnet cannot afford to let any of them live to tell tales, and their best bet is to all stick together.

If the heroes agree to take al Mir along, his first recommendation is that they all pack up and leave town immediately. Then, on the road, he presents two options for resolving their common troubles. Both involve seeking the realm of Har' Akir, where he was born.

The first option is to seek out Ankhtepot himself and beg for mercy. Al Mir believes that he can convince the darklord that he had no knowledge of his parents' rebellious plans, and that he does not share them in any way. He will offer to swear allegiance to Ankhtepot if the darklord will rescind the werejackal's death sentence. As friends of al Mir, the heroes should the be free from danger as well.

The second option is to return to the ruins of al Mir's old temple to restore his former power and to collect a holy item with which to destroy the mummy. That accomplished, al Mir believes that Ankhtepot will not dare send any other agents after him, lest the darklord lose them as well.

Who will pity the snake charmer bitten by a serpent, or any who go near wild beasts?

—Ecclesiasticus 12:13
Apocrypha

BIOGRAPHY

heneya was born in the distant realm of Zakhara, a desert land of genies, sultans, and tropical oases. She is the fruit of an unholy union between a human woman and an elder serpent. Neither truly woman nor truly beast, Sheneya is a thoroughly evil creature who uses her unique talents for murder and assassination.

Appearance

Sheneya is an extraordinarily thin woman who stands some five and a half feet tall. Her skin is dark and tightly stretched over her bones. Her eyes gleam blackly and dart about constantly, as if ever wary.

Although Sheneya does not feel comfortable wearing clothes, she recognizes their importance in human society. She tends to favor whatever outfit helps her to blend in, paying no attention to color or style, and generally looking somewhat disheveled.

The most obvious evidence of Sheneya's unique background is a complete lack of hair from head to toe. From a distance, it may seem that her head is shaven, but up close it is obvious that Sheneya actually has no hair. Her other distinctive trait is an extremely low body temperature, roughly half that of a normal human. Anyone who touches her bare skin notices that she feels cold to the touch, and characters using infravision can see the difference. This has led more than one doomed adventurer to assume that Sheneya is some sort of undead creature.

Sheneya

Maledictive Werecobra, Chaotic Evil

Armor Class	7, 5, or 3	Str	11
Movement	15	Dex	16
Level/Hit Dice	4+2	Con	12
Hit Points	25	Int	15
THAC0	17	Wis	13
Morale	Steady (10)	Cha	16
No. of Attacks	1		
Damage/Attack	1d3 (bite)		
Special Attacks	Poison and enthralling		
Special Defenses	Hit only by ivory and +1 or better magical weapons		
Magic Resistance	Immune to charm or enchantment/charm spells		

Background

Sheneya's parents, Jandi and Alleya, were entertainers who traveled the sands of Zakhara in search of adventure and gold. Theirs was a stormy relationship, and they were known to quarrel loudly with some regularity.

During their travels, the couple met a mysterious nomad who offered them magical secrets for charming snakes. He gave his name as Hister but would say nothing of his past. Hister was, in fact, an agent of the almost mythical Grand Snakemaster (see "Snakes" in the MONSTROUS MANUAL tome), who had taken the guise of a man. In exchange for his secrets, Hister asked that Alleya bear his child. He explained that he was growing old and wanted to leave the world some offspring.

The deal completed, the disguised serpent went on its way. Sheneya's parents made good use of the powers they had gained, and their act became renown throughout the land. The couple's fame and fortune—

Sheneya

like the child in Alleya's womb, Sheneya—grew with each passing month.

When the time came for Alleya to deliver, however, trouble arose. As she entered labor, a terrible fever wracked her body. Minutes after Sheneya was born, Alleya died.

An examination of the body revealed that Alleya had been poisoned. Knowing that the couple was prone to loud arguments, the authorities grew suspicious. Investigating further, they learned that the child was not Jandi's. This, they thought, was certainly motive enough for a man to attempt murder of both his wife and a bastard child. They eventually beheaded Jandi for Alleya's death, although he protested his innocence to the last.

As no one else appeared to claim her, Sheneya was placed in the care of a man who professed to be her uncle. Thus it was that she was reunited with the sinister creature who had sired her. Hister explained to Sheneya that she was a unique creature, one who would do the bidding of the Grand Snakemaster in the world of men. In time, she would be rewarded for her loyalty and efforts with power over men and serpents alike.

Current Sketch

Sheneya believes that she has a great destiny to fulfill, although exactly what it is she does not know. She is convinced, however, that one day both men and serpents will be hers to command. Most of her life is now spent researching ancient lore and learning the secrets of mankind. She is especially interested in human stories involving serpents in general and the Grand Snakemaster in particular. When the day comes for that creature's plans come about, Sheneya intends to be ready.

Personality

Sheneya is a cold and cunning woman, utterly emotionless and without compassion. She has no respect for life other than her own, and anyone who crosses her is likely to wind up poisoned in the night. Although the years have brought her a greater understanding of human society, she is still uncomfortable when dealing with people. Most notice that there is something odd about her manner and speech.

Combat

Sheneya prefers to avoid violence except when her opponents are helpless. Although she usually accomplishes this by means of her enthralling dance, she has also been known to use sedatives and other measures to gain the upper hand. Still, whatever the situation, Sheneya is a dangerous opponent.

Weapons not made of ivory or imbued with a magical enchantment of at least +1 cannot harm her.

Also, the very blood in her veins is so infused with deadly venom that it makes Sheneya immune to all other poisons. Indeed, so lethal is her blood that it is treated as poison itself. In game terms, it is considered a type K poison (contact; 2d4 minutes; 5/0) if it comes into contact with exposed flesh, or a type I poison (ingested; 2d6 minutes; 30/15) if ingested. If Sheneya's blood were injected directly into someone's veins, it would be treated as a Type E (injected; immediate; death/20) poison.

Sheneya has mastered a mesmerizing dance that affects all those within 60 feet who watch her gyrations. This attack, which she calls the "Dance of the Cobra," requires onlookers to pass a saving throw vs. paralysis or be enthralled until 1d6 rounds after it ends. The dance's sensual nature is such that a –2 penalty is applied to the saving throw.

Because her mind is neither human nor serpentine, Sheneya is immune to all spells from the sphere of Charm and the Enchantment/Charm school. The sole exception is the *snake charm* spell, which requires her to make a saving throw vs. spell. Failure leaves her stunned for 1d4 rounds.

Human Aspect

When Sheneya is attacked in her human form, she generally plays the part of a helpless woman. She makes every effort to appear meek and timid, defending herself more with shrieks of fear and alarm than actual blows.

If this tactic fails to gain mercy, she either attacks with her magical glass *dagger +1* or transforms into one of her more dangerous aspects. As a rule, she chooses the latter only when she is unobserved or has no other choice.

In her human aspect, her Armor Class is 7. This changes when Sheneya assumes either of her other shapes.

Hybrid Aspect

When in the shape of a snake-woman, Sheneya can be very deadly indeed. Her skin is covered by a fine layer of glistening scales, giving her a natural Armor Class of 5.

When Sheneya attacks in her hybrid aspect, she does so with her deadly bite. While this attack inflicts only 1d4 points of damage, it allows her to inject a powerful venom into the veins of her enemies. They must pass a saving throw vs. death or be slain in 1d4+1 rounds by this poison unless appropriate healing measures are undertaken. A penalty is applied to this roll, equal to the number of points of damage the bit inflicted. Thus, someone bitten for 2 points makes the saving throw at a –2 penalty.

Anyone not slain by the poison still feels its effects. On the round immediately after being bitten, a wave of weakness and nausea sweeps over the victim, cutting his Strength, Dexterity, and Constitution scores in half.

This change may indirectly affect attack and damage rolls, Armor Class adjustments, and even bonus hit points. The effects last for one day per point of damage inflicted by the bite. Those bitten more than once find that the duration is extended by the additional points of damage inflicted, though there is no further reduction in ability scores.

Giant Cobra Aspect

Sheneya's third form is that of a giant cobra. In this guise, Sheneya attacks only with her bite. This inflicts 1d4 points of damage and injects a toxin identical to the one described above. Because of the great speed with which she strikes in this form, Sheneya receives a –2 bonus on her initiative. The scales that cover her in this form give her a natural Armor Class of 3.

KISS OF THE SERPENT WOMAN

This adventure sends the characters into an ancient temple in search of a mysterious relic. The woman who hires them to recover it is none other than Sheneya, and she has no intention of paying them off with anything but her deadly serpent's kiss.

Introduction

This adventure can be set in almost any domain that has an area of heavy forest, thick jungles, or even steaming swamps. In order to begin the adventure, the heroes must be available to accept an offer of employment.

Other than Sheneya, there is only one important NPC in this adventure, and even he is destined to die early on. His name is Skoll and he is sent to act as a guide for the party. Once they have reached their destination, Skoll dies in the first of the temple's many traps. This saves the Dungeon Master the trouble of having to portray Skoll through the rest of the adventure, and it also makes clear to the party just how deadly this place can be.

Scene I: The Lost Expedition

This adventure begins with the heroes being contacted by Sheneya. She comes to them timidly, acting weak and frail. Sheneya tells them that she is a scholar whose expertise is in antiquities. Some time ago, she discovered a forgotten temple hidden in the heart of a nearby jungle. This place, which she calls the "Stone Serpent," is spoken of in arcane tomes. It is reported to have been the center of a serpent cult that vanished over two hundred years ago.

Sheneya says that she led an expedition to the temple and entered its antechamber but could explore no further, as she was immediately stricken with a curse. Ever since then, her health has been failing. All of her hair has fallen out, and she grows colder every day. If the heroes examine her, they find this loss of hair and lowered temperature to be true. (They have no way of knowing that she is a werecobra and these are her normal conditions.)

Sheneya says she believes the only way this awful curse can be lifted is to recover a serpent idol deep within the temple and take it to a healer. (Actually, she wants this idol in order to enact a ritual to the Grand Snakemaster.) She begs the player characters to go to the ruined temple and return this idol to her. But she warns the group to be extremely careful in their exploration, for the temple is rumored to be filled with deadly traps. Also, legend would have it to be a haven for serpents, and the party should harm none they find within it.

As payment for their services, Sheneya offers the heroes nothing up front. She has, she explains, no real wealth; every copper piece she had was spent on the first expedition. If the heroes assist her, however, she offers them half the value of any relics brought back from the Stone Serpent. (She is willing to dicker on this percentage, offering whatever is necessary to get them to agree.) In addition, she swears eternal friendship to them. (Of course, this is another lie.)

To aid the group, Sheneya offers two things. The first of these is a jade key, carved in the likeness of a fanged serpent. It opens the entrance of the temple. The second is the services of a guide, Skoll. He knows the area, and she has instructed him carefully as to how to find the temple, for she is too weak to lead the party there herself.

Assuming the heroes agree to this adventure, the trip to the temple should take a few days, during which time the Dungeon Master can toss a few wilderness encounters in the group's path. These should reflect the nature of the terrain through which the heroes are traveling. In swamps, for example, alligators and carnivorous plants might be encountered. The Dungeon Master should work to make this terrain seem untamed and extremely dangerous, which would explain why it is so little traveled.

For his part, Skoll turns out to be a gloomy companion. He bemoans every difficulty along the trail, regularly expressing the opinion that this expedition is doomed to failure and that all its members are sure to die before it ends. If asked why he agreed to come along, he answers that he needs the money to win himself a wife.

Scene II: The Stone Serpent

When the party finally arrives at last at the Stone Serpent, read the following text aloud.

SHENEYA

Looming out of a tangle of mossy vines, a vast pile of crumbling gray stone rises before you, fashioned to resemble a coiled serpent.

Its massive head reaches halfway down that bulk, casting a sightless gaze of evil upon you. Its forked tongue stretches forth to form a stairway, leading to a wide mouth locked in a vicious snarl. The parted lips reveal needle-sharp iron teeth forming a great portcullis, which blocks access to a dark tunnel beyond.

A dank mist seeps out from between those fangs, carrying a chill from inside the earth, and with it the reek of poison, and the stench of death.

When the player characters investigate this stone structure, they discover that the mouth is the only entrance. In the left corner of the serpent's jaw, there is a keyhole worked within the rock, just large enough for the jade serpent key the party carries. When the key is inserted and turned, the iron teeth grind slowly open, retracting into the upper and lower jaws. The key must be left within the keyhole for the portcullis to remain open.

Once the party has entered the serpent's mouth, continue with the following narrative.

The foul odors you smelled from outside are much thicker within, enough so to make your head swim. Along the walls are painted twisting patterns of serpentine shapes, so intertwined that it is impossible to say where one begins and the next ends. To your blurring eyes, they seem to writhe almost as if alive.

As you take a few moments to let your dizziness pass, there is a sudden grinding of metal on stone, and the heavy fangs of the Stone Serpent crash shut behind you! When they come together, the ringing of metal on metal echoes loudly through the air, bringing fragments of stone and dust from above to shower down upon your heads.

The entire structure of the temple groans for a few seconds, as if in danger of collapsing in upon itself. But at last it settles, and silence descends once again.

Then, from outside the portcullis, there comes the sound of a woman's mocking laughter. It is the voice of Sheneya!

"I told you the temple was deadly, heroes," she says. "Enough so that I must guarantee you do your best to overcome it. Bring me the idol, and I will open the gate to release you. Fail me, and your bones will remain here to welcome the next expedition I recruit."

The heroes have little choice at this point but to obey. While they could attempt to break through the gate, especially if they have a few muscular warriors, any dwarves in the party note that this could be dangerous, for the stone is old and could collapse upon them. What's more, Sheneya remains outside to attack them as they work. It would seem, then, that the safest route is to proceed into the temple.

As the party moves deeper into the structure, its ancient, decrepit nature is obvious at every turn, in thick layers of dust and curtains of cobwebs, besides the crumbling stone itself.

Worse, the place is a den of snakes of every sort. With each step, the heroes must avoid trampling upon one or more. Fortunately, these serpents seem lethargic and do not strike unless they are stepped upon.

The map on the next page and the key that follows reveal the details of the Stone Serpent's interior.

1. The Serpent's Mouth

This is the entry chamber to the temple, which the heroes have already entered. A tunnel at the back of this chamber leads deeper into the temple, like a yawning throat.

2. Dart Trap

At this point in the tunnel, the party comes across a pressure plate in the floor that serves to trigger a trap. The plate is five feet on a side and will not activate unless over 200 pounds of weight is placed upon it. Once this limit is exceeded, however, a shower of spring loaded darts is hurled through the air. If that happens, every character must make a successful a saving throw vs. breath weapon or be struck by 1d8 darts. Although their toxin has long ago lost its potency, the darts still cause 1 point of damage each. There is a 2% chance per point of damage inflicted that any wounded character contracts a debilitating disease (per the *cause disease* spell).

3. Red Vapors

At this point, the tunnel expands to form a large chamber. The following narrative can be read to describe it.

You have come upon a large, square chamber. The walls are crumbling and yellow but also encrusted with strange scarlet patches. Whether or not this contamination has anything to do with the bitter odor hanging in the air is impossible to say.

At the center of this chamber is a large iron statue fashioned to resemble a serpent rearing preparing to

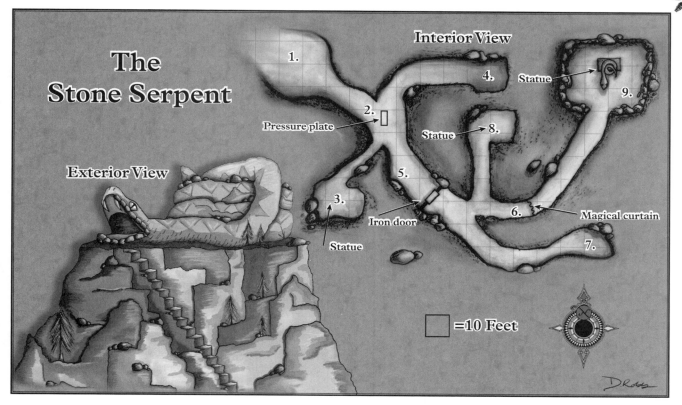

The Stone Serpent

Exterior View

Interior View

1.

2. Pressure plate

3. Statue

Iron door

4. Statue

5.

6.

7.

8. Statue

9.

Statue

Magical curtain

☐ =10 Feet

strike. It's eyes are gleaming emeralds that seem to glare at you malevolently.

A careful search of this statue, once the dust has been removed, reveals a pair of indentations in the top of its base, roughly the size of its emerald "eyes." Below these is the outline of a small compartment in the side. Once discovered, this can be opened easily with the edge of dagger or other tool. Inside this hidden cache is an iron key. If the drawer is opened without removing the serpent's emerald eyes and setting them into the indentations, however, a torrent of red vapors pours forth from the statue's mouth. These smell bitter and cause anyone in the room to cough and sneeze.

The Dungeon Master should instruct everyone here to make a saving throw vs. poison, although there is actually no immediate danger from these fumes. The scarlet mists are merely one component of a deadly chemical mixture. The Dungeon Master should keep track of which characters failed their saving throws in this room. (Skoll can be assumed to have failed.) It becomes important when they find the jade statue in room 10. Note that a *neutralize poison* spell negates the effects of the gas.

The emeralds are worth 100 gold pieces each.

4. Lightning Trap

As the characters move down this tunnel, they find that it comes to a dead end. This is also the first sign that they find of Sheneya's last party.

The walls of the tunnel here are blackened and burnt, as if a great torrent of fire had coursed through the tunnel. A trio of bodies, each charred almost down to the skeleton, lie crumpled upon the floor. So severe was the inferno that claimed these explorers that metal clasps, weapons, and the like are partially melted. From their positions, it is easy to tell that these men died in agony.

Strangely, the floor is as swarming with serpents here as anywhere else within the temple. They coil in an out among the scorched bones, apparently oblivious to any danger. Whatever the trap that lies here, it seems the snakes are immune to it.

This section of the tunnel is protected by an unusual magical construction. If anyone enters this area under the influence of a magical spell (not the effect of a magical item), they set off a deadly trap. Every such

character is struck by a bolt of lightning that inflicts 6d6 points of damage. A saving throw vs. breath weapon cuts this damage in half.

After these strokes of electrical energy are discharged, it takes a full hour for the charge to build up again. Until that time, it's safe for the characters to explore this area.

5. Spike Pit

At this point, the heroes come upon another deadly trap. Luckily for them, it has already been triggered. It is here that most of Sheneya's last party was wiped out.

The tunnel suddenly drops away here at the lip of deep pit. After a fall of some fifty feet, the floor of the cavity is covered with two-foot-high stone spikes. Half a dozen men are impaled upon these deadly spires. Fragments of thin stone are scattered around them, showing that they were all the victims of a false floor.

On the opposite side of this pit, some fifteen feet away, an iron door is set into stone wall. A coiling serpent is carved into the stone around the door. There is no edge around the trap, however, so reaching that distant portal will be very difficult.

Once the heroes find some way of reaching the door, they'll need to use the key from area 3 to open the door. Exactly how they accomplish this is up to the players. Should anything go wrong, however, the fall onto the spikes inflicts a full 10d10 points of damage.

6. Curtain of Light

When the heroes get through the door at area 5, they'll quickly come upon another dangerous site.

A curtain of blue-white light blocks your progress at this point, shimmering like a serpent's scales. It radiates no heat but does crackle and hiss like an endless series of static discharges. The smell of a summer storm seems to hang in the air about it.

Any metal object taken through this curtain is affected as if by a *disintegrate* spell. A normal saving throw is allowed, with magical items receiving a bonus equal to their magical "plus" or a +2 if no such adjustment is associated with them. The heroes are free to pass through the curtain unaffected. Only metal is vulnerable to this effect, and it begins to spark when brought near the barrier.

The barrier can be temporarily eliminated by a *dispel magic*. When the spell is cast, the curtain vanishes for a number of rounds equal to the level of the caster.

Once the barrier has been passed, the heroes see a brass door set into the stone. A carved serpent coils about the portal, looking very much like it might come to life at any moment. This door cannot be opened without the key from area 8.

7. Invisible Flame

As the heroes move down this tunnel, they enter a region of odorless, colorless, flammable gas. Any open flame here has a 50% chance per round of setting off a catastrophic explosion. This blast is like that created by a *fireball,* inflicting 6d6 points of damage to everyone in the area. A successful saving throw vs. breath weapon reduces the damage inflicted by half.

Fortunately, there are a few clues to indicate this trap. First, this is the only part of the temple not crawling with serpents. Like other living creatures, snakes cannot breathe well in this gas-filled corridor, so they avoid it. If the heroes note this fact and still proceed, their next clue is a growing dizziness as their own breathing is affected. At the same time, any flames they carry grow brighter, fed by wisps of the gas. If the heroes continue further while carrying open flames, they risk setting off the explosion.

8. The Jade Dragon

At this point, the characters come upon a chamber filled with a churning white mist. It may be that the players will take this to be the very Mists of Ravenloft themselves, but this is not the case. In truth, this is the second part of the deadly chemical elixir first encountered in area 3.

The tunnel widens here to create a fairly large chamber. Something stands in the chamber's center, but it cannot be seen clearly. A thick fog fills this place.

The thing at the center of the room is a brass serpent very much like the statue found in area 3. It has brightly gleaming ruby eyes, but there is no sign of a hidden cache. If the eyes are removed, however, one will be found to have a brass key affixed to its back.

Anyone who enters this area must make a saving throw vs. poison. Failures should be noted, just as in area 3, but no obvious effects are felt at this time. (Again, Skoll should be assumed to fail the roll. Remember that the mist can be countered by a *neutralize poison* spell.)

9. The Jade Serpent

This crudely hewn chamber has a most unsettlingly primitive look to it. At its heart is a two-foot-long serpent carved of jade and set with black pearls for eyes. This shining snake stands atop a cube of gray stone some three feet on a side. A series of patterns is carved into the floor, looping intricately around the serpent and its pedestal. In order to reach the prize that has drawn you to this place, you'll have to pass across these arcane patterns.

The patterns set into the floor are not at all dangerous; they are intended to draw attention away from a deadly trap. As any member of the party draws close to the jade dragon, he begins to glow. At first, he gives off a faint red light. As the distance to the statue decreases, this glow brightens and intensifies, turning next orange, then bright yellow. If anyone actually touches the statue, his glow swells to an almost blinding white. This light can be smothered at any time by a *dispel magic* or *darkness* spell.

The real trap in this place is triggered by the pedestal upon which the serpent statue stands. When the weight of the statue is removed from the block, a counterbalance is released, which in turn opens hundreds of tiny holes in the ceiling. From these openings, thin wisps of azure vapor trickle downward. Heavier than air, they pass over everyone in the chamber, then gather on the floor to form a knee-deep fog of deepest blue. At this point, the saving throws attempted in areas 3 and 8 come into play.

The guide Skoll and any other characters who failed both saving throws are suddenly convulsed with agony as the blue vapors touch their skin. Seconds later, their flesh begins to dissolve from their bones, like a snail melting from being touched by salt. If a *dispel magic* or *neutralize poison* is cast upon them right away, they survive, although the deformation caused by the exposure results in a loss of 1 point of Charisma for every round that passes before the appropriate spell is cast (up to a maximum of 4 lost points). If no such magic is available, these characters are reduced to piles of bones lying in puddles of pink ooze. The sight of so horrible a death can call for fear or even horror checks from those watching.

Characters who failed the saving throw in area 3 but succeeded at the other are less severely affected. As soon as the blue vapor touches them, red blisters bloat upon their flesh. This is the first symptom of a deadly disease (as described under the *cause disease* spell). Only a *cure disease* spell can keep these blisters from growing worse and worse. As long as the blisters are in evidence, these characters are subject to nervous trembling that reduces their Dexterity score by 2 points.

Characters who failed the saving throw in area 8, but who succeeded at the saving throw in area 3, find the blue vapors choking and caustic, causing lasting damage to their lungs. Until such time as a *cure disease* spell is cast upon them, they will constantly wheeze and gasp for breath. This has the effect of reducing their Constitution score by 2.

There is no effect at all on those who passed (or neutralized) both saving throws. Such characters have somehow shrugged off the toxins of this evil place.

Scene IV: The Serpent's Reward

Having gained the jade serpent statue, the party must escape the temple. Unfortunately, they have one more peril to overcome. As the heroes carry the statue back through the temple, its presence awaken the serpents from their lethargy, and they arise to attack these desecrators of their home. The heroes have to battle every step of the way back to the temple's entrance. (The Dungeon Master should choose the number and type of snakes to suit the condition of the party at this point.)

Sheneya waits for the group at the mouth of the temple. She is content to trade them their freedom in return for the jade serpent. She turns the key far enough to open the portcullis only a few feet, then commands the heroes to set the statue outside on the stone steps, while they remain inside. She warns that if any of the heroes try to slip out before she has the statue, she will close the portcullis on them, cutting them in half.

Meanwhile, of course, the heroes are continually beset by snakes within the temple. They do not have much of a position from which to bargain.

If the group obeys her commands, Sheneya leaves the portcullis partly open, allowing the heroes to crawl out through it and escape the temple. In the meantime, she makes good her own escape from their wrath. If necessary, she transforms into her giant cobra form and burrows underground until the group has quit the area.

Recurrence

As a master assassin, Sheneya can be show up in almost any adventure as a seemingly random encounter. Most player characters have certainly made a lot of enemies in the world, and any one of them might hire this deadly woman to put paid to them. By the same token, any time the heroes come across an artifact with a serpent theme, it might easily draw the attention of Sheneya, who tries to devise some way to wrest it from them.

If the heroes somehow managed to get away with the jade serpent in this adventure, Sheneya is certainly determined to take it from them. She feels that it's an important part of her heritage. Of course, in this adventure it's nothing more than a jade statue. If the Dungeon Master wishes it to be more than that, it could become the heart of numerous scenarios.

Professor Arcanus

But man, proud man, like an angry ape,
Plays such fantastic tricks before high heaven
As make the angels weep.

—William Shakespeare
Measure for Measure

Biography

Professor Arcanus is the master of a traveling road show featuring "authentic relics of the occult." In truth, most of the items in his show are fakes (though good ones). Those that are real, however, are very dangerous indeed—though Arcanus may not recognize just how much so.

Arcanus was born Randal duPree of Dementlieu, but that name was set aside nearly a decade ago when he became an entertainer. He now lives wholly in the role of Professor Arcanus, "Master of the Mystic Arts and Keeper of Forgotten Treasures."

Prof. Arcanus

Maledictive Weregorilla, Chaotic Good

Armor Class	6	Str	19
Movement	12	Dex	14
Level/Hit Dice	4+1	Con	19
Hit Points	25	Int	14
THAC0	17	Wis	14
Morale	Elite (14)	Cha	17
No. of Attacks	3		
Damage/Attack	1d3 (fist)/1d3 (fist)/1d6 (bite)		
Special Attacks	Roar		
Special Defenses	Hit only by silver and +1 or better magical weapons		
Magic Resistance	Nil		

Appearance

Professor Arcanus is a short, heavy man. At first glance he seems overweight, but actually he is barrel-chested and muscular. He has a round face, which adds to the impression of obesity. His features are heavy and accented by a prominent forehead under which his dark eyes gleam. He has dark, black hair, swept back and oiled so as to produce a prominent widow's peak. His eyebrows are thick and bushy, as are the mustache and goatee he sports. Arcanus wears a monocle, although this is strictly an affectation, for the lens is nothing more than plain glass.

When Arcanus goes about in public he wears the same costume that he uses for his performances. This is a sleek, black suit with a blood-red rose in the lapel. He wears a short black cape, which is lined with crimson fabric. He often wears a top hat, but this is frequently carried in his hand and used as a prop during his show. By the same token, he carries a slender walking stick at all times. The head of this cane is a fist-sized, red stone that sparkles like a perfect ruby.

Background

Professor Arcanus was born to a family of modest means in the city of Port-a-Lucine. When he was a young man, his parents took him to see a show put on by a traveling band of Vistani. This was his first exposure to show business, and Arcanus was instantly smitten, for two reasons. The first was simply the grandeur of the show: the dancers, the knife throwers, the jugglers, and all the other entertainers. The second, and far more important, was the impression made on him by Nadja the Seer.

Professor Arcanus

Nadja was a fortuneteller whose exotic beauty claimed his heart the moment Arcanus laid eyes on her. So great was his fascination with her that the young man returned to the show day after day. On the last day of the show, Arcanus stood at the edge of the camp and watched the Vistani packing up. A tear came to his eye at the thought that he would never see Nadja again. After several strong drinks, he determined to visit her. He would profess his love and she—he was certain—would fall into his arms.

When he reached Nadja's vardo, however, things did not go as he expected. Not only did Nadja reject him, she laughed in his face. If she could do no better than a drunken child, she said, better she should die an old maid. Enraged, Arcanus vowed that she would love him or none other. He forced himself upon her, ignoring her cries.

Moments later, Arcanus felt strong hands on his arms and found himself hauled away from the woman. As she did her best to rearrange her torn clothing, the men of the tribe dragged Arcanus to the center of the camp. There, he was lashed spread-eagled between four tent stakes while the Vistani decided his fate.

At dawn, the tribe gathered around him. The time had come for his judgment. Without a word, two muscular young men came forward. Nadja, bruises marring her beautiful face, stepped up behind them. An old woman pronounced his sentence.

"Your actions have revealed your true nature," she said,. "As payment for your crime, you shall become that which you already are."

With that, the young men bent low over Arcanus and tore open his shirt. They drew long knives across his chest in a painful "X." Then Nadja stepped forward, glaring at him with raw hatred. Arcanus started to speak, to explain that he had been drunk, when she spat in his face. Then she produced a small flask of crimson liquid and poured it into the intersecting knife wounds. It burned like acid, wringing cries of agony from the young man. Before long, the pain became so great that he lost consciousness. When he awoke, the Vistani had gone.

The nature of his punishment soon became clear. Whenever injured or in pain, Arcanus now ran the risk of transforming into a dangerous beast, one that hungered for blood and violence. It soon became apparent that he could not remain in Port-a-Lucine. Packing a few belongings, the sorrowful young man took to the road.

As he traveled, Arcanus saw many wondrous things. Some were majestic and awe-inspiring, like the Balinoks' peaks. Others were ominous and frightening, like the howling of wolves in the forests of Kartakass. This discovery of wonders rekindled his early fascination for show business to shape a new life. Arcanus determined to become a one-man show, to bring marvels to other people.

Current Sketch

Professor Arcanus is a showman first, last, and always. He travels the misty lands of the Core, stopping at every town to open up his wagon and display his wonders.

Arcanus is constantly looking for new wonders to add to his exhibit. He has a good eye for fakes and can be assumed to have a 75% chance of recognizing real magical items when they are shown to him. This doesn't mean that every item on display in his show is real, however. Just because he knows that his *Skeleton of Baron Metus* is a fake doesn't mean he won't show it anyway.

Personality

Arcanus is an extroverted man, well practiced in the art of appearing mysterious. For example, he replies to questions he can't (or won't) answer with comments like: "The sands of time have yet to reveal that" or "the Mists shall hide such information until they feel the time is right."

Arcanus is a naturally curious man, especially in matters of the occult. He likes to investigate mysteries, always hoping to discover either an object that can be displayed in his show or a cure for his lycanthropy.

Combat

Arcanus changes form far less frequently than most werebeasts. In battle, the chance that he transforms is based upon the damage he has suffered. At the end of each round, his chance of changing form is equal to the damage he has suffered thus far.

In either form, Arcanus can be struck only by wooden weapons or those with at least a +1 magical bonus.

Human Aspect

In human form, Arcanus tries to avoid combat, claiming that such is unbecoming a gentleman. If pressed, however, he is a fairly powerful enemy. He retains a fraction of his lycanthropic strength in human form, allowing him to strike twice per round, inflicting 1d3 points of damage with each blow. (This does not spread his lycanthropy.)

Over the years, Arcanus has mastered the art of mesmerism. In game terms, he can use this power three times per day, but only if he has some manner of focus with him. Usually, he uses the gleaming stone on his walking stick, but any other shiny object will do. The effects of this talent mimic those of the *hypnotism* spell, save that it affects only one subject.

Gorilla Aspect

When transformed into a gorilla, Arcanus is a savage and fierce beast who hungers for blood and combat. In this form he can attack thrice per round. The first two attacks are blows from his savage fists, which inflict 1d3 points of damage each. He follows these up with a bite that inflicts 1d4 points of damage and has a chance of infecting his enemy with lycanthropy.

In his gorilla form Arcanus has the ability to utter a powerful howl that echoes through the air, touching the simian roots in all humans. Those who hear this roar for the first time must make a fear check. Failure has the normal effects indicated in the *Domains of Dread* book. Those who have heard this roar before are entitled to a +2 bonus on the check, as are demihumans. Humanoids need not make a check, as the gorilla's roar has no effect upon such bestial creatures.

Anyone who contracts lycanthropy from Arcanus becomes a carnivorous ape (as described in the MONSTROUS MANUAL tome). Although technically werebeasts, these creatures cannot change shape. They feel no loyalty to their creator but are not openly hostile to him. They dwell in the wilds, preying on animals and men alike. Only when they are killed does it become apparent that they were once men.

Exhibits

Professor Arcanus has a large collection of occult items. Some are authentic and others are nothing more than clever fakes. While Arcanus generally knows which are which, he has been fooled by a few imitations and failed to recognize one or two prizes in his archives.

The following list indicates some of Arcanus' most popular displays. Most of these are on display at any given time, as well as a dozen or so others.

The Skeleton of Duke Gundar

Though Arcanus doesn't realize it, these are actually the remains of Duke Gundar, an ancient vampire who used to rule the domain of Gundarak before the Grand Conjunction. The wooden stake driven through the ribs is the only thing keeping him from returning to life. If anyone were foolish enough to draw forth the stake, the vampire would begin to regenerate at once. Before long, it would rise again and begin to prey upon the living.

The Phylactery of Lord Azalin

Arcanus touts this as "the source of Lord Azalin's power." It is in the shape of a silver crown. While he knows this is not the genuine article, Arcanus bought this relic from a darkling band several weeks ago.

The Spellbook of Ar-Shickanus

According to Arcanus, this leather-bound tome is a powerful relic recovered from the ruins of a castle in Hazlan. In truth, it's nothing more than a random collection of notes about magic and spellcasting. There are no great secrets hidden in this book, but it certainly looks impressive. In addition, the ink has faded to a brownish color, and Arcanus insists that it was written in blood. He knows better, of course, but he won't own up to such knowledge.

The Brain of Rudolph van Richten

One of the more striking exhibits in the show is a brain floating in a pale green elixir. Arcanus insists that this is the brain of the great scholar Dr. Rudolph van Richten. Again, this is a fraud. In truth, this is the brain of a murderer who was captured and executed in Falkovnia. Indeed, Arcanus used to display it as *The Murderer's Brain,* but it didn't draw much attention. He recently hit on the idea of passing it off as Van Richten's, and that has made it a much bigger success.

The Hand of Vecna

The name of this relic is less well known on the Demiplane of Dread than it is on the world of Oerth. Still, Arcanus always gives a frightening oratory about the terrible lich king and his dreadful power. The hand is displayed in a large glass box, where it scrambles back and forth striving constantly to escape.

It this a fake? Yes and no. The hand is certainly not the relic that Arcanus claims it to be. It is, however, a crawling claw (as described in the MONSTROUS MANUAL tome). If the hand were stolen or released, its evil nature would lead it to begin attacking people.

The Book of the Dead

Arcanus claims to have brought this book from the distant desert realm of Sebua. In truth, he bought it from a book seller in Martira Bay. The writing looks very much like the hieroglyphs used by the nations of The Burning Lands, but anyone who is familiar with those places will instantly recognize it as a fake.

Lycanthrope Blood

Arcanus claims that this collection of a dozen different glass vials contains blood taken from a variety of werebeasts. Each is labeled with the name of the person from whom it is supposed to have been drawn and a brief description. For example, one of the vials is marked *Jacob Santori, The Werewolf of Nova Vaasa: He killed fifteen strong men before being slain with a silver arrow.*

These vials are exactly what Arcanus claims them to be. If questioned about them, he evidences a keen interest in the topic of werebeasts, quizzing his guests in turn as to what they might know about the subject.

Interestingly enough, none of these samples makes any mention of a weregorilla.

The Soul Blade

This is a brightly polished dagger with a 12-sided ruby set into its hilt. A sign claims that this weapon steals the souls of those who look too deeply into it. In truth, this is the domain of Aggarath (as described in *The Forgotten Terror*). For those who do not have that adventure, this gem can be treated as a *mirror of life trapping*. Only someone who is stabbed with this weapon will be drawn into the gem.

MISSING BONES

n this adventure, the heroes visit Professor Arcanus's traveling magic show and witness a man heckling the professor. The next day, the fellow and his wife turn up dead. The heroes recognize the marks of a vampire's feeding and discover that one of Arcanus's exhibits—the skeleton of Duke Gundar—is missing. But the local watch suspects the professor for the crime. If the heroes cannot clear his name, Arcanus is likely to hang.

Introduction

This adventure can take place just about anywhere in Ravenloft, for Arcanus wanders the domains at will. When he reaches a village or city, he unpacks his exhibits and puts on a show, remaining until local interest wanes.

Scene I: Traveling Magic Show

The adventure begins when the heroes visit Professor Arcanus's show. They may encounter it accidentally, or they might have seen his handbills sought it out. When they arrive, read the following text aloud.

As you reach town near sundown this evening, you come upon a large wagon, decorated with sinister runes, carven bones, and dramatic glyphs. The whole affair is obviously intended to shock and frighten common folk. To adventurers like yourselves, its attempt to appear ominous and dire is almost comical.

The proprietor, the man who calls himself Professor Arcanus, stands before the open wagon, putting on a

show in the last golden rays of the sun. A barrel-chested and intelligent-looking man, Arcanus performs his act with a considerable flourish and charisma. As you watch, the audience is delighted by his sleight of hand and simple stage magic. But if Arcanus truly knows anything of the supernatural, it doesn't show in his performance.

This part of the show goes on for about ten minutes, with the audience constantly bursting into cheers and applause. There is one dissenting opinion, however. A young farmer, obviously the worse for drink, shouts out rude comments. Arcanus takes these in stride, apparently as used to hecklers as any other performer.

His prestidigitation complete, the "professor" now begins to display the mystical artifacts advertised in his handbills. He presents them one at a time, providing a colorful story for each. Meanwhile the young farmer's scoffing turns to outright personal insults.

Eventually, the farmer's words grow so offensive that others in the crowd become angry. A few punches are thrown, and suddenly a good old-fashioned brawl erupts. (No one is seriously hurt in this skirmish, and no one draws weapons.) By the time this brawl peters out, Arcanus has packed up his show for the night. He spares time for a brief conversation if the heroes seek him out; otherwise, the events of the night draw to a close.

Scene II: Jaybe Wakes the Dead

Next morning, the heroes are awakened by watchmen hammering at their door. Read the following text aloud.

"We're looking for Professor Arcanus," one watchman says, glancing furtively about the room. The left side of his head sports a livid bruise, and his left eye is swollen shut.

"Have you seen him?" the other demands, his hand tense on the hilt of the sword at his hip. His tunic is torn, revealing bloody welts across his right shoulder.

"He's wanted for murder," the first continues, "and likely something worse. That heckling last night must have got under his skin. We found the heckler and his wife dead near Arcanus's wagon this morning. When we tried to arrest the professor, he changed into a great beast with huge fangs, then knocked us down and fled.

"We're gathering all the able-bodied to hunt him down before he kills again. So you'd better get your gear ready."

The Apparent Evidence

If the heroes ask, they learn that the bodies of the farmer and his wife are being held at the local watch office. Examination reveals to the group that the man was indeed torn limb from limb, while the woman is completely bloodless. The mark of fangs upon her throat make it evident that she was a vampire's victim. Obviously, that same vampire killed her husband. Given the watchmen's story, it would certainly seem that Arcanus is that vampire.

An Overlooked Clue

If the heroes investigate Arcanus's wagon, they note one other significant fact: Both the stake and bones from the display marked "The Skeleton of Duke Gundar" are missing. A search of the grounds around the wagon turns up the stake, trampled into the blood-soaked ground where the farmer's body was discovered.

The Actual Events

While the town watch is convinced that Arcanus murdered the heckler and his wife out of anger and bloodlust, the truth is a bit more complicated than that.

The couple sneaked back to the wagon late last night to prove how fake the exhibits were, and the farmer drew the stake from the vampire's coffin. The vampire revived while the man stood bragging, slew the foolish fellow, and fed upon the woman, then slipped away into the night.

When the guardsmen found the bodies and sought to arrest Professor Arcanus, they were a bit too brutal in their treatment. When Arcanus protested, the first watchman clouted him with an oaken club "to teach him some manners." Arcanus saw red, transformed involuntarily into his gorilla aspect, and laid the pair low, then escaped.

Scene III: Vampire Hunt!

If the heroes have accepted the watchmen's story at face value, they most likely will be hunting for Professor Arcanus at this point, believing him to be a vampire. On the other hand, if they recall having seen the professor perform his act in the light of the setting sun, they should realize that he probably could not be a vampire. Further, if they discovered that the bones of Duke Gundar are missing, they may deduce what actually happened to the farmer and his wife. Of course, the mystery of the Arcanus's transformation into a "great beast, with huge fangs" remains to be explained. It does demonstrate, however, that there is more to the man than appears at first glance.

In either case, the professor's next action is to contact the heroes, asking them to help find and capture the vampire. He slips into their room while they are out that day, and leaves a written message for them.

I could not help but notice you in the audience last night; you stand out from the locals. By now you must have noticed the missing bones of Duke Gundar and have realized that I, who walk about by day, could not be a creature of the night.

Yet we are all in deadly danger! While the local watch beats about the bush looking for me, a real monster prowls about to kill at will. If you would help me to defeat it, meet me at the crossroads outside of town tonight at midnight.

Professor Arcanus

If the heroes have already concluded that Arcanus must be innocent, this note serves as a pat upon the back. On the other hand, if they missed this obvious evidence, they should feel chagrined and all the more ready to help this falsely accused man.

If the heroes meet with Arcanus, he can tell them how he bought Gundar's body from Gabrielle Aderre, leader of the Invidian rebels. He didn't realize the possible danger involved. Together, Arcanus and the heroes can track the weakened vampire as it slowly begins to recover its strength. It has holed itself up in some nearby caves. In the resulting battle, the Dungeon Master should arrange for things to go against the heroes at first. Then, as hope seems lost, Arcanus is wounded and transforms into a weregorilla, thereby revealing his secret to the heroes.

If Gundar survives the encounter, he heads directly for his former home, Castle Hunadora. No longer trapped within his domain, he is free to travel about at will, so he will soon try to search out Dr. Dominiani, who betrayed him and caused his death.

Recurrence

There are many ways in which Professor Arcanus can lead the heroes to future adventures. He might ask their help in recovering an object to add to his show. Or he might instead ask that they help him to destroy something that he fears is too dangerous too keep. He might even ask their aid in obtaining a cure for his lycanthropy.

Further, Arcanus can be used as an link to the adventure *The Forgotten Terror*. After all, the magical dagger *Aggarath* rests in his hands.

> *It can be said that all vile acts are done to satisfy hunger.*
>
> —Maxim Gorky
> *Enemies*

BIOGRAPHY

Mother Fury is a dangerous woman who heads a monastic order hidden in the forests of Kartakass. Her teachings call for men and women to renounce their civilized nature and embrace the beast within them. She makes no pretense of being anything other than a feral creature, although she discloses the full truth about her heritage only to her followers.

Appearance

This striking woman has three forms. Among normal men and women, she takes human shape. Within the walls of her cloister, she wears her hybrid aspect. In the woods outside those walls, she runs in the aspect of a dire wolf.

Human Aspect

In human form, Mother Fury is nearly six feet tall. She has brown hair shot with silver streaks. Her cunning eyes seem to miss no detail. She possesses a wide mouth, but her lips are thin. When she smiles, unnaturally sharp canines flash. Often her expression is distant and impassive, but in moments of great passion, her eyes blaze with light and her countenance grows animated.

Mother Fury and her disciples wear a loose habit of dark gray. This has a hood that can be draped to shadow the face. Wolf fur adorns the collar and cuffs, while an ebony sash cinches the waist. A string of wolf's teeth loops downward from this sash to a pocket on the hip.

Hybrid Aspect

In hybrid form, Mother Fury stands a bit taller than in her human aspect. Her silver-shot brown hair now covers her whole body. Her brows jut forward, and her jaws protrude to form a snout full of deadly sharp teeth. Her dark eyes flash constantly with reflected light. As a half-wolf, she sprouts dangerous claws from her hands. This makes it difficult for her to handle objects: She suffers a –2 penalty to Dexterity checks. This does not detract from her combat ability, however.

Dire Wolf Aspect

Like all loup-garou, when Mother Fury takes wolf form she becomes a dire wolf. Measuring fully eight feet from snout to tail, she is a truly deadly creature, combining all the savagery of a normal lupine, the massive bulk of a dire wolf, and the unnatural toughness of a werebeast.

Mother Fury

True Mountain Loup-Garou, Chaotic Evil

Armor Class	3	Str	18/00
Movement	12, 15, or 18	Dex	17
Level/Hit Dice	7	Con	18
Hit Points	48	Int	12
THAC0	13	Wis	10
Morale	Elite (14)	Cha	15
No. of Attacks	3 or 1		
Damage/Attack	1d4/1d4 (claws) and 2d4 (bite) or 2d4 (bite)		
Special Attacks	Surprise, spell use		
Special Defenses	Hit only by gold and +1 or better magical weapons, regeneration		
Magic Resistance	40%		

Mother Fury

MOTHER FURY

Background

Mother Fury was born in heavily forested Kartakass. Through her early years, she lived as a dire wolf, hunting and killing with wild abandon. Seldom did she assume either of her other forms. She held humans and their like in contempt, mere prey to be slaughtered and eaten.

Near her twentieth year, however, the werebeast found herself facing something new. She attacked a party of skilled adventurers, and they very nearly destroyed her.

Afterward, while licking her wounds, Mother Fury decided that there might be more to such creatures than she had assumed. For the first time, she embraced the human side of her heritage. Over the next few months, she gathered a group of aggressive men and women around her. These folk came to revere her power and, in time, a fanatical cult formed around Mother Fury.

Current Sketch

Mother Fury and her followers occupy a cave complex along the Kartakass-Hazlan border. Here, they celebrate the wilderness and the brutal struggle of predator and prey. What began as a simple love of savagery has grown into a something of a religion.

Over the course of each month, the cult members undertake rituals of hunting, battle, and feasting. The culminating ceremony comes when the moon is full above the Balinoks. Then, a captured human or demihuman is released into the wild, and a random cult member has until dawn to find and kill him. If the tracker fails, the hunted is recaptured and "blessed" with membership in the order. No one is allowed to refuse this honor.

Personality

Mother Fury and her followers live for the thrill of hunting and death. They savor the taste of blood and raw flesh, especially that of intelligent creatures. Although they eat cooked meat, they have no taste for plants.

A temperamental woman, Mother Fury is prone to fits of black fury but is equally lavish with her affection. She has come to rely upon her emotions and instincts more than her intelligence, and she sees little reason to rein them in.

Combat

While Mother Fury is dangerous in all her aspects, she favors battle in her full wolf shape. In this form, her bestial rage is at its greatest and the sensations of violence are untempered by human emotions. In her other forms, however, her fantastic Strength score gives her a bonus of +3 on all attack rolls and +6 on damage rolls. (These bonuses do not apply in her dire wolf form.)

In all forms, Mother Fury is immune to damage from most weapons. Only those made from gold inflict their normal damage. Magical weapons can injure her but do damage equal only to their magical *plus*. Thus, a *sword +2* inflicts only two points of damage when it hits her. Magical weapons with no associated bonus, and blessed ones, cause her only a single point of damage with each blow.

In any of her forms, Mother Fury heals swiftly. At the end of any round, she recovers 1 point of damage. This does not apply to injuries caused by gold weapons, which heal at the normal rate of 1 point per day.

Human Aspect

In human form, Mother Fury is able to deliver a painful bite with her sharp canines. This attack inflicts 1d4 points of damage and carries with it the danger of lycanthropic infection. She never makes use of weapons. She preaches that these dilute the thrill of combat, and true warriors long to taste the blood of their enemies.

Mother Fury can cast spells when in this form. Her ability is similar to that of a 7th-level druid. The spells she normally has ready are: (1st) *cure light wounds, detect good, pass without trace;* (2nd) *charm person or mammal, heat metal, speak with animals;* (3rd) *hold animals, spike growth;* (4th) *call woodland beings.*

Hybrid Aspect

This form is Mother Fury's most horrific, for it combines her human cunning with the savage ferocity of a wolf. When she attacks in this form, she is able to impose a −1 penalty on her enemies' surprise rolls. She strikes with two clawed hands (each inflicting 1d4 points of damage) and a deadly bite (which does 2d4 points of damage).

Dire Wolf Aspect

Like all loup-garou, in full bestial aspect Mother Fury becomes a dire wolf. In this shape, her powerful bite does 2d4 points of damage. Anyone bitten has a chance of contracting the dread disease. In this aspect, Mother Fury is able to move very quickly and strike without warning. As such, anyone who encounters her in this guise suffers a −2 penalty on their normal surprise rolls.

Offspring

Those who contract lycanthropy from Mother Fury have only two aspects: human and dire wolf. They change shapes when she unleashes a special howl. This call has its effect at distances of up to a mile.

> **Mother Fury's Followers (lowland loup-garou):** AC 4; MV 12 (human) or 18 (wolf); HD 5+4; hp 30 each; THAC0 15; #AT 1; Dmg 1d4 (human) or 2d4 (wolf); SA Surprise and lycanthropy; SD hit only by gold and +1 or better magical weapons; SZ M (6' tall/long); ML Elite (13–14); Int Avg (8–10); MR 20%; AL CE; XP 2,000.
>
> Notes: These creatures impose a –2 penalty on their opponent's surprise rolls and are so strong that they gain a +3 on attack and +6 on damage rolls in human form. Like any werebeast, they can transmit lycanthropy with their bite.

THE HOWLING CLAN

 his adventure pits the heroes against Mother Fury and her werebeast followers, in order to rescue a friend who has been forced to join the cult. To succeed, the heroes will be forced eventually to fight for their lives in an savage arena of blood and fury.

Note: The Dungeon Master might decide to use one of the heroes as the person who is abducted and inducted, instead of an NPC friend. In this case, that hero's capture, infection, and escape can be run as a one-on-one scenario in preparation for this adventure. The DM should take care, however, to choose a player who won't feel uncomfortable having his character in such a position—whose hero won't die fighting rather than play cagey and wait for an opportunity to escape.

Introduction

This adventure is intended to take place in the heavily wooded domain of Kartakass, home to Mother Fury and her cult of beast-worshiping lycanthropes. If need be, however, it can be moved to any similar location—the more remote and heavily wooded, the better.

Prior to the adventure, Mother Fury's followers came upon a friend of the player characters and captured him to use in their monthly celebration of the hunt. To their surprise, however, that character managed to elude his hunter until daybreak. Joyously, the rest of the cult tracked down the quarry and returned with him to receive Mother Fury's transforming bite.

Mother Fury and her disciples were soon to be surprised again, however. At the first opportunity, the new member fled the cult. Though the others soon gave chase, their quarry put his newfound lycanthropic powers to good use and eluded them all, escaping the woods and returning to civilization. As the adventure opens, this character bursts in upon the player characters as they sit at breakfast, and breathlessly begs for their help.

The Dungeon Master should choose for this role some NPC close enough to the player characters that they are willing to go through great travail to aid him.

Note: If the Dungeon Master is running this introduction as a separate, one-on-one scenario with one of the heroes, the events should occur as follow.

1. The hero, alone, is set upon by wolves. Although he is hopelessly outnumbered, the brutes wrestle him down rather than killing him. Then they drag him off to meet their leader, Mother Fury.
2. Mother Fury tells the hero that he is to take part in a very special ceremony of hunter and hunted. She explains the rules: He is to be released a half hour before his pursuer; only one disciple shall hunt him; and if the hero can survive until daybreak, he will be allowed to live.
3. The hero is released into the woods, naked, and spends the night playing a dangerous game of cat-and-mouse with the werebeast who hunts him. The DM should press the player to come up with plans to shake off his pursuer, rewarding clever ones with howls of frustration from the werebeast, and punishing poor ones with narrow escapes and a growing collection of wounds.
4. At last the hero sees dawn break over the forest. With it, he hears the lone howl of his beaten foe.
5. Just as the hero breathes a sigh of relief, however, the howls of other werebeasts echo the first, and the entire pack joins the pursuit. With so many hunters, the quarry is doomed to be captured again, whatever he might do.
6. Dragged back to the cloister, the hero faces Mother Fury, who explains that he has proven himself worthy to join the pack. With that, she bites him, and the fever of infection begins.
7. Some days later, the hero has an unguarded moment in which to flee the cloister. Again, there is a hunt, but this time the hero has a werebeast's strength, stamina, and speed upon which to rely. Armed with those and his own determination, he flees the forest to seek help. Still, his only hope for a cure is to return with friends to destroy Mother Fury and her cult.

Scene I: A Breakfast Visitor

This adventure begins with the heroes learning of their friend's recent trouble. To set the stage, choose a time when the group has spent the evening camping out of doors, then read the following text aloud to the players.

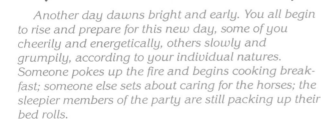

Another day dawns bright and early. You all begin to rise and prepare for this new day, some of you cheerily and energetically, others slowly and grumpily, according to your individual natures. Someone pokes up the fire and begins cooking break- fast; someone else sets about caring for the horses; the sleepier members of the party are still packing up their bed rolls.

Then, unexpectedly, you all hear the sound of something rushing through the underbrush, headed right toward your camp! Being seasoned warriors, you come quickly to the alert, drawing weapons and preparing for a fight. The brush parts, and a savage- looking figure lurches forward!

The Dungeon Master should give the player charac- ters a moment to think that they are about to be at- tacked before revealing that the figure is actually a friend of theirs. That friend, however, is in a condition they've never seen him in before: naked and bedraggled, pant- ing heavily and covered with welts and scratches.

Taking a shaky breath, this friend gasps, "Get ready! I'm being followed. They'll be here any second!"

Hardly have these words been uttered than a pack of dire wolves (a few of Mother Fury's disciples) arrives. They battle the heroes for a few rounds, then fade back into the woods, apparently discouraged for now. The Dungeon Master should set the number of cult members to be sufficient to give the heroes a bit of a fright, while remaining few enough that it seems reasonable for them to give up the fight fairly quickly.

Battle ended for now, the intended quarry begs for an escort back to town, offering to explain the situation along the way. Along the route, he fills the party in on his trouble, and asks for their help in finding a solution—a cure for his dread disease, and freedom from the cult to which he belongs unwillingly.

Assuming the player characters do not themselves know how to cure a case of lycanthropy, they need to find a knowledgeable priest to talk with once they reach civilization again. Finding a priest with the requisite information can be as easy or difficult as the Dungeon Master desires. The party might be referred from one scholar to another, perhaps even traveling great distances, before learning what they need to know. Or, if time demands, they might be allowed to discover their answer from the very first priest they go to see.

In either case, however, the answer the heroes re- ceive in the end is this: Before a cure can be attempted, the victim must destroy the source of the infection; he must kill Mother Fury. Of course, killing her also de- stroys the cult that seeks to hold him in thrall.

Scene II: The Wolf's Den

As the PCs make their way to Mother Fury's stronghold, led by their infected friend, they are shadowed by a great number of large, dangerous-looking wolves. These creatures range around the party in all directions but remain always at the limits of sight, slipping into the undergrowth whenever spotted. The Dungeon Master should work to convey an ominous sense of menace to their presence as they trail the heroes.

Whatever the heroes might suspect, however, the werebeasts are actually here as something of a protec- tive escort. Mother Fury has made clear to her disciples that she wants these adventurers to reach her lair un- hindered. As a matter of fact, the cultists even chip in and help if the heroes have trouble overcoming any dangers they encounter along the way. Also, of course, their presence makes it clear that the party isn't going to sneak up on Mother Fury's cloister, no matter how they might try.

The player characters' friend seems tense and feverish during this trip, as if wrestling with an inner demon. From his agitated appearance, it isn't immediately apparent which of the two will win that inner battle. This should give the heroes something extra to worry about, besides their lupine escort.

Along the way, the Dungeon Master should toss a few wilderness encounters at the party. None of these should involve wolves or lycanthropes, however, because of the cult's influence. Good encounters for these woods might instead include giant spiders and maybe even an evil treant. Anything else that serves to convey the wild, untamed nature of the region is a good possibility, though the DM should avoid encounters that are overtly magical in nature, or events that might overshadow the coming conflict with Mother Fury and her folk.

After a day of travel through the woods, the heroes are led at last by their friend to the opening of a large cave. The rock outcropping into which this cavern leads has been roughly carved into the shape of a wolf's head. This is the entrance to Mother Fury's underground lair. At its mouth, the party is greeted by a quartet of powerfully built, savage-looking individuals.

"Mother Fury has been expecting you," these werebeasts say. They lead the group into the tunnel, through countless twists and turns, to a large chamber furnished with fur rugs. Stores of water and fresh, raw meat have been placed here, and a small fire burns in a crude hearth. The heroes are told that Mother Fury will see them soon and that they must await her here. Leaving, the cultists draw a heavy gate across the chamber entrance and lock it. Two remain outside the doorway as guards. For a time, the heroes are left to rest and eat in preparation for their meeting with the disciples' leader.

Scene III: The Arena

Some time later, Mother Fury sends for the group. Read the following text aloud.

The four cultists escort you to an immense chamber fitfully lit by torches. It resembles nothing so much as a vast arena. On a platform a dozen feet above the floor, seated upon a rough stone throne, the matriarch of this order gazes down upon you.

"My lost child has returned, I see," she says, grinning in savage humor. "And he has brought me gifts of sport and food." Her eyes pass hungrily over each of you in turn, then return to the infected one. Under her gaze, his body trembles with suppressed tension. Sweat springs out upon him, carrying the scent of the wolf.

The Dungeon Master should play this scene so that the heroes can hardly help but debate the wisdom of their coming. It should occur to them that there is at least a possibility that the dread disease has progressed too far in their friend, that they have been duped into following him like lambs to the slaughter. Even if this victim is one of the player characters, the others should be made to worry that perhaps the werebeast nature is running too strong right now for him to keep it suppressed. As these thoughts pass through their minds, their friend stands trembling with the strain of working to retain his control.

If the heroes are impulsive, they are liable to draw their weapons right now and attack the cultists. If not, Mother Fury initiates the battle, loosing her transforming howl. Read the following text aloud.

For a moment all is silent. Then from her seat above you, Mother Fury throws back her head and looses a wild, ululating howl, a cry that could come from no wholly human throat. It echoes throughout the stone caverns, stirring something primal in all of you. This is the cry of the night, the shout of the hunter, the howl of the wolf.

One by one, a dozen other voices join Mother Fury's. And as each voice is added, another of the cultists steps forward to undergo a horrifying transformation. Limbs pop and shift, fur sprouts from flesh, and human faces transform into the ravening countenances of wolves. Even your friend succumbs to this call at last and begins to change before your very eyes.

With the transformation of the heroes' friend, the cultists leap to the attack. Mother Fury watches the fight for several rounds, relishing the sight of so much blood and savagery, then joins in herself at a dramatically appropriate time.

Should things begin to go badly for the cult, Mother Fury is not above turning tail and fleeing, though she does not do this until most of her followers have been defeated. If she does flee, any remaining cult members try to cover her escape, then follow her if they can.

Should things begin to turn out badly for the player characters instead, they also have the option to try to escape. In this case, they are pursued through the forest by Mother Fury and her disciples. The DM should handle this situation as a nightmarish running battle. The loup garou harry the group all the way through the forest, howling constantly, attacking every time the heroes stop to catch their breath, using classic wolf pack tactics to strike at them from the shadows and then slip away again just as quickly. Unless the heroes bungle somehow, however, they should eventually escape the forest and regain civilization. They can return later to try again to best Mother Fury, or perhaps they may seek some other way of breaking the curse. Of course, there may be more members of the party who are afflicted now. . . .

As an alternative, if the Dungeon Master judges that the players can handle the thought of having their characters captured, this may be an option during the heroes' attempted escape. In this case, while the pursuing wolves prove too much for the heroes to escape, Mother Fury commands that the heroes not be killed, *as long as they were valiant in the battle.* (She does not hesitate to let cowards die.) The wounded heroes are then held captive until the dread disease has incubated within them, at which time they are initiated into her cult.

If Mother Fury has a blind spot, it is in that she always assumes that a person, once infected with her lycanthropy, will choose to revel in his savagery and so will welcome life within her cloister. Of course, this leaves the heroes with the option of trying to escape and find a cure later.

Recurrence

If the heroes bested Mother Fury and her disciples, any of the werebeasts who escape are certain to return to plague the group later with attempts at revenge. Of course, having been bested once, they aren't likely to play fair at all but will choose a moment when the heroes are already weak and in trouble to make their attack.

If instead the heroes merely escaped the cult, Mother Fury commands that they be hunted down and destroyed, to prevent word of her group being spread far and wide. In this case, she might employ any sort of agent to track the party, or hire assassins to attack it, besides her own disciples.

HENRI MILTON

All the soarings of my mind begin in my blood.

—Rainer Maria Rilke
Wartime Letters

BIOGRAPHY

enri Milton is an artist—sort of. He's a werebeast who has discovered a magical relic of great interest. Milton has a small ceramic tablet (*Picalinni's Palette*, described later) covered with fell runes. When blood is poured onto the palette and it is left alone over night next to a blank canvas, a magical process causes a remarkable (if disturbing) painting to appear on the canvas. The pigments from which the image forms are, Milton is certain, distilled from the blood he pours in the bowl.

Milton is driven by a desire to be recognized as the greatest artist in the Domains of Dread. Actually, he is not without talent himself. Rather than refine that skill, however, he has opted to make use of this hideous item.

This decision, made in haste and without regard for consequence, has driven Milton fully into the clutches of evil. Experience has shown him that only the blood of a freshly murdered man or woman will fuel the magical process that is winning him the fame he so desires.

Henri Milton

Henri Milton

Maledictive Wereboar, Chaotic Evil

Armor Class	4	Str	19
Movement	12	Dex	15
Level/Hit Dice	5+2	Con	17
Hit Points	45	Int	11
THAC0	15	Wis	13
Morale	Elite (13)	Cha	8
No. of Attacks	1		
Damage/Attack	2d6 or by weapon (1d6)		
Special Attacks	Nil		
Special Defenses	Hit only by silver and +1 or better magical weapons		
Magic Resistance	Nil		

Appearance

In all of his aspects, Milton appears somewhat disheveled and unkempt. This might seem to be a reflection of the guilt that gnaws eternally at his soul, but in truth that is not the case. Milton's personal hygiene has never been good; he was every bit as untidy long before he found the accursed bowl and became a lycanthrope.

Human Aspect

Henri Milton is not a tall man. Indeed, he only stands about six inches over five feet, while his poor posture makes him seem even shorter. His belly is a bit too round, the result of a tendency to glut himself at meal time. He often smells of liquor and always has terrible breath.

Milton's ugly face is flat and wide. His eyes are small, weak, and watery. His nose is too broad, as if he were a professional fighter, and his lips are thick. Spotty stubble almost always adorns his chin.
The clothes Milton wears are intended to make him look stylish and elegant. Perhaps, on a better man, they would do just that. But on this dirty little fellow, they seem thoroughly out of place, while even slightly out of fashion. Milton lacks the ability to wear elegance well and always seems uncomfortable, like a pig trussed up in a man's clothing.

Hybrid Aspect

In his hybrid form, Milton is actually a bit taller than as a human. His posture is far worse, however, so he appears to be a good deal shorter. His brow is flattened over dark eyes and his elongated ears are swept back angrily. Jagged tusks emerge from the sides of his mouth and saliva drools constantly from his lips.

In this form, Milton snorts constantly and moves about with a shuffling gate. He sways from the side to side, looking as if he were about to topple over at any moment. This gangly appearance belies the fact, however, that he is fairly swift and agile when need be.

A stench follows Milton in this form, as of a pig that has wallowed in its own filth.

Background

Henri Milton was born in the northern city of Il Aluk, although his parents were natives of Invidia. His father was a stone mason who earned a comfortable living, but his shrewish mother insisted upon living beyond their means. Milton grew up in a home marked by constant tension and occasional domestic violence.

As a boy, young Henri sought release from his troubles through the arts. Although his father looked with favor upon the boy's efforts, especially his attempts at sculpture, his mother only mocked them. It was her belief that he should find a job that paid well, no matter how unsatisfying it might be.

As his sixteenth birthday neared, young Henri expressed his desire to travel to Invidia and attend the College d'Art at Karina. His father supported the idea, recognizing that the boy had talent, but his mother did not. They had left Invidia behind, she insisted, and there was no call for any member of their family to return there.

That night, the young man listened as his parents fought about the matter. Their dispute grew more and more heated until it finally erupted into violence. With tears in his eyes, Henri fell into a fitful sleep.

The next morning, Henri's father told the boy that his mother had left them. Although he did not press the matter, Henri assumed then (and still believes to this day) that the fight ended with her death. His father insisted that he set out at once for Invidia, further convincing the lad that he was hiding something. Having little affection for his mother, however, Henri took his father's words to heart and left Il Aluk forever.

Henri's trip south passed without incident and the boy soon found himself aboard a river boat drifting toward Karina. When he arrived at the town, he made his way at once to the College d'Art. Enrollment left him almost penniless, but fortunately the school provided room and board as well as education.

Sadly, Henri Milton would never make his mark as an artist. He had a modicum of talent, true, but he lacked the spark of greatness. He could find work painting portraits and such, but he would never produce the masterpieces that he yearned to create.

Less than a year after he first enrolled in the College d'Art, Milton left it behind. He sought work in Karina but found none of any merit. He worked odd jobs to keep from starving but only barely succeeded. In time, he took a position as a freight handler on a riverboat. While it was not glamorous work, the pay was good. It was exactly the sort of job his mother had envisioned for him.

After a year or so of this work, Milton met a passenger who was traveling to Karina to attend the College d'Art. In many ways, this youth reminded Milton of himself at a younger age. But this young man had true talent. He showed Milton several of his paintings, and there could be no doubt of the fact.

And yet, there was something odd about the boy's work. His paintings possessed a macabre element that disturbed Milton. There was a violence in them that stirred up memories of his trouble past. Deducing that he might have much in common with the young man, he approached the passenger to discuss the matter. Quite by accident, he discovered the youth's secret—he saw *Picalinni's Palette* and knew at once that this treasure must be his.

Milton stole the magical item and fled the ship at Mortigny. He made his way northward by land and settled in Pont-a-Museau, where he has resided ever since.

Almost at once, he began to paint, allowing the magic of the *palette* to guide his brush. Although he believed that the magic of *Picalinni's Palette* was his to command, he did not understand its true nature. With each canvas he painted, the cursed thing tightened its grip upon his mind.

Current Sketch

Henri Milton is determined to become a famous artist. For most of his life, this has seemed an impossible dream. Since the discovery of *Picalinni's Palette*, however, it appears to have come into his grasp.

Milton keeps a small apartment with an attached studio in one of Pont-a-Museau's poorer districts. He has begun to sell his paintings, which are described by critics as "disturbing glimpses into mankind's bestial nature," and is gradually becoming a respected artist.

Urged on by the evil of the *palette*, however, he has begun to dabble in more macabre media than mere paints. The last several models employed by Milton have vanished, and people are beginning to whisper dark rumors about him.

Personality

Henri Milton's life is a study in tragedy. His troubled childhood shaped him into a disturbed youth whose one great dream was dangled before him and then snatched away. He is now beginning to acquire something of the fame that he has always hungered for, but in his heart

Picalinni's Palette

This magic item is a dangerous object created nearly two decades ago. It was fashioned by an order of monks in the domain of Sri Raji, at the behest of the noted artist Jaspor Picalinni. Picalinni had traveled to Sri Raji to study that culture's unusual art and architecture. So offensive was he, however, that the craftsmen who created the *palette* wove a fell curse into it.

Picalinni had no great wishes for the *palette,* only that it be decorated with symbols and icons reflecting the land of Sri Raji. It was to be nothing more than an idle curiosity, a mere souvenir of his journey. Little did he know that it would eventually come to destroy him.

The *palette* appears as a flat, ceramic boar with a thumb-hole and several depressions around its edge in which paint can be mixed. Images of tigers, boars, monkeys, and other jungle animals decorate it, along with sinister magical runes.

If paint is mixed in the *palette,* an artist is compelled to paint pictures of ever-greater savagery. Over the course of a month or so, he becomes obsessed with frightening, bestial pictures of death, destruction, and evils too great to look upon. This is further reflected in a gradual change of the artist's alignment. At the end of each week in which he uses the *palette* even once, a saving throw vs. spell is required. If this roll fails, the artist's alignment shifts one step toward chaotic evil (first along the law/chaos axis, then along the good/evil).

When the artist becomes chaotic evil, he grows frustrated with his work. At this time, the idea occurs to him that new media exist in which he might work— among these is fresh blood. In time, the desire to give in to this compulsion is too strong to resist.

The artist quickly discovers that the canvases he paints using blood and *Picalinni's Palette* are masterpieces. True, they are horrific and macabre, but they are undeniably works of absolute genius. Any one of them can be sold for a good fee, and the desire to paint more grows with each completed work.

However, each painting completed in this manner requires another saving throw vs. polymorph. As these are failed, the artist gradually transforms into a werebeast and then, in time, he becomes trapped in an animal form.

After the first such failed throw, the artist becomes more bestial and offensive in his human form. This lowers his Charisma by 2 points but has no other effect.

After the second throw is failed, the artist transforms into a wereboar hybrid each time he begins to paint. He reverts to his true form (and collapses exhausted) after 2d4 hours of frantic work.

When the third saving throw is failed, the artist is permanently transformed into a hybrid wereboar. At the same time, his mind collapses into an almost bestial state (although some lucid moments emerge). From this point on, he is little more than a wild beast. He travels about in violent rages until something happens to end his life.

Wereboars created by *Picalinni's Palette* cannot spread the disease of lycanthropy. Only when the relic at the root of these problems changes hands is the curse passed on. On that note, an artist does not willingly give up the *palette* after failing the first saving throw. If the object is taken from him, he retains whatever alignment he presently has and is subject to whatever curse had befallen him to that point.

he knows that it is not his own doing. Beyond that, the magic of *Picalinni's Palette* has tainted his soul, driving him to the brink of madness as it makes ready to destroy him.

Milton spends most of his time locked away in his studio, trying to paint. He continually fights to avoid using the magical *palette,* aware on some level that it is destroying him. Without its help, however, none of his work is satisfactory. Thus, like a man who has allowed himself to become addicted to a dangerous drug, he is constantly drawn back to a thing he now hates.

In order to acquire the blood to feed his artistic expression, Milton lures young men and women to his studio with the promise that he will immortalize them on canvas. He begins his work using a normal palette and paints, but eventually resorts to the dread magical relic when his expectations and visions are not met.

Combat

Henri Milton is a dangerous opponent, not because of any great skill with weapons or tactics but because of his base savagery. While the exact nature of any battle with him depends upon the form in which he finds himself, there is one characteristic that is true of both his aspects: No weapon can harm Henri Milton unless it is either fashioned of silver or magical in some way. All other arms simply bounce harmlessly off his tough hide.

Human Aspect

In his human guise, Milton is not used to battle. He fights with whatever weapon is at hand, generally inflicting 1d6 or 1d4 points of damage. As a rule, he tries to flee any combat while in this form. If he can't get away, he'll beg and grovel in order to avoid violence. Only as a last resort does he engage in combat.

Hybrid Aspect

Whenever he begins to paint, Milton is forced into his hybrid aspect. It is in this shape, that of a half-man/half-boar, that he is truly dangerous. All of the anger and rage that young Milton has accumulated over the years is channeled into a killing fury.

In wereboar form, Milton attacks with a combination of powerful blows, painful bites, and tusk thrusts. All told, these inflict 2d6 points of damage in battle.

A Bloody Canvas

his adventure draws the characters into contact with Henri Milton, Ravenloft's most talented artist. (Or so he would seem.) The events that surround this encounter involve a series of paintings created with *Picalinni's Palette* and the blood of a mad man. The artworks resulting from this disturbing mixture are so horrific that no man may look upon them without himself being driven to the brink of madness.

Introduction

The adventure is set in the city of Pont-a-Museau, where Milton maintains a small residence. His home serves as both living quarters and art studio. Recently, as his fame has increased, the artist has added a small, private gallery to the back of the building. The room where this work is exhibited is kept locked at all times, and the collection within can be viewed only by invitation. These paintings are the works upon which this adventure centers.

In addition to Milton, the adventure features one other major NPC.

Boris Stanielle

Boris Stanielle is the young lad from whom Milton stole the *palette*. He has been driven mad by his consuming need to recover that treasure. Like Milton, Stanielle is assumed to have failed two saving throws thus far. Consequently, he transforms into a hybrid wereboar whenever he begins to paint or grows highly emotional.

Scene I: Madman's Curse

As the adventure opens, the heroes are walking down a city street in Pont-a-Museau one evening, minding their own business. Unexpectedly, a raving madman bursts out of a dark alley and tries to strangle the nearest of

them. (Statistics for madmen are given in the *Monstrous Compendium: Ravenloft Appendix I.*) The attacker is a middle-aged man, prosperously dressed, but he howls and growls like some sort of a wild beast and is clearly bent upon murder. Although the heroes cannot know it yet, his mind has been destroyed by the bestial nature of Milton's latest artworks, and it may be impossible for him to ever think rationally again.

Drawn by the sounds of battle, a pair of night watchmen come rushing to the scene just as the player characters subdue the madman. The watchmen recognize the fellow as a local businessman named Ghorman—a wealthy philanthropist, patron of the arts, and generally well-loved figure in the town. They are astonished to find him involved in a brawl, and they immediately assume that the player characters set upon him to rob him, rather than that he attacked them.

If the heroes merely subdued this businessman, they can avoid trouble with the watchmen by pointing out the insane gleam in his eyes, the froth upon his lips, and the mad curses he babbles. If, instead, the PCs killed him, they have to do some fast talking to convince the watchmen of their innocence. (As taking the life of another person when it could be avoided is pretty close to an evil act, if the heroes didn't at least try to restrain or capture the madman, the Dungeon Master may justified in requiring a powers check.)

One thing that eventually works in the party's favor is that Ghorman's family, when it learns of his madness, seeks to hush things up and avoid a scandal. Consequently, they do not press to have the heroes prosecuted for their "attack" on the businessman.

The Dungeon Master can use the family in any of a number of different ways to draw the heroes further into the adventure. If the heroes are prone to helping those in distress, Ghorman might have a young son or daughter who is desperate to learn what foul events occurred to drive his or her father mad. If, on the other hand, they feel at all guilty about their battle with Ghorman, his family might stare accusingly at these "ruffians" into whose hands the father fell. If Ghorman survived his battle with the player characters, they might even be hired by the family to learn what so affected him, perhaps in the hope of discovering a cure to his madness.

Alternatively, the town watch might even suggest that the heroes conduct an investigation so as to prove their own innocence in the events. After all, even if the family doesn't plan to press charges, the town fathers still might decide to. These politicians might even view the player characters as convenient scapegoats.

Scene II: On the Madman's Trail

Once the heroes have decided to investigate Ghorman's behavior (whatever their reasons), they can trace fairly easily the businessman's actions on the day that he

attacked them. He left a detailed schedule of appointments among his papers, and this can be obtained by either fair means or foul.

Although only one of the appointments listed is significant, the Dungeon Master might introduce a few others to give the heroes more of a sense of investigation. Some of these could be red herrings. For instance, Ghorman might have had a meeting with some men who wanted him to invest in their business. The heroes learn that when he refused to invest, the tone of the meeting turned angry. That could lead them to suspect that perhaps one of those businessmen somehow struck back at Ghorman by driving him mad. Other items on Ghorman's schedule might include a trip to the barber, a visit to an orphanage, and a trip to the bank, just to name a few.

The significant event on Ghorman's schedule, however, was a visit to an art gallery. Ghorman's money paid for this exhibit, which features the work of a half dozen local artists. As luck would have it, the art on display includes canvases by both Stanielle and Milton. While Stanielle is well aware that his rival's paintings are being shown, Milton has not visited the gallery since the show opened and so has no idea that the man from whom he stole the *palette* has tracked him down.

When the heroes visit the gallery that evening (it isn't open until late), they meet Boris Stanielle. He seems a nice enough fellow, although a bit nervous, not unusual for someone with an artistic temperament. The nature of his paintings, which depict brutal killings and other scenes of carnage and mayhem, should offer a more disturbing insight into his character.

Over the course of the conversation, Stanielle points the heroes' investigation toward Milton. It is his intent to set the group upon Milton's trail, then slip in and regain the *palette* while is rival is occupied with them.

The heroes learn two important things during this encounter. The first is that Stanielle and Milton seem to have identical techniques and styles. (Indeed, an expert examination of their canvases would say that all of these works were painted by the same hand. The only real difference is the signatures.) The second—which comes to light during their conversation with Stanielle—is that Ghorman went to visit Milton last night. It seems that the businessman found Milton's absence at the show disturbing, and heard second hand that the artist was working feverishly on a new group of paintings. He asked the gallery manager for directions to Milton's home, and said that he intended to stop by and visit the artist.

Scene III: The Eye of Madness

When the heroes travel to Milton's home, they discover find that he is gone. The entire place is dark, even the studio and gallery. The artist is, in fact, out searching for a new model. He's prowling the streets, seeking a beautiful young woman to lure back to his studio.

No doubt the characters will want to explore the building, especially the private gallery. In looking through the residential part of the building, they find nothing unusual. The only thing they learn for certain is that the artist is sloppy, seems to have little interest in cleaning up after himself, and generally lives like a pig.

An examination of Milton's studio reveals nothing too interesting at first. The place has an easel, several unused canvases, and the usual assortment of paints and such. A more careful examination, however, turns up the fact that the paints are little used, which is clearly unusual. More disturbing, however, is the realization that there are no unfinished or drying paintings anywhere in the studio. From the evidence, it would seem that Milton has not raised a brush in months. An especially astute hero might discover bloody red stains on the floor, but it ought to be difficult to say for sure that these are not just dried paint.

If they enter the gallery itself, the heroes put themselves in unexpected danger. Here, Milton has placed no fewer than eight painting on display. Each is kept behind red silk curtains.

Unlike the other paintings created by Milton, these works were produced when the artist poured the blood of a madman onto his magical *palette*. They are even more disturbing and horrific than those on display at the gallery. It is impossible to say exactly what any of these canvases depicts. They are covered with swirls and patters that seem to bring a different, but equally awful picture, to the mind of each viewer.

Anyone who draws back the curtains and looks upon one of the paintings must make a madness check. Those who look at more than one painting suffer a –1 penalty to the check for every painting after the first. Thus, the second painting viewed requires a check with a –1 penalty, the third a check with a –2 penalty, and so on.

As the characters are exploring the gallery, Milton returns to his studio with an attractive young woman in tow. It is apparent that she is either drugged or very drunk, as she offers no resistance as the artist sets about his work.

First, Milton places a blank canvas on an easel. Then, he recovers the *palette* from a hidden niche within his fireplace. Finally, he recovers a large knife and makes ready to murder the unsuspecting woman. It is assumed that the heroes step in to stop him at this point.

As soon as the heroes seek to intervene, Milton undergoes transformation into a wereboar. This change should happen even as the party steps forward to act, making for a dramatic surprise. A fierce battle almost certainly follows. Although the heroes might believe that they must protect Milton's "model," this isn't the case. He offers her no further threat, intent as he is upon dealing with the heroes.

Recognizing quickly that he is in over his head in this battle, Milton retreats into his private studio, knocking over easels and canvases along the way, in an effort to slow pursuit. Any heroes who follow him into this place are exposed to painting after painting as Milton rips down the red curtains covering them. To avoid having a painting catch his eye, each hero in this room must pass a saving throw vs. paralysis each round. Unfortunately, attempting to battle Milton without looking at the paintings imposes a –4 penalty on all of the heroes' attack and damage rolls.

If Ghorman becomes mortally wounded, his last act is to set torch to the paintings, which begins an awful conflagration within the building. Flames race through the private studio from painting to painting, curtain to curtain, and quickly spread through the rooms beyond. Canvas, paint, thinner, and the like make a highly volatile source of fuel, and within minutes the entire building is transformed into a virtual inferno.

At this point, Boris Stanielle arrives on the scene, obviously quite agitated. After a quick look around the scene, he screams, "No!" and dashes into the burning building, intent upon recovering the *palette*—though the

heroes are not likely to understand his motivations at this time. Moments later, the building's roof collapses, sealing his fate.

As the roof falls in, thick cloud of black smoke belches high into the night sky, hellishly lit by the flames below. Titanic faces seem to writhe madly in this smoke cloud, mouthing gibberish as they ascend. Again, the heroes must avert their eyes to avoid making a madness check. Even then, beneath the roaring of the flames, they seem to hear the demented cries and howls of the damned. In the days that follow, the town of Pont-a-Museau discovers more than one citizen who was driven to insanity by viewing this scene from afar.

After the battle, the heroes should certainly be able to figure out what happened to Ghorman. What they choose to do with that knowledge is up to them. The mad paintings have been destroyed, leaving them no hard evidence. Then again, the cloud itself is evidence of a sort, for those who might choose to believe. Perhaps the town fathers might be convinced that the artist kept a store of horrible drugs in his home, and used them to drive Ghorman mad to keep him from interfering. Such a theory could also explain the effects of the smoke cloud upon the citizenry of the town.

Recurrence

The possibilities for further adventures involving *Picalinni's palette* depend upon the party's actions during this scenario.

If the heroes deduced from Milton's behavior that the source of the evil was not the artist himself but rather the *palette* he was preparing to use, they may have made a point of capturing the *palette* during their battle with him. Of course, such items have a way of captivating the mind, so it might be that one of the heroes now becomes fixated with owning it himself.

If they did not recover the *palette*, it now lies among the ashes of Milton's home, waiting to be found by someone else later on. In this case, it may not be long before the heroes again hear of a famous painter of disturbing works, and view pieces that bear a distinct resemblance to those of Milton and Stanielle.

Finally, the events of this scenario can also be reflected in the lingering effects of any failed madness check on the part of the heroes. It might be that the Dungeon Master can arrange for the treatment of any such illness to require the destruction of *Picalinni's Palette*. Of course, in order to destroy the evil item, the player characters have to find it again. . . .

Vjorn Horstman

The strongest man on earth is he who stands most alone.

—Henrik Ibsen
An Enemy of the People

Biography

Although Dr. Horstman is classed as a wizard, he is not actually a spellcaster. In truth, he is a brilliant scientist who has always been fascinated with the subject of lycanthropy. Although his earlier work was dedicated to finding a cure for the dread disease, his more recent studies have been of a far less noble nature.

Horstman has developed a special strain of the disease that transforms its victim into a werebeast for one hour. At the end of this time, the person reverts to normal. Although the disease has been burned out of his body, that isn't evident. Most people who suffer the treatment believe that they have been infected with normal lycanthropy.

Appearance

Horstman stands just under six feet in height, but he is so gaunt that he appears to be rather taller. His flesh is drawn tight across protruding cheek bones, and his eyes have a sunken, tired look. All things considered, his countenance bears as much resemblance to a skull as to a living face.

Horstman has bushy eyebrows, a high forehead, and not so much as a wisp of hair on his spotted scalp. A laboratory accident destroyed his left eye many years ago. Being a man of little vanity, he has done nothing to hide this deformity. Thus, his left eye is a sickly white orb without iris or pupil. He never covers this disturbing sight with a patch, and takes no notice if someone stares at it upon meeting him.

When encountered outside of his laboratory, Horstman wears the clothes of a gentleman. He favors a dark gray or black jacket with a white or yellow cravat or ascot. He is as likely to wear a low, wide hat as not.

In his lab, the doctor generally wears a simple white shirt and matching pants. Over these, he wears a light brown, leather apron. Slender gloves, made of the same leather, cover his hands nearly to the elbows.

Dr. Vjorn Horstman

7th-level Human Wizard, Lawful Evil

Armor Class	9	Str	12
Movement	12	Dex	15
Level/Hit Dice	7	Con	11
Hit Points	30	Int	18
THAC0	18	Wis	17
Morale	Elite (14)	Cha	7
No. of Attacks	3		
Damage/Attack	By weapon (1d4)		
Special Attacks	Cause lycanthropy		
Special Defenses	Immune to lycanthropy		
Magic Resistance	Nil		

Background

Vjorn Horstman was born to a powerful family in the domain of Falkovnia. His father was an important general, and the Horstman family enjoyed a comfortable lifestyle. As a young man, he received an excellent education but also learned to hold the lower classes in contempt.

In school, Horstman devoured all courses related to science and medicine but held all others in disdain. He showed great promise, his keen mind being tempered by cunning insight and shrewd judgment. To a man, however, his instructors felt that he was utterly lacking in compassion or kindness. His cold disposition frightened them, but fear of his powerful father kept them from challenging the lad.

Vjorn Horstman

When his schooling was completed, Horstman was immediately given a position with Falkovnia's Ministry of Science. For the first few years, his work was of only passing interest or importance. He longed for more, however, and pursued his own studies in the dead of night. It was during this time that Horstman first became interested in the study of lycanthropy.

A series of unusually brutal killings were taking place within the rarefied circle of the nobility. Although Horstman was not assigned to look into the matter, he did so on his own. While the Royal Guard failed to apprehend the killer, Horstman tracked her down. He discovered that a minor serving girl in one of the noble houses had become infected with the dread disease.

Under Horstman's guidance, the girl was captured and the killings ended. While most assumed that the young scientist had seen to the destruction of the woman, this was in fact not the case. Instead, he had sealed her up in a hidden chamber of his private laboratory. Over the course of the next few months, he conducted horrific experiments on the captive lycanthrope.

As the years passed, Horstman continued to pursue this field of study. He captured, studied, and eventually dissected numerous werebeasts. At the same time, his position within the government improved until—shortly before his thirty-fifth birthday—he was appointed Falkovnia's Minister of Science. He holds this post still, using its power to conduct horrific experiments upon criminals, political prisoners, and anyone else who runs afoul of Falkovnia's darklord.

Current Sketch

Horstman's official position is Minister of Science, but the doctor's work also includes the duties of an executioner and torturer. These extra responsibilities suit Horstman well, for they provide him with more subjects (victims, really) for his sadistic experiments.

The doctor's current goal is to find a way in which the bestial nature of a person can be released and then controlled. In this way, Horstman hopes to develop an elite cadre of powerful beast-warriors for Vlad Drakov. In the course of this research he has discovered his *primal serum* (described below). Although it is not yet perfected, Horstman feels that the final formula for this dreadful concoction will soon be his.

Horstman has no political ambitions himself, although others may not believe this. Drakov has him watched constantly, out of fear that the scientist may turn his deadly intellect against his master. This is unlikely, however, as political power holds no fascination for the evil Dr. Horstman.

Personality

In his younger days, Horstman was not truly evil. His interest in science outweighed any love for his fellow man, however, and he eventually began to look upon all his fellows as little more than laboratory mice. As he gradually lost his humanity, a darker nature surfaced within him. Whether this is the cause or result of his current experiments is impossible to say.

As things stand now, Horstman is the very model of a sadistic mad scientist. To him other people are nothing more than subjects to be studied, manipulated, and eventually dissected. He cares nothing for the pain he inflicts or the suffering he brings to the world. A dozen deaths are not too great a price to pay if it brings about the successful end to a research project.

Combat

Horstman is not a dangerous foe in a fight. He is an older man, far more used to the laboratory than the battlefield. If attacked in a place with chemicals and such at hand, however, there is a good chance that he spots some weapon to use in his defense (such as a vial of acid).

Horstman is seldom encountered without his two bodyguards. Although he has little use for them, they are a result of the government office he holds, and he must tolerate their presence. These men are elite members of Falkovnia's military (5th-level warriors wearing banded mail [AC 4] and carrying broadswords [2d4/1d6]). They fight to the death in Horstman's defense, never checking morale unless some manner of magic or the like is used on them.

Primal Serum

Horstman's greatest invention is the *primal serum*. This fluid is very thin, even thinner than water, yet somehow oily to the touch. The secret of its creation is known only to Horstman, although anyone can use it once it has been manufactured.

Primal serum comes in a variety of formulas, each of which transforms the recipient into a werebeast of that type for one hour. To date, Horstman has been able to brew a *serum* for werebat, wererat, werewolf, werejackal, wereboar, weretiger, and werebear. He is experimenting with potions that create non-mammalian werebeasts, like weresharks or werecrocodiles, but has had no success in those fields yet. In all cases, Horstman's victims assume a hybrid aspect.

To produce one dose (about an ounce) of *primal serum,* Horstman requires some ten pounds of tissue from the type of animal that will be mimicked. Thus, ten pounds of rat flesh is required to manufacture one does of a serum that will transform a person into a wererat. The actual process of manufacture requires a special sort of still created by Horstman and takes one day per dose. No more than one dose can be produced at any one time. Once created, a dose of *primal serum* remains efficacious for one month. At the end of this time, it sours and becomes a deadly poison (Class J).

Vjorn Horstman

Once a dose of *primal serum* is created, it can be either injected or ingested. In either case, a saving throw vs. poison is allowed to escape the effects of the elixir. If the serum is injected, a –4 penalty is applied to this roll. An injection of *primal serum* takes effect in 1d4 minutes. This onset time is tripled if the fluid is ingested.

The Unnatural

 his adventure takes place in the city of Lekar, capital of Falkovnia. It begins when the heroes show mercy to a pitiful creature, spawned from one of Dr. Horstman's sinister experiments. That simple act draws them into a series of horrifying encounters involving Horstman and his search for the secrets of lycanthropy. In the end, the player characters learn firsthand why Falkovnia is one of the most dreadful of all Ravenloft's domains.

Introduction

In order for this adventure to begin, the player characters need to be in the city of Lekar (or a similar place, if the adventure is being run outside of Ravenloft). The heroes do not have to seek out this adventure; instead it will come to them.

The Dark Men

The only important nonplayer characters that the heroes meet during the course of this adventure are the Dark Men. These twisted creatures, the survivors of Horstman's early experiments into the nature of lycanthropy, dwell in the maze of sewer tunnels lying beneath the city. For the most part, these creatures keep to themselves. From time to time, however, they are forced to raid the surface world for supplies. Rumors abound within the city that the things are cannibals, dragging unfortunates into the depths to feed upon them.

In game terms, these creatures have the same statistics as the broken ones described in the *Ravenloft Monstrous Compendium®: Appendix I.*

Scene I: The Wounded Thing

As the adventure begins, the heroes stumble upon a disturbing event. While crossing a bridge near the outskirts of the city, they hear from below the unexpected sounds of harsh laughter, accompanied by pitiful cries of pain. When they investigate, they discover the following.

A pair of soldiers—cruel-looking men with scarred faces and dirty uniforms—are lurking in the darkness beneath the bridge. They laugh cruelly, jabbing with their swords at something you can't yet see. Not far from where they stand, the wide opening of a sewer tunnel pours a steady flow of thick sludge into the stream. The odor of corruption and decay issuing from inside is so strong that it threatens to overcome you.

There is a sudden burst of activity, and the thing that so amuses the guards lurches into view. It is a twisted little creature, more or less human, but bent and bestial looking. From its small size and its facial features, it seems but a child. Dark blood leaks from several sword wounds on the creature's body and one eye is swollen shut.

As soon as it spies you, the creature tries to change its course. It stumbles sideways, and one of the guards grabs it by the shoulder. Barking a laugh, he throws the creature down into the sewage. It screams like a child as it falls, whimpers for an instant afterward, then lies still.

Seeing this, one of the soldiers spits on the little thing in disgust. "Bah!" he curses at his companion. "Yu'v gone an' killed it!"

In truth, the creature is not dead. The soldiers realize this in a few moments if the heroes don't take action to distract them. As soon as they see that it's still alive, they start to torture the poor thing again.

It is important that the heroes be given the clear impression that this creature, deformed and horrible though it may appear, is hardly more than a babe. The Dungeon Master must make certain that they do not assume it to be a goblin or other evil beastie.

The little creature is one of the Dark Men who haunt the sewers beneath Lekar. This particular example of that pitiful race is a child, having only half the Hit Dice of an adult. He got himself lost in the sewers and eventually found his way to the surface world. Curious, he came out to look around. Unfortunately for him, the soldiers spotted him immediately. Before he could return to the safety of the sewers, they caught him. That was nearly an hour ago. Since that time, they have amused themselves by beating the creature and pricking him with their swords.

Assuming that the heroes do something to drive off the soldiers, they can provide medical aid to the poor child. He is very weak, having only 1d4 hit points left, and is bleeding badly. Just as the heroes rouse him, the soldiers return with reinforcements, intent upon punishing them for their interference. Panicked, the beast child stumbles away and vanishes into the mouth of the sewer tunnel. Bleeding as he is, it should be obvious to the heroes that he cannot last long without further treatment. That fact and the horde of soldiers closing in upon the party ought to be enough incentive for the heroes to follow the creature into the sewers. If necessary, the little creature beckons for the heroes to follow.

K. M°Cann

Scene II: The Dark Men

When the heroes follow the wounded child, they enter the domain of the Dark Men. Read the following text.

The stench within this underground labyrinth is staggering, but eventually your noses lose their sensitivity to it. Still, the dank air seems to work its way inside your clothing, leaving a sticky film upon your skin underneath. A turbid stream of ankle-deep water flows at your feet, gurgling obscenely as it passes. Condensation drips from the "ceiling," adding a steady chorus of plopping sounds that echo into the dark distance. Occasionally, a deep rumble or heavy slither reaches your ears from one side passage or another. There is no telling what the source of these sounds is, however.

Soon you discover the little beast-man again. He lies unconscious behind a tangle of pallid roots that has broken through the sewer wall. Obviously, weakness finally overcame him. Fortunately, he is still breathing, though shallowly.

A few *cure light wounds* or similar spells get the child back on his feet. By now he recognizes that the heroes are helping, and he does not fear them. He thanks them in a garbled version of the language of Falkovnia, and his limited vocabulary makes it clear that he is, indeed, hardly more than a toddler.

At this point, however, the heroes hear a whisper of movement from all around and discover that they are surrounded by dozens of bestial humanoids. The largest informs them in a guttural voice that they have trespassed into the realm of the Dark Men, then commands them to hand over their weapons and accompany him to the Seat of Judgement. Unless the heroes wish to fight their way through dozens of these creatures, they must obey. As an incentive to peaceful compliance, their little friend takes their hands one after another, and gazes imploringly up at them all. Then, at a harsh command from the leader, he goes to join the other Dark Men.

Some time later, the group is brought into the chamber known as the Throne of Judgement. Read the following text aloud.

Your captors lead you into a chamber that must once have served as a collecting pool for the sewers.

Rough tunnels have been dug into the perimeter near floor level, however, allowing the water to drain away into the lower reaches of the city's sewers. The room is lit by greenish flames spouting from a crack in the floor's center. Apparently, that crevice leads to the source of some strange, flammable gas.

Just beyond the fire pit, a rough throne stands, built from mismatched stone blocks. It is splotched and stained with moisture and lichens. Upon it sits a loathsome, bloated being that seems a mix of human and toad. The creature gazes impassively at you through mismatched eyes as the leader of your captors makes his report. Their guttural voices speak rapidly, making it impossible for you to understand their conversation, though you recognize a word here and there.

Suddenly, the figure on the throne smacks the other on the head.

"Give them back their weapons," the toad-thing growls. "They've done nothing to deserve our suspicion. The opposite, in fact."

Quickly, the other Dark Men move to comply with their leader's orders. The heroes are given their weapons; stone blocks are dragged forward to serve them as seats; and they are brought food and drink to refresh themselves. (The food is a fleshy gray substance that can't quite be identified, while the drink is tepid water in stone bowls.)

The being on the throne introduces himself simply as "the Leader" and relates to the heroes the story of the Dark Men, telling them of the evil Dr. Horstman and his awful experiments. All of the Dark Men were once human, he says, though many have lost much of their humanity. The child the heroes saved is the first of these creatures to be born within the sewers rather than created in Horstman's lab. He represents the future of their race.

Still, the Leader explains, Horstman continues to create others of their kind. Even now, there are pitiful wretches languishing in his cages, the subjects of experiments the like of which still haunt all Dark Men's nightmares. The Leader says that the Dark Men want to end Horstman's career. They have a plan to invade the lab, rescue its victims, and bring the doctor back for judgment. They know of a hidden way into an alley near the lab, but have feared that their appearance would raise an alarm before they could get sufficient numbers into the building. They would stand a better chance of success if true humans were to lead them.

Scene III: The Monster's Den

If the heroes are willing to help with this plan, the Dark Men put it into action immediately.

First, they outfit the heroes with uniforms of the town watch, which they have captured from careless guards. Then they lead the heroes upward through the sewer tunnels to a spot near street level. There, removing a few loose blocks from a sewer wall, they open an entry into an alley beside Horstman's house. After the heroes clamber up to guard the alley's mouth—their presence as "watchmen" discouraging any citizens from approaching—a score of Dark Men enters the alley behind them.

Next, the heroes must gain entrance to the doctor's house itself. Here again, their "borrowed" uniforms help. They need to come up with some excuse to give to the door guard, but the Dungeon Master should be lenient in judging its apparent validity. Faced with this large a band of "watchmen," that guard believes just about any story they tell him, at least sufficiently to open the door for them.

Once the door is open, the heroes' way is clear. The Dark Men pour out of the alley and rush into Dr. Horstman's house right behind the player characters.

What follows is a fairly one-sided battle. The house's defenders are thoroughly outnumbered and quite unprepared for battle. Further, the Dark Men are driven by years of helpless rage. This is their opportunity to vent it, and they do so with abandon. Read the following text aloud at this point.

The Dark Men follow you joyfully into Dr. Horstman's house. Though they remain silent from the alley to the door, once inside the house they break out in a savage chorus of howls, growls, grunts, and whistles.

Like a deadly whirlwind, they rush through the building with reckless abandon, propelling you before them, and destroying everything in their path. Their bestial natures seem to dominate their minds. You watch the house's defenders fall helplessly to their attack, torn, gored, savaged, and trampled. True men die screaming beneath the paws and hooves of beasts.

You can hardly help but ask yourself if you are on the right side of this battle.

The carnage continues until at last the heroes find themselves before the door to the lab itself. Two of the largest Dark Men burst the door and rush into the room beyond. A cacophony of enraged animal cries greet them. Then the heroes are pushed into the room by the press of Dark Men from behind. Inside, they discover that Dr. Horstman is not without his final defenses. Read the following text aloud.

If the horror was great before, the vision that greets you inside the lab is even worse.

A pair of metal tables stands in the center of the room, bearing the most recent of the doctor's experiments. Atop each is a naked human figure bleeding from numerous surgical incisions and surrounded by various animal parts—eyes, claws, even beaks and wings, as well as internal organs. Apparently, Dr. Horstman was in the process of experimental grafts when your "friends" burst the door. One of the victims lies motionless, apparently dead; the other still whimpers and twitches fitfully.

As for the two Dark Men who preceded you into the lab, one is locked in mortal combat with an enormous wolfman; the other wrestles on the floor with a huge tiger that bears human eyes and ears.

A line of iron cages stands along the back wall, most containing the results of prior experiments, creatures the Dark Men have come to rescue and claim as their own. At the room's back corner, a cadaverous man in white clothes and a bloody leather smock cringes inside a cage, a dying beast thing at his feet. You recognize the thin man as Dr. Horstman from the description the leader of the Dark Men gave you. Apparently Horstman locked himself in the cage for protection.

As you and your Dark Men companions open the other cages, releasing their inhabitants, the doctor lifts a glass tube to his lips and blows.

Horstman has just shot at one of the heroes with a dart containing his *prime elixir.* As quickly as he can, he reloads and shoots as many of them as possible (4/round). Unable to exit the room because of the press of Dark Men behind them, the heroes are ultimately unable to avoid these darts. As each is hit, he immediately undergoes transformation into a werebeast of the Dungeon Master's choice. He remembers nothing else from that point, until regaining human form an hour later.

Of course, those heroes who are hit last have a few moments to see what happens to the first victims. These new werebeasts begin to attack anyone within reach, friend or foe. Facing their complete ferocity, the Dark Men are forced to flee the building.

When the heroes return to their senses an hour later, each is in a different part of Horstman's house, spattered with blood, and surrounded by the bodies of various human defenders and Dark Men alike. No other living thing remains in the building. The player characters can only conclude that, in their savagery, they slew anyone who remained within these walls.

All things considered, it is probably a good thing if the heroes leave town at this point. Otherwise they stand the risk of being discovered by the city watch and imprisoned. After all, Dr. Horstman was an important figure, and the player characters were clearly involved in his disappearance.

If the heroes decide to visit the Dark Men once more before leaving town, they find the tunnels with which they are acquainted now abandoned, as is the chamber of the Throne of Judgement. Those tunnels leading deeper into the sewers have been collapsed, preventing the party from proceeding any further. Apparently, the Dark Men have retreated further underground, and they do not want to be followed. Considering their losses at Horstman's house, that sentiment should not be surprising.

Recurrence

If the Dungeon Master desires, it is just possible that Dr. Horstman might somehow escape the Dark Men, to plague the heroes later. More likely, however, is the prospect of some other budding scientist recovering Horstman's notes and following up on the doctor's work. He might actually succeed in creating a small army of werecreatures, as Horstman attempted to do, and begin using them to take power in the area. Naturally, should the heroes get wind of such a person, they have every incentive to put a stop to his plans. Otherwise all the blood they spilled while fighting to thwart Horstman will seem to have been in vain.

It is possible, as well, that even the Dark Men may return to the campaign at some later date. For now, they fear the player characters, due to the mayhem these heroes caused while under the influence of the *prime serum.* In time, however, their thankfulness for the heroes' aid against the evil Dr. Horstman may come to outweigh their current fearfulness. Further, their culture may begin to spread to other underground locations, and legends of the heroes and the help they once gave may will certainly be carried along with it. Consequently, at some point in the future, the player characters may even find themselves sought out by the Dark Men once again, to help defeat another great evil—this time perhaps a threat from the subterranean world.

For now, however, the heroes are likely to be consumed with worry about having been injected with the *prime serum.* They have no way of knowing that its effects were only temporary, so they probably believe that they have been infected with lycanthropy. Assuming that the heroes set out to seek a cure, the Dungeon Master is free to lead them either to a good-hearted soul who—after some puzzlement—informs them that they are not werebeasts, or perhaps to a more sinister individual, who recognizes the truth but uses their confusion to send the heroes off on all sorts of quests, ostensibly for their own good, but actually for his own gain.

Let your conscience be your guide.

Sandover

God sends meat and the Devil sends cooks.

—English Proverb

Biography

andovor is a most unusual man born in the island domain of Souragne. He has become a werecrocodile as a result of his devotion to the reptile god Merrshaulk. He lives deep in Souragne's great swamp, where he is the master of a tribe of reptile men. These hearty but diminutive creatures worship Sandovor as an avatar of their god.

For the most part, Sandovor and his people keep to themselves. They live their lives in the swamp, worshiping their reptilian god, catching fish or birds, and working on the construction of an impressive step pyramid. From time to time, however, when their faith demands a sacrifice, they slither forth. People who travel too near the swamps at these times run the risk of being taken by these folk.

Appearance

In his human aspect, Sandovor is unnaturally tall, reaching a height of nearly seven feet. His skin is dark and tanned, although he spends little time out of doors. His eyes are coal black and seem to have an almost

Sandover

supernatural light about them. His head is bald, although whether this is the result of natural heredity or a side effect of his lycanthropic nature is difficult to say.

Sandovor is fond of leather clothes, favoring soft, buckskin-like materials fashioned from the hides of various reptiles. He has a fondness for darker colors, which he adorns with bright jewelry. He has a large collection of gold jewelry, much of which is decorated with various green stones such as jade and emerald.

When he transforms into a crocodile, Sandovor is a truly impressive sight. From the tip of his snout to the end of his tail he stretches fully 25 feet long. A snap of his powerful jaws can split logs in two, and a sweep of his heavy tail can crush bones.

Sandovor

Maledictive Werecrocodile, Neutral Evil

Armor Class	5	Str	18
Movement	12	Dex	14
Level/Hit Dice	4+2	Con	17
Hit Points	32	Int	15
THAC0	17	Wis	15
Morale	Avg (10)	Cha	12
No. of Attacks	2		
Damage/Attack	2d6 (bite) and 1d12+1 (tail); or by weapon		
Special Attacks	Spell use		
Special Defenses	Hit only by silver and +1 or better magical weapons, immune to poisons & toxins		
Magic Resistance	Nil		

Background

Sandovor was born in Port d'Elhour, a village in the island domain of Souragne. His father was a combination tanner and tailor who worked the hides of animals into leather clothing. The man occasionally did his own trapping but normally turned this duty (which he found distasteful) over to his son.

As young Sandovor grew into manhood, he found himself fascinated by the creatures that lived in the swamps. In particular, however, he was interested in the mighty crocodiles that lurked within its murky waters.

Sandovor's interest in crocs led him to undertake regular trips into the swamps. During these expeditions, he would place traps for his father and then set about watching for his favorite creatures. From time to time, he would find crocodile eggs and hatch them out, but he always felt sympathy for the little creatures and released them back into the wilds of the swamp.

During one of his hunting forays, Sandovor stumbled upon a group of unusual people. They were small, not much bigger than halflings, and had complexions so dark that they almost vanished into the shadows. These strange people were chanting softly, playing eerie flutes, and dancing hypnotically.

As he approached closer, Sandovor saw that the creatures were ringed by an audience of mighty crocodiles. These creatures were mesmerized by the little men and their strange ritual. And as he watched, Sandovor found himself captivated as well. Of a sudden, a wave of pain washed over his body. Sandovor cried out, betraying his presence, and tried to flee. Before he had taken a dozen paces, however, the pain was joined by uncontrollable muscle spasms. He staggered, fell, and lost consciousness.

Or so he thought.

Actually, the eerie music touched something deep inside Sandovor. As a result, he underwent a transformation. His inner spirit—what the reptile men would call his totem—had been aroused and was now ascendant. He had become that which he had so long admired, a gigantic crocodile.

In time, Sandovor returned to his human shape. He found himself in a tiny grass hut, part of a diminutive village hidden away at the heart of the swamp. Any fear he might have had of the little people quickly faded when he realized that they viewed him as some sort of a god. "Many men have the spirit of the crocodile dwelling within them," he was later told, "but those whose bodies house a giant reptile are rare indeed." Sandovor soon came to serve as the reptile folk's high priest of the god Merrshaulk. He abandoned any notion of returning to his old life.

Sandovor knows little of the land from which his adopted people came. He has mastered their language and learned their stories but has no first-hand experience of the swamps where they lived before wandering into the Mists. What researches he had conducted outside the tribe have led him to believe that the reptile men came originally from another world, one where they built great step pyramids and lived among steaming jungles.

Current Sketch

For the most part, Sandovor is content to rule over his people and the small region they have claimed for themselves. Having long been worshiped as a god, it may be that even he has come to believe this. At the very least, he presents himself as an avatar of Merrshaulk, the god of the reptile men. As such, Sandovor demands regular sacrifices from his followers, something that they are only too happy to supply. Once per month, generally when the moon is darkest, they go out to seek him a victim, preferably a child. This sacrifice is eaten by the reptile folk in a ceremonial feast.

Over the course of the past few years, Sandovor has commanded his people to begin construction of a stone pyramid similar to those found in their home land. This grand structure has been slow to arise, although the high priest's magic has greatly aided its construction. When completed, it is to serve as both a temple and palace.

Personality

As high priest of Merrshaulk, Sandovor demands absolute loyalty from the reptile men. For the most part, these reptile people are only too happy to obey their master. In return for their loyalty, Sandovor takes good care of the clan. He allows no one to harm or wrong it without feeling the vengeance of the "Crocodile Priest."

Combat

A highly intelligent man, Sandovor is a dangerous enemy. What's more, his shapechanging ability and growing mastery of priestly magic combine to make him extremely deadly. In either of his forms, Sandovor is immune to damage from any weapon that is not made from silver or imbued with a +1 or better enchantment. He is also immune to poisons or toxins of any sort, although he can still contract diseases and infections.

Human Aspect

In his human shape, Sandovor seldom engages in battle. He commands his followers, who act as 1st-level fighters, to fight his battles for him. When he does join in a battle, however, he shows no trace of mercy. If engaging in physical combat, the high priest depends upon a *dagger of venom* that he wears at all times. This weapon functions exactly as described in the *Dungeon Master's Guide*.

More often, however, Sandovor employs his magical powers to lash out at his enemies. He has the spellcasting abilities of a 7th-level priest of Merrshaulk (see *DMGR4: Monster Mythology*, or treat Sandover as a standard priest who favors water-based spells if *Monster Mythology* isn't available). This gives him major access to the all, animal, divination, healing (reversed only), and plant spheres, as well as minor access to the chaos, charm, and combat spheres. When he casts a *sticks to snakes* spell, the reptiles created are always poisonous. Sandovor can't turn or command undead and never wears any form of armor. Although his beliefs allow him to employ any weapon, he uses only the *dagger of venom* described above.

Crocodile Aspect

When Sandovor assumes his totemic crocodile aspect, he strikes with crushing jaws and deadly tail. His bite

inflict 2d6 points of damage, and his tail causes 1d12+2 points.

Those bitten by Sandovor risk contracting lycanthropy and transforming into crocodiles whenever a they hear the playing of a flute. A saving throw vs. polymorph is required for them to remain in human form. If the flute is not one created by the reptile men, a +4 bonus is applied to the saving throw. If it was made by Sandovor himself (or another priest of Merrshaulk), a –4 penalty is applied instead. The transformation lasts for a number of hours equal to 20 minus the Wisdom score of the victim.

THE VIPER'S GRASP

This adventure takes place in the domain of Souragne, near the village of Port d'Elhour. If the Dungeon Master prefers to place it outside of the realm of Ravenloft, then any similar region of tropical swamps and bayous will suffice.

The events described in this scenario center around Sandovor's attempt to conduct a large voodoo ceremony. In order to bring this sinister ritual to its fruition, the high priest must sacrifice dozens of spirits to the reptile-god he worships. Actually, however, the victims are not to be killed outright. Rather, they are transformed into sub-human reptile men—to labor as nearly mindless slaves toward the completion of the reptile people's great pyramid.

Introduction

How and why the heroes are in Souragne is of little importance to this adventure. All that really matters is that they are not in the middle of some important quest that will require them to move on quickly.

For the purposes of this text, however, the assumption is made that the heroes have come to Port d'Elhour in response to a summons from an old acquaintance, a fellow by the name of Jakobi. If desired, the Dungeon Master can replace Jakobi with any similar character from his prior campaign.

This adventure is divided into two major parts. The first of these involves a raft expedition into the swamps that dominate northern Souragne. It features encounters with the many dangerous creatures that dwell in these dismal expanses. In addition, the hostile environment itself comes into play.

The conclusion of the adventure takes place within the hidden city of the reptile men. Here, the heroes must free the prisoners and fend off the attacks of their captors. With a little luck, they'll be able to buy the escaping men and women enough time to get away.

Scene I: Jakobi's Letter

The adventure begins when the heroes receive a letter from an old friend. It requests that they travel to Port d'Elhour to offer assistance against some unnamed threat. The Dungeon Master can read the following text aloud.

The heat of Souragne causes sweat to trickle constantly down your face and back. Your clothing clings to you uncomfortably. Thick, humid air fights your very efforts to breathe. Not for the first time, you wonder at the wisdom of obeying the strange letter that has brought you to this inhospitable place.

It was a simple enough communiqué: A request for assistance on the letterhead of an old friend named Jakobi. Although it has been many years since you last spoke with the young man, his quick smile and sense of humor comes readily back to mind.

Jakobi's letter contained no details about the trouble he faces. It is that absence that you find most distressing.

The heroes have no trouble in finding Jakobi's home. Their old friend has a small estate on the outskirts of Port d'Elhour. In addition to a residence just large enough to house his family and a handful of servants, the property supports a large area of cultivated land thick with coffee shrubs.

Unfortunately, Jakobi isn't here to meet the player characters when they arrive. Indeed, they learn that their friend hasn't been seen in several days. The party can gain this information from Jakobi's wife, Genette. She is extremely upset, and she pleads with the heroes to find her husband. The following narrative presents the information she supplies them.

"A week ago, my 'usband went out into the fields with the laborers—but they none of them never come back. I look and look for some sign of what 'appened to them, an' I don' find nothing.

"One of the laborer's wives, she is a seer. She says that they have gone into the swamps—that they 'ave been taken by something that isn't 'uman. We been 'earing stories about such things for a while, that's why my 'usband send for you. It was 'is idea that you could find out what it was all about.

"Now 'e is gone. You will 'elp 'im, won't you? You will find my Jakobi?"

It is difficult to refuse Genette, considering that the woman is so obviously distraught. Even if Jakobi were not an old friend, the heroes should almost certainly be willing to take up this challenge.

If they seek out the woman Genette described as a seer, the heroes are in for a most unusual encounter. The slender woman is disturbing, to say the least. She seems to look through people as she talks to them, and she often carries on conversations with people who aren't there. If asked about the men who vanished from Jakobi's estate, she offers the following story.

"Many ha' been taken since last the moon was full. Men and women, old and young, no one is safe from those who dwell in the swamps. If you would save them, you must act quickly. There are only three days left before the moon is full again. When that 'appens, those who were taken will be lost.

"In my dreams I 'ave seen a stone pyramid rising from the tangled vines of the swamp. In this place dwells an evil thing whose thirst for blood 'as taken our loved ones away from us. Find this structure and you will find those you seek—or you will find death."

There isn't too much left for the heroes to learn or do before heading into the swamps. All that remains is for them to come up with some plan to find the stone pyramid the seer woman has mentioned. Pretty much any plan they might conceive of ought to fit the bill. If they decide to hire a native guide, he can speculate as to where it must be and the lead them to it. If they are relying on divination spells or a magical item, these suffice. Even the gut instincts of a ranger or druid could do the trick.

If the heroes have decided to hire a guide, they need to do so quickly, however. They must keep in mind that the full moon marks the start of Sandovor's ritual and the doom of his prisoners. Under the circumstances, a guide can be hired, but only at a great cost.

Beyond this, the party need only buy some provisions, rent a few rafts, and then head off into the choking miasma that hangs over the swamps.

Scene II: Crossing the Swamps

The next phase of the adventure can be as brief or as extended as the Dungeon Master desires. What is important is that the player characters come to respect the swamp and the many hazards that it presents. The encounters detailed in this section serve as examples of the sorts of things the Dungeon Master can toss their way.

- **Crocodiles!** Perhaps the most dangerous of the swamp's natural predators are the great reptiles that drift slowly about just beneath its surface. To these ravenous beasts, a raft full of adventurers is a tempting target. These creatures are described in the *Monstrous Manual,* and the number appearing should be based upon the strength of the party.
- **Invisible Death:** Traveling through an unusually still area of the marsh, the party might come into an area thick with vampire moss and dark trees. Both of these terrors are detailed in the *Monstrous Compendium Annual: Volume One.* These two menaces combine to make this area especially deadly. The dark trees withhold their own attack for as long as possible, allowing the vampire moss to weaken the adventurers. At the last possible moment, just as it seems that the heroes will get away, the dark trees then attack.
- **Attacks by Undead:** The swamps of Souragne are said to be filled with undead. Zombies and ghouls (usually lacedons and sea zombies) have been known to set upon adventuring parties, adding to their own ranks through their gruesome attacks. When using these creatures, the Dungeon Master should play up the eerie silence of their approach. Zombies might rise from out of the waters around the rafts, as if the party has disturbed the site of an ancient battle. Ghouls might then join in the attack, leaping from dens hidden within the roots of cyprus trees. Descriptions and statistics for both of these creatures are listed in the *Monstrous Manual.*
- **Fire and Snakes:** Swamps are swarming with all sorts of reptiles, among them many species of serpent. Strangely enough, the vegetation of a swamp is also prone to wild fires, especially after several hot days with no rain. All it takes is one stroke of lighting to begin a blaze that puts both human and animal at risk. This encounter combines the threat of snakes and fire into one. As the party travels, it is suddenly overrun by a wave of panicked snakes that lash out at everything in their path. The heroes experience several very tense moments as serpents poisonous and not sweep over their rafts. Just as this threat ends and the heroes breathe a sigh of relief, they smell smoke on the wind and learn what it was that panicked the serpents. Unless they get to cover quickly, they are destined to roast alive!

Scene III: City of the Reptile Men

On the last day of the month, the heroes finally discover the village of the reptile men. This encounter is prefaced by a change in the nature of the swamp. The party must give up its rafts and proceed on foot. After traveling like this for a few hours, they come upon the outskirts of the village. It is assumed to be just after sunset when they arrive, so Sandovor's ritual is just beginning.

The Dungeon Master can read the following narrative to get this part of the adventure rolling.

Just ahead , the dense vegetation of the swamp suddenly thins. A large expanse of more or less dry soil, ringed by the dark forms of cypress trees and tangled vines, surrounds a half-completed stone pyramid. There is something sinister in that simple, terraced shape—a feeling of alien evil that cannot be denied.

A large plain of polished stone stretches away from the looming structure to meet a great, circular well. Green flames leap from this pit, rising high into the air and painting the whole place with a disturbing emerald light. Dozens of tiny grass and clay huts flank these structures, throwing weird, prancing shadows that stretch to the edges of the swamp.

All of this is overshadowed, however, by the sight of several dozen men and women standing perfectly still upon the stone plain. These are clearly the villagers you have been seeking, but there is something clearly wrong with them. They don't move or talk—indeed, it seems that they don't even blink or breathe. Could it be that you have arrived too late? Are these poor souls already lost?

As soon as this narrative is completed, the air is filled with the eerie keening of a primitive flute. In answer to this piercing summons, the reptile men begin to emerge from their grass huts. If the heroes think to ask, the DM can tell the players that this music is coming from within the pyramid itself. If they don't, however, its source remains a mystery.

The Dungeon Master should determine how many of these creatures are present, basing that number upon the strength of the party. All things considered, it should be possible for the heroes to defeat this tribe, but only after a long and difficult battle.

Exactly what the heroes do at this point will shape the end of this adventure. There are a few important points that the DM needs to keep in mind, however.

The Reptile Men

The diminutive reptile men oppose any action by the party but can be driven into the swamps by a display of great force. This is especially true if the heroes are seen to effectively oppose Sandovor himself. In game terms, these people can be treated as goblins.

The Prisoners

All of the men and women standing on the stone plain have been injected with a drug fashioned from some of the plants found in the swamp. This has the effect of turning them into mindless zombies. They are not actually undead, however, and can't be turned by clerics.

If the heroes attack the village, they have to be careful to avoid harming the prisoners. After all, these folk aren't able to defend themselves in any way.

Sandovor

When the party first arrives, the master of this place is hidden away inside his pyramid. If the heroes decide to carry the attack to him, they have to enter that stone structure. Inside, the Dungeon Master should have them crawl through an expanse of narrow tunnels, all of which are populated with various reptiles—many poisonous to touch or armed with venomous fangs—before they reach the chamber in which Sandovor resides.

Sandovor leaves the pyramid to attack the heroes if it becomes apparent that many of his beloved reptile men are being destroyed. When he does, however, he emerges in his giant crocodile form. The impression that the player characters will no doubt receive is that they have angered some giant reptile that resides inside the temple.

Chain of Events

If the heroes do not take any action, the ritual proceeds uninterrupted. The reptile men gather around their prisoners, flanking the stone plane. As soon as the last of them reaches this position, the flickering of the green flames change to a hypnotic strobing.

This draws the mesmerized folk forward, step by step, until they begin to topple into the well. While this might appear to be a deadly mishap, it is actually worse than that. Those who fall into the green flame are not destroyed; rather, they are transformed into sub-human reptile men (with the same game statistics as kobolds, but of only semi-intelligence).

Uninvited Guests

There are two ways for the heroes to react to this situation. They may make an overt strike against the village of the reptile men or they might resort to a more subtle infiltration of the pyramid.

In the former case, they find that the spirit of these little folk is far greater than their size. The Dungeon Master should keep in mind that these creatures look upon their leader as nothing less than a god. When battling in his name, they have no fear of death, for they are certain of their eternal reward. In answer to their faith, they are supported in battle at first by Sandovor's priestly magic and then by the supposed avatar's very presence in giant crocodile form.

If the heroes decide to infiltrate the temple, instead, events proceed a little differently. As mentioned above,

they have to sneak through narrow tunnels (large enough for dwarves, gnomes, or halflings to walk along but very cramped for larger characters) until they reach the center of the structure. While they could conceivably just climb the side of this unfinished structure in order to gain its center, this would put them in full view of the reptile men, which would precipitate a battle.

Temple Design: If the Dungeon Master desires to create a map of the temple, he should keep in mind that the structure is only half finished. The upper tiers are missing entirely. Those chambers currently existing within the lower half are intended for worship, for shelter of the high priest, and for storage of his treasures.

The chambers for worship lie near the outer rim of the temple, but have small tunnels leading deeper into its mass, to allow the favored among the faithful to come view their "god" within his central chambers. Those central chambers are built for Sandovor's comfort, so they are of a more normal size. The temple's treasure chambers are fairly well hidden even now, and all are trapped by deadfalls.

Complicating the entire network, however, are temporary partitions designed to hold walls and ceilings in place until construction is complete. Consequently, the heroes should find their exploration of the temple fairly confusing. Passages that should not exist in the final structure remain open for the moment, and many that should exist are temporarily blocked off.

Both of these approaches offer potential for success. If the heroes can press this werecrocodile into a bargaining position, he releases his prisoners. Of course, this doesn't mean that he won't try to obtain more in another month, or otherwise harass the people of Souragne.

The success of other actions must be decided by the Dungeon Master. In all matters, however, it must be remembered that the reptile men and their master think very highly of themselves. They feel that the power of Merrshaulk is on their side and, given this, that only a great enemy need be bargained with. All others are simply to be destroyed.

Recurrence

After the events described above are concluded, Sandovor will return to the construction of his great pyramid, using only his followers. Now that the locals know of the temple's presence, tensions rise between the humans and the reptile men. The heroes may very well find themselves called back to participate in a full-scale war.

If in some later adventure the heroes come into possession of an important relic, one sacred to Merrshaulk, Sandovor might dispatch his people to retrieve it. Similarly, he might contact the heroes and ask them to recover such a thing for him. If the item is important enough, the reptile lord might even promise in exchange never again to prey upon the folk of Souragne.

He who incites strife is worse

than he who takes part in it.

—Aesop
Fables

BIOGRAPHY

Hilde Borganov is wife to the burgomaster of Tidemore, a small fishing village on the western coast of Necropolis. Here, where the shadows of the Mountains of Misery stretch toward the Nocturnal Sea, this couple overseas a community of seemingly normal folk. Despite its innocent appearances, however, Tidemore is a dark and sinister place. Hilde has gradually infected the well over half the population with the dread disease of lycanthropy. Under her guidance, this sleepy village has become a deadly trap waiting to snare innocent sailors.

Appearance

As a true lycanthrope, Hilde Borganov is able to assume three distinct forms. In each she bears a distinctive white scar, the mark of an encounter with an enchanted harpoon.

Hilde Borganov

Human Aspect

Hilde favors her human form above all others. She is an attractive woman, though not truly beautiful. Of average height, she carries perhaps a few too many pounds. Her hair is blue-black and generally worn in a bun, held in place by two long, bone pins. Her eyes are a dull black set against whites with a faint blue tint to them.

A jagged white scar runs along the back of Hilde's neck, starting behind the right ear and curving under the chin. Hilde hides this injury beneath a flowing green scarf reminiscent of drifting kelp fronds. Along with the scarf, she favors flowing skirts of blue and green beneath frilly white blouses. Her whole ensemble calls up images of the sea and its foam-crested waves.

Those who touch Hilde may note that something is amiss with this woman. Although her features do not betray her true nature, the rubbery texture of her skin may serve to alert a careful observer.

Hybrid Aspect

In this form, Hilde appears as a grotesque combination of human and manta. Her body is flattened and distorted spreading out into the angular form of a ray. Her skin becomes a rubbery black in color on her back, shading to an off-white on her front. The semblance of a face is visible near upper edge of her body, but her features are greatly distorted, and cannot be recognize as those of Hilde Borganov. From the base of her spine stretches a long, slender tail, wholly black in color and ending in a bony barb that can deliver a painful sting.

Spindly arms and legs dangle from beneath the aquatic wings of Hilde's hybrid body. Although these allow the werebeast to walk on land and manipulate objects, they are weak. Hilde has a movement rate of only 6 in this form, and her arms act as if her Strength score were only 6.

Hilde's distinctive scar runs along the back of the hybrid form's right fin. It begins near her spine and then fades away.

Ray Aspect

Hilde's tertiary aspect is that of a somewhat oversized stingray. In this shape, Hilde can glide gracefully beneath the waves without attracting attention. Her back is an even black color, marred by the white scar that begins near her spine and then forks toward the tip of her right fin. Her under surface is white.

Hilde Borganov

True Wereray, Lawful Evil

Armor Class	5	Str	12
Movement	12, Sw 12	Dex	15
Level/Hit Dice	5	Con	12
Hit Points	30	Int	16
THAC0	15	Wis	13
Morale	Steady (12)	Cha	15
No. of Attacks	1		
Damage/Attack	1d8 or by weapon		
Special Attacks	Sting		
Special Defenses	Hit only by coral or sea shell and +1 or better magical weapons		
Magic Resistance	Nil		

Background

Hilde Borganov was born to a wandering clan of true wererays that dwelt in the storm-tossed waters of the Nocturnal Sea, near a place known as Selbstmorde Reef. Many a ship met an early end atop these jagged, undersea peaks, giving up their crews to feed the sharks and barracuda as well as the hungry wererays.

Some time after Hilde had reached adulthood, her people were attacked and destroyed by an assembly of surface dwellers wielding magic and magical weapons. She escaped and fled the region. For nearly a year, she searched for some place to settle. Then just as despair was about to overcome her, Hilde stumbled upon a most unusual discovery. From a distance, it seemed to be a sunken human city. As she explored further, however, its strange architecture brought her to believe that it had been created by something terribly inhuman.

Worse, at the city's center, Hilde found a squat, stone temple bearing disturbing runes and hieroglyphs. Although the rest of the city was in ruins, this place was sealed against the sea and appeared to be intact. In years since that time, Hilde has studied the temple and its surrounding ruins, and has researched legends on the land nearby. She believes that a fell race of creatures slumbers inside the temple. From her studies, she has learned that the beings called themselves the Shay-lot, though whether that refers to their race, their city, or their nation, she does not know.

Although she knows relatively little about the history of the Shay-lot, Hilde has great plans for their future. One day soon she hopes to find a way to release these forgotten creatures from their temple. When that day comes, Hilde believes, she will take her place as their leader and lead them in a war against the surface dwellers. When the coastal cities are in flames, Hilde's slaughtered clan will be avenged.

Current Sketch

In order to pursue her plans, Hilde has taken up residence in the human village of Tidemore. Over the past few years she has infected over half the population with lycanthropy. Her victims were carefully chosen. To a man (or woman), they are pliable folk who could be bullied, bribed, or otherwise coerced into following her orders. Through these puppets, Hilde has come to rule the village.

The remaining citizens of Tidemore are aware that things are not right in their community. The fact that their temple has been converted to the worship of some ancient and forgotten god of the sea is sufficient proof, but accompanying that is the strange behavior of their most prominent citizens. Those who suspect or have discovered the worst are unwilling to take action against Hilde and her followers out of fear for their own lives.

Personality

Hilde is a clever and scheming woman. She directs the actions of her followers carefully, guiding them in the exploration and restoration of the sunken city. Since her discovery of the Shay-lot, Hilde has become more and more obsessed with them—especially their obscene religion. Their strange ways seem to have infected her mind, driving her to the brink of madness.

Travelers who come to Tidemore are judged carefully by Hilde. If they appear to be a threat, they are lured to sea and destroyed. If they are of no value to her, they are sacrificed to satisfy the hunger of her aquatic spawn. If they might prove useful, they are attacked and infected with her lycanthropy.

Combat

Hilde dislikes combat unless the odds are in her favor. Since this is almost always the case around Tidemore, she appears to be far more bloodthirsty here than she might in other places. Hilde is able to breathe water or air with equal ease, even in her human aspect. She retains her full personality and intelligence in each of her forms.

Weapons made from coral and sea shells are effective against Hilde in any of her guises, as are magical ones with at least a +1 enchantment.

Human Aspect

In her human form, Hilde is only as dangerous as the weapon she wields. As a rule, she maintains the illusion that she is nothing more than a simple burgomaster's wife. Thus, she seldom has any weapon at hand.

Hybrid Aspect

In her hybrid shape, Hilde uses her barbed tail like a whip to inflict 1d8 points of damage with each successful strike. Anyone hit is injected with venom. Unless a successful saving throw vs. poison is made, the victim is paralyzed and in terrible pain for 1d4 turns. Hilde often leaves those she stings to drown, enjoying their horror.

Hilde can deliver a painful bite when in this form, although she seldom makes use of this attack. When she does, each successful bite inflicts 1d4 points of damage. She can bite one victim while stinging another but cannot direct both attacks at the same target.

Ray Aspect

As a ray, Hilde can employ her stinger and bite, just as in hybrid form. In addition, she can settle onto the sea floor and cover herself with sand. Thus disguised she is effectively concealed as if by an *invisibility* spell.

The Forgotten Ones

 his adventure depicts the events that transpire when the heroes find their way into Tidemore. Once here, they are confronted by a strange community of frightened people, mysterious rituals, and perhaps even ultimate darkness. As the adventure proceeds, the heroes learn of the existence of the Shay-lot, their sunken city, and Hilde's sinister plan to revive them. Only as events near their end, however, do the heroes discover the secret of Hilde's lycanthropic nature.

Introduction

At the start of this adventure, the heroes are assumed to be at sea. For the purposes of this scenario, their vessel is called *Seafarer* (although that can be changed as the Dungeon Master desires).

Ideally, this adventure should be used as an interlude within a larger one, so that Tidemore is but one port of call during the voyage of *Seafarer*. It is best if that larger adventure puts a little pressure on the player characters to keep things moving along. At the same time, however, the Dungeon Master must strike a balance so that this pressure in no way overshadows the events to follow.

Scene I: Storm at Sea

It matters little for this adventure whether the player characters are mere passengers or are actually the masters of *Seafarer*. In either case, the fate of the vessel must be very important to them. After all, if the ship is lost there is every reason to believe that they will go down with it. Beyond that, damage to the ship threatens the prompt completion of their current mission.

As *Seafarer* makes her way across the Nocturnal Sea, a powerful storm whips up. This gale is a great one, strong enough to do severe damage to the ship. The following boxed copy can be read at the start of the adventure to describe the onset of the storm and hint at its looming effects.

As the sun begins to sink in the west, dark gray clouds pile up across the horizon. Ominous reds wash over those looming thunderheads, and the air grows suddenly still and cool. The rising moon vanishes quickly behind a ceiling of churning gray. And then the rain begins.

There is no gradual building of a storm, no rising wind or slowly increasing precipitation. Rather, one minute all is calm, and the next, a torrential downfall hammers across the deck. Stiff winds sweep from out of nowhere, howling like beasts from hell and clawing at the canvas sails. The masts creak dangerously, rocking with every blast. As the crew dashes about the deck, working frantically to secure lines, furl the sails, and strike the rigging, deadly waves swell up to slap at the hull.

If the heroes are not in Ravenloft at the start of this adventure, this storm can serve well to bring them into the Demiplane of Dread.

During the course of the storm, the Dungeon Master should include one or more of the following events. Each serves well to indicate both the severity of the storm and the damage being suffered by the ship.

- **Lightning Strike:** Lightning causes a large piece of mast and rigging to collapse, trapping a crew member. If the heroes act quickly, they can save his life. If they delay, however, the sailor is lost. If the Dungeon Master wishes, a player character might take the place of the pinned NPC.
- **Death Below the Waterline:** As the storm rages, the ship is tossed to and fro. At one point this action opens a crack in the ship's hull. This break is beneath the waterline, allowing the chill waters of the sea to rush into the ship. If the heroes don't act quickly, the vessel may soon vanish beneath the waves.
- **Man Overboard!** With the ship tossing back and forth in the grip of wave and wind, those aboard *Seafarer* are in constant danger. Even as they fight to keep the ship afloat, the deadly surf drags a man from the decks. As with the collapsing mast, this event centers around the rescue of an NPC sailor. If the Dungeon Master wishes, he can threaten one of the heroes, instead.

If the heroes take action that is both prompt and appropriate, they should be rewarded with success and experience points. If they delay or don't think their actions through, however, disaster may be their only recompense.

Scene II: Unsafe Haven

For many hours, the heroes join with the crew of *Seafarer* to battle the storm. By dawn, it has blown itself out and a well-deserved rest can be had by all.

Shortly before dawn, the storm breathes its last. As the sun rises, a deep blue sky spreads above the ship. The last vestiges of the great storm, a few scattered gunmetal clouds, seem to evaporate as you watch.

Seafarer has survived, but she's badly wounded. She lists hard to one side, her hull leaking in several places and her hold's slowly filling with water. It seems just possible that the storm will win in the end.

A cry of "Land Ho!" from the lookouts offers sudden hope, however. Far to the east, a jagged coastline runs north and south. With the aid of a spyglass, the captain peruses this coast, then reports that a small village is nestled there. The promise of skilled shipwrights can be seen in wooden docks that jut out into the waves.

As *Seafarer* makes her way to anchorage, the crew observes fishing boats traveling outward from the docks. These row along silently beneath the warm light of the rising sun, their crews gazing coldly upon the crippled ship. They return no signals, answer no calls, and don't even respond to waving sailors.

By the time *Seafarer* reaches dock, a small party of villagers has gathered there. Lines are thrown and secured by grim-faced hands who make no effort to communicate. By the time *Seafarer* is securely moored, a few official-looking folk have arrived on the dock.

When you step onto the wooden quay, the dockhands back away. As one, they return to other tasks. At the same time, however, another knot of people moves forward. Their clothes are somber, but mark them as people of wealth and, presumably, influence.

"Welcome to Tidemore," says a heavy man. He offers a wide, easy smile. "My name is Borganov, and I am the burgomeister here. These five are the members of the town council. We don't get visitors here often, but I imagine that your stop wasn't planned."

In the conversation that follows, the Dungeon Master should make certain that the following things take place.

First, arrangements are made for *Seafarer* to be repaired. This won't require much haggling, as the repairs are a source of considerable income for the town.

Second, an observant hero should notice that the mayor and his companions don't look well. It's difficult for the hero to say for certain what's wrong, apart from the fact that their complexions seem a bit gray.

Anyone who directs his attention to the dock workers notices that they do not share the unusual pallor of the mayor and his companions. Still, they look a bit frightened and are certainly intimidated by something.

Scene III: Strange People

At some point, the player characters will probably want to make contact with the common folk of Tidemore. In all likelihood, this means striking up a conversation with one of the local laborers working to repair *Seafarer*. It's also possible that at least one of the heroes will want to sneak into town and snoop around a bit.

If the heroes don't initiate this themselves, the Dungeon Master can force the issue by having one of the crew repairing *Seafarer* injured. As they provide medical care, the workman offer up important information.

In either of these cases, they learn some very important things.

About the Mayor

First, the heroes learn that the mayor and his companions are greatly feared by the common folk of the town. Although no two stories agree exactly, the following boxed text can be read to sum up what the heroes are told.

"I shouldn't be telling you this. The Mayor or the Chief Constable wouldn't like it. I don' know for sure what's about them, but it ain't safe for me to be talking about it. Mind you, it wasn't always this way.

"Nearly two years ago, something happened. I think the real mayor was killed or carried away or something. I don't know the truth behind the matter, but I've heard stories. People say they've seen the mayor—indeed, all the important folk of Tidemore—going down to the sea at night. They've struck a bargain with something sinister, something that lives beneath the waves.

"If you don't believe me, just take a look at the temple. It's not a place that's fit for human beings anymore."

A more detailed investigation reveals that the same sorts of stories are told about every important figure in the town. The general populace is clearly cowed.

The Temple

If one of the heroes makes his way to the temple near Tidemore's center, he discovers a most ominous sight. The temple around which the village has grown is not what it should be. The following boxed text can be read to the players whose heroes who make their way here.

The church that rises before you is offensive to mind and spirit alike. While it is clear that this place was once a common enough temple, where sailors, fishermen, and their folk could gather to seek the blessings of the sea, a terrible change has been wrought.

Twisted figures of coral—creatures that look like horrible unions of fish and men—seem to guard the place. Every window has been sealed with metal shutters and painted over with thick black lacquer. Fell hieroglyphs—offensive depictions of strange, aquatic creatures and black rituals—cover the door-way. Evil fairly hangs in the air, weighing heavily upon your spirits.

The heroes can attempt to enter the temple at this point in the adventure, but there isn't much of value for them to find. The walls are covered with disturbingly alien murals depicting strange undersea scenes. Also, Hilde keeps a few macabre articles and instruments inside the temple, which she uses to conduct religious services, and there are also a few tablets bearing bizarre pictograms from the sunken temple. But the heroes have no way of knowing what meaning these strange symbols and items might hold.

The group doesn't have much time to investigate, however, before the coral guardians of the temple come to life to drive out these invaders. Although these should be described as strange creatures of coral and sea shell, these guardians can be treated as gargoyles or stone golems. For what it's worth, the weapons they carry can be very valuable later in battling Hilde and the other wererays.

Scene IV: Midnight Service

By now, the heroes may well realize that it is in their best interests for *Seafarer* and her crew to get out of town. But Hilde Borganov has other plans for them all.

The only reason she is allowing *Seafarer* to be repaired at all is because she perceives that the craft is valuable to her efforts. Up to now, she has been recovering material from the sea floor using only the small fishing boats of Tidemore. With a real sailing ship as a base, she can accelerate her efforts.

This means, however, that the crew of the ship (including the heroes) must be either destroyed or made into Hilde's followers. Exactly how the wereray goes about this depends upon the actions of the heroes. It is her intent to convert them at the temple. (If this plan fails, however, she waits for them aboard *Seafarer,* as described in Scene V of this adventure.)

To work their transformation, Hilde instructs the mayor to bring the heroes to the temple for a midnight service. This is presented as an invitation but turns into an attempted abduction if the heroes don't comply. Unless they break free, the heroes are destined to attend the service.

If the heroes come of their own free will, they likely suspect foul play, but there is no solid evidence of perfidy in the actions of their hosts. Once the heroes enter the temple, however, the doors are sealed behind them. Escape is virtually impossible.

Inside the unholy sanctuary, Hilde Borganov introduces herself to the heroes as high priestess. She tells them of the sunken city she has found and of her plan to release the monsters slumbering there. She presents this information as if it were wonderful news. To the heroes, she should seem quite mad. They have no way of knowing that she is a wereray, of course, and may even suspect that they have stumbled upon the machinations of a sea spawn.

Her speech made, Hilde begins the service in earnest. At first, the sights and sounds confronting the heroes seem to be only offensive and evil. Before long, however, it become clear that the things they are seeing were not meant for human eyes. The strange various chants and songs of this unholy order begin to prey upon their minds. Indeed, every hero who observes these rituals must make a madness check. The effects of a failed check do not manifest for several days, but once these sinister seeds are planted it is difficult to uproot them.

As the frantic service reaches its peak, the floor opens beneath the heroes and drops them into a flooded sea cave below, where they are attacked by waiting wererays. This should be a desperate battle, one that the heroes have little chance of winning. Their best hope lies in escape.

As they battle, the heroes note that the tide is going out, revealing a partially submerged passage to the sea. If they are willing to swim underwater partway, while fighting off pursuing wererays, they eventually find themselves upon the sea shore.

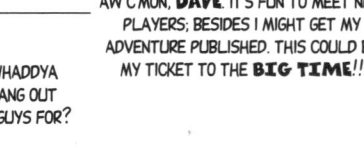

Scene V: Ship of the Damned

If the heroes avoided attending the midnight service, or after they have faced the wererays and escaped, they will certainly want to make their way back to *Seafarer*, hoping to leave this accursed place.

Unfortunately, the situation is worse than they know. While they were occupied with the invitation to visit the temple, another group of wererays made its way aboard *Seafarer* and attacked the crew. One after another, the sailors were either killed or infected with lycanthropy.

Headlong to Oblivion

If the heroes race back to the ship without caution, they rush straight into Hilde's grip. After all, once they are aboard the *Seafarer*, the infected crew can attack when they least expect it.

Taking Care

With a little bit of caution, however, the heroes have a good chance of survival. This is especially true if they befriended any of the laborers working on the ship.

As the heroes make their way back to *Seafarer*, one of the townsfolk seeks them out. He is alarmed, even terrified, and tells them that death awaits them on the ship. With a little effort, the heroes can learn what has happened to *Seafarer's* crew. Beyond that, they can reveal what they know of the wererays, and as a result might even recruit some of the locals as something of a militia.

Aboard Seafarer

With or without local seamen in tow, the heroes eventually return to *Seafarer*. Once they arrive, the Dungeon Master has to decide exactly how events unfold.

If the crew of the ship is composed mostly of minor NPCs, then the DM can assume that they have all been either killed or converted into followers of Hilde. In this case, the heroes have quite a battle ahead of them. While things might seem to be normal at first, the newest of Hilde's minions try to destroy the heroes at the earliest opportunity.

If they can manage it, they split the heroes up and strike them down one at a time. Only if this isn't possible do they risk an all-out attack. In any battle against wererays, an effort is made to knock the heroes into the sea, where they can be attacked more easily.

Scene VI: Setting Sail

Once the corrupted crew has been dealt with, the PCs will likely want to get clear of port at once. This can be a very dramatic scene, with lines being cut and sails raised even as Tidemore's wereray militia swarms onto the dock.

The most dangerous part of the heroes' escape has yet to materialize, however. As the ship is leaving port, the Dungeon Master should read the following text.

A brisk wind rolls across the deck, filling the sails and driving Seafarer away from the dock. Waves lap gently at the ship, and gulls circle on all sides. At first, these familiar sounds are safe and reassuring.

But then a distant and ominous echo begins to fill the air. What is at first too faint to hear clearly soon becomes unmistakable. Another foreboding ceremony is being conducted within Tidemore's obscene temple.

As if in answer to these dark sounds, the sea around the ship begins to churn madly. Even a casual glance at the waters reveals clearly that the dark sea is alive with sharks and rays.

Before long, Hilde herself leads a group of wererays aboard the ship. They intend to take no prisoners this time, killing everyone. This battle should be one in which the heroes are hard pressed just to stay alive. Coupled with the sight of their new allies falling left and right, this should be more than enough to make even the most hardened adventurers tremble.

In the end, as the coast of Necropolis falls away in the distance, the heroes should finally succeed in driving off their attackers. Hilde herself dives overboard the moment that things look bad for her side.

Recurrence

There are a number of ways for the events in this adventure to surface again in future sessions of play. Perhaps the most obvious of these involves the Shay-lot and their sunken city.

There's no reason for the heroes to visit the Sunken City, or even to learn its location, during the course of this adventure. Indeed, by keeping it a secret, the Dungeon Master leaves himself an interesting place to which the heroes can return.

The exact nature of the Shay-lot is also left undetermined. Bits and pieces of their culture, all of which seem evil and offensive to characters of any alignment, may be found. These might even include magical items, all of which carry heavy curses with them.

If Hilde survives, she is all the more determined to raise this sunken city quickly. She infects the lycanthropy everyone remaining in town, then moves the entire population under the waves. Anyone returning to visit Tidemore finds it deserted. Meanwhile, the wererays continue to labor at their obscene mission. . . .